Sea Change in Crimson

Ray Pace

Creole Belle Publishing

Sea Change in Crimson is a work of fiction.

"They all laughed at Christopher Columbus." — Ira Gershwin

"I like Florida. Everything is in the 80`s. The temperatures, the ages and the IQs." -- George Carlin

For Travis, Spenser, and Hawk.

We know what he means. Jacky's the boss. He pays well, and he even likes us. There's also a hint. Uncle Billy has a fishing boat. Marlin-fishing anyone? Now, if I can just remember who the hell Uncle Billy is. Is he that old goat who got drunk at Muriel and Jacky's wedding? The one that passed out with his head stuck in a slice of the wedding cake. Or is Uncle Billy the guy who kept his sunglasses on all evening at the wedding reception? The guy who would duck behind people when the photographer came around?

Maybe Uncle Billy isn't a relative at all. He could be a Chicago uncle. Chicago uncles are a special breed, trusted friends involved in common interests, both legal and not so legal. It's not uncommon in Chicago to have an Uncle Eli who runs a liquor store where the cigarettes have no tax stamps. If you ask Uncle Eli who's handling action on the Derby, he might point you to Uncle Carlos at Juarez Tacos. If you ask Uncle Carlos where you can buy a small Ruger for your lady's protection, he might send you to Uncle Lerrone. He operates out of a soul food place on the Southside.

I think about all the "uncles" I've known as I stare out the window at the red striped port side engine and the red light on the wingtip. Below that is darkness. I'm guessing we must be somewhere over Oklahoma or Arkansas. I wonder if they do Uncles down there. I think they do Bubbas.

Then I think no. Maybe we're over Texas or Louisiana? There must be a way to tell the difference. And then I fall asleep.

Just before the final approach to Fort Lauderdale, I wake up. There's a beautiful red sun coming up through a cloud bank over the Atlantic.

"Wake up, Sunshine." I poke Jimmy. "You're missing the best part of the trip."

"Jesus." Jimmy jerks to life. "Look at all the boats."

There are hundreds of boats in the waterways. Most are tied to a pier. Some are already moving out for a day's fishing on the Gulf Stream. I look again. Some of the boats going down the canals look like cars. Then I realize. They are cars. The streets are flooded.

"Must have been a hell of a rain," Jimmy says.

Soon, we're on the ground at the car rental place. The guy at the counter has our reservation. We get in the jitney, and he takes us to an all-wheel-drive Jeep.

"Good choice of cars," the rental guy says as we pull toward the Jeep through a large puddle of water. "You shouldn't have any trouble navigating our streets."

Chapter

August 20

The red-eye from Vegas to Fort Lauderdale takes off in the dark. scheduled to land about sunrise. I could look up the exact tim my boarding pass, but I'd disturb my fellow jet lag victims by rumm through the overhead luggage bin. I'm tired. I'd probably grab the w carry-on and get accused of purse-snatching. The rest of our stuff is locked gun case below us in luggage. We're bringing our two Glocks i South Florida doesn't have enough "If it bleeds, it leads" stories for th news.

Okay, I'm in a bad mood. I'm sitting next to a snoring Jimmy Cox. F dropped off as we taxied for take-off from LAS. I tried to tell him the of Vegas as we left was beautiful. If you didn't know better, you'd sw there was water down there and boats next to houses. I wanted him to and compare it to when we fly into Fort Lauderdale. It's supposed to sunrise when we arrive. He'll see real boats in canals. Not the hot, du streets of Vegas that dead-end into the desert.

Do I hear him mumble, "Whatever," and continue his snore? I can't The flight attendant interrupts to say the cabin lights are being turne If I want to read, I can use the overhead lamp I always get confused wit so-called fresh air nozzle. Before I can reply, she's down the aisle, repe her announcement. She's another mechanical part of the product "Fl from Las Vegas to Fort Lauderdale."

I decide to sit in darkness and think about our mission to Florida.

"I want you guys to go see Uncle Billy in South Florida," Jacky said in phone call from Chicago. "He needs help unloading real estate down t So, Jimmy's legal advice and Nick's talent for, uh .... You guys know w I mean."

"How much rain have you had?" I ask.

"None," he says. "This is a king tide. Seawater comes up through the ground."

We head south on Federal Highway toward Miami. A sign announces, "Meyer's Deli." It's a nice-looking restaurant, with few cars in the lot due to most of it being flooded.

"Hey, we got a Jeep," Jimmy says. "Pull in. I'm hungry."

I find a dry place to park near the front door. We make it into the restaurant without having to wade. The deli has six other people in booths.

"Great to see you guys," our waitress says. She's a solidly built woman who looks like she's lived a happy life for the past seventy years. She has one of those gravel voices that make you think she's telling you a dirty joke.

"I hope you like the way Meyer washed down the parking lot today," she says. "It's an added attraction. A little saltwater never hurt anyone."

"Sadie looks at the bright side of things," the guy behind the counter says. "The Dolphins are having their usual doofus of a season. Sadie tells people at least they won't have to worry about packing for the Super Bowl."

"Meyer blows our dough on season tickets to the Dolphin's fiasco," Sadie says. "He's tried giving them to customers. Everyone holds their noses and runs the other way."

"It's true," Meyer says. "Sadie and Meyer go and suffer through the games. You wouldn't believe how bad they are. Last week we both fell asleep in the fourth quarter."

We order eggs and lox with coffee and juice. Sadie brings a basket of warm onion rolls and butter for starters.

"This king tide flooding?" Jimmy asks. "Does it do this often?"

"Too often," Sadie says. "We're trying to sell before it gets any worse. We're thinking maybe New Mexico. Someplace up from the sea. Where you guys from?"

"Vegas," I say.

"That's a possibility, too." Sadie pours fresh coffee into our cups. "We have friends in Henderson in the Green Valley area. Meyer loves his golf."

"Good place for it," I say. "You two would fit right in."

She leaves to bring coffee to the other tables.

"Rising ocean water could be Uncle Billy's problem trying to unload the property," I say.

Jimmy butters an onion roll, dips it in his coffee, and looks up.

"I read the emails Jacky sent. Uncle Billy has a bigger problem than king tides. Cuban sharks are trying to force him out."

Chapter 2

We leave the friendly vibes of Meyer's Deli and head south on Federal Highway. We swing over to the beach and drive through seawater ponds covering half the road. Jacky said to stop first at Coral Surf Beach & Tennis Club. That's where Harry and Colette Feldstein live. Harry's expecting us. He has advice about dealing with Uncle Billy.

Coral Surf Beach & Tennis Club sits twenty stories high on the ocean side of A1A. The security guy at the gate rings Harry. We get the go-ahead to park and head for the elevators. I punch the button for fourteen and see there's no button for thirteen. Jimmy notices.

"We're really going to the thirteenth floor," he says. "Already, it's our lucky day."

"Hey, we drove here without drowning."

Jimmy's about to answer when the elevator doors open. Harry is waiting for us at the entrance to the apartment. He's wearing sandals, jogging shorts, and a Chicago Bears T-shirt. His bald head has a deep tan, and his grey beard stubble has crumbs stuck in it.

"You two bums, get in here," he says. "I haven't seen you two since we got together in Cabo."

We get punches on the arm from Harry and a hug and a perfumed air kiss from Colette, who's dressed in a pink tennis outfit.

"I left some cafe and croissants for you guys out on the balcony," she says. "I have to run—tennis lesson. I'm getting quite good. Harry, we should take the boys out for dinner."

Colette grabs her tennis racket, wiggles her butt, and disappears along with her French accent.

On the balcony, the view is magnificent. The deep blue ocean has small waves. Sailboats glide just outside the surf line. Below is a large swimming pool. On the side are six tennis courts.

Something's missing.

Jimmy says it first.

"Where the hell's the beach?"

"It comes and goes," Harry says. "This global warming stuff ain't bullshit. They come around for a handout to replace the sand now and then. There's still a small pathway next to the buildings at low tide. That's the only time I can jog along the beach."

"How bad is it?" I ask.

"I'm waiting for the right price," Harry says. "Believe it or not, the prices are going up on these units. Companies buy into it. Good place for their execs to R&R. If the whole thing falls into the ocean, they'll write it off. You look at all that young stuff tanning around the pool. They're here to relax all those hard-working execs."

"Working gals?" Jimmy asks.

"No, not in Miami." Harry winks. "You think this is Vegas? No, those hard-working execs in their sixties all have 22-year-old girlfriends. They're all named Tammy, Brandy, and Candy."

"You sell this joint. Where are you gonna go?" I ask.

"Baja, or Puerto Vallarta. I figure we're already in a banana republic. We might as well get more bananas for our buck. Colette's all for it. She worries about the damn building keeling over."

"What chance of that?" Jimmy asks.

"Engineers have told me that it won't happen for another ten years, maybe longer. But there's something wrong here if you think about it. The building is sitting in saltwater. Hell, the foundation was probably poured using a mix of sand and seawater. I know what that can do to rebar. I tell Colette, we get our price, and it's hasta la vista. If you don't mind walking through saltwater or waiting for a category five hurricane, it's a great place to live."

Harry pours more coffee and tells some favorite Chicago stories. Drunk politicians, crooked cops, and shady deals are the main features.

We respond with similar Vegas stories.

"I thought Chicago had the market cornered on all that," he says, "But then I moved down here. The talk about what to do about rising seawater keeps you spinning. Everyone has a plan involving large pumps, tons of cement, and millions of bucks. It's Rube Goldberg double talk. Somehow saltwater becomes fresh water after it's pumped through miles of pipe and canals. It's being treated. The only treatment I see is the taxpayer getting the double-talk shuffle."

We laugh, sip our coffees, and look out over the ocean.

"Hey," Harry says. "You guys didn't come here to listen to me bitch. You need to know about Billy before you get into something you weren't expecting."

"Anything you can help us with," I say. "We've both been trying to place Billy. Was he at Jacky and Muriel's wedding? I'm thinking he was the drunk who put his face in the cake or the guy in sunglasses who avoided the photographer."

"No," Harry says. "That was the Finkel brothers, a couple of clowns. Leo and Joel. They run a brokerage firm on La Salle Street. Cleaned up on mortgage default policies back in oh-eight. Billy wasn't at the wedding. He had car trouble. Just outside Nashville, the Feds found a couple bales of pot in the trunk of his Mustang."

"Ouch," Jimmy says.

"Billy later walked on that one. He even vowed to go straight, and by the looks of it, he's staying pretty clean. By the looks of it. *Capisce?*"

We both nod.

"Anyhow, a few years back, he got hold of the Sea Chanty. It's one of those leftovers from the fifties. A dozen small units around a pool with a lot of tiki bar decorations. It's got a small boat dock out back on one of those canals that get you to the ocean. He managed to rent to tourists and a few locals. For a while, things looked good."

"Okay, Harry," Jimmy says. "You know how to tell a story. Things didn't stay good, did they?"

"He got hassled over the name, for starters. Some other outfit was using Sea Chanty. So, he changed it to Sea Shanty. No go. Next was Sea Change. I don't know what it's called now. He changed the sign to keep from being sued."

"Jacky says he needs some help to move the property," Jimmy says. "I'll be happy to look over any deal, but I hear that there's a Cuban shark in the water. What's up?"

"Billy's got the Sea Change or whatever it's called, plus property down in the Keys," Harry says. "They call it Maroon Key. I've looked on the map and can't find it. That doesn't mean it's not there. The Keys are Fantasy Land. Some parties, though, are getting too serious. One of the parties is Cesar Fuentes. He's a hot-shot politician who says global warming is a fraud. His family fled with suitcases full of other people's money as Castro took control of Havana. They've been doing a variation of that act ever since."

"If Fuentes makes the right offer," I ask, "what's the problem? Billy sells out both places and heads off to do whatever?"

"There's more than one shark," Harry says. "There's the Haitian Henri Boyer. He's an alumnus of the *Tonton Macoute*, Papa Doc Duvalier's secret police. He runs a chain of Haitian restaurants and a couple of massage parlors. His favorite sport is voodoo."

"Sounds like a wonderful addition to the prayer meeting," I say. "Anyone else?"

"Vinnie Malone. He's out of New Orleans. The best I can tell is he runs dope on shrimp boats. He parties hard at the clubs on South Beach."

"All these guys are after the Sea Change?" Jimmy asks, "What's so special?"

"Maybe they're after Maroon Key. They've all made offers that Billy can't refuse. He either sells to them or else. Right now, he's stalling them."

"How's he doing that?" I ask.

"He's telling them that a heavyweight Chicago outfit is backing him. If they give the okay on the deal, things will go smooth. If not, people might get hurt."

"So, who's this Chicago outfit?" I ask.

Harry pours more coffee into our cups, shakes his head, and laughs.

"I think he means you and Jimmy."

Chapter 3

"This Uncle Billy problem could be bigger than what we bargained for," Jimmy says. He steers the Jeep through puddles of seawater. "I thought this was just some hard-nosed negotiating with semi-legit businesspeople."

"I thought all businesspeople were semi-legit," I say. "We should at least look to see what kind of a dump this Sea Change place is.'"

A dog-with-bone growl comes from the driver's seat. A minute goes by.

"Okay," Jimmy says. "You talked me into it. If I get killed, Cassandra will kick your ass."

Jimmy's right. His wife would kick my ass. I look at the directions Harry wrote for us.

"Take the next right. It's supposed to be at the end, by the water."

"I'm guessing it's now called the Sea Chang," Jimmy says as we park. His brilliant deduction comes from the sign above the arched entrance. The 'E' has been covered with paint. There's something else noteworthy. A cop car with its lights flashing is in one of the parking places. Next to it is another vehicle, Animal Control.

"You don't suppose they're here to grab Uncle Billy?" Jimmy says.

I'm about to respond when loud shouts from a woman fill the neighborhood. We jump out of the Jeep to look.

"You two are the stupidest bastards I've ever met," she says. "You think this thing strolled down Collins Avenue? Or rode a taxi here? No, somebody put it in the goddamn pool."

Her blond hair is soaked, and water drips from her skin. She stands barefooted in her red two-piece swimsuit. Blood trickles down her leg from below her knee. She's in the face of a fat cop who's holding her back from the animal control guy. Two women stand behind her, ready to swing shuffleboard sticks. A man is ready, too. He's holding a red fire ax.

The animal control guy is busy. There's a five-foot-long alligator stuck in a noose at the end of a pole. It's acting up, hissing, and trying to roll.

"Never thought I'd see something like this on my vacation," the guy with the fire ax says.

"Get used to it," one of the shuffleboard women says. "Florida doesn't have cockroaches. They call them Palmetto Bugs. Probably call this gator an overgrown gecko."

The cop tries to explain how the gator arrived.

"Could've come down the Miami River from the Glades," he says to the wet blonde in the red two-piece. "They're all over. Got into the Bay and made its way up into your canal."

"And then what?" she asks. "Pulled a key out of its wallet and opened the gate on the dock?"

The cop shrugs and turns to see how the animal control guy is doing.

"Anything I can help you with, Charlie? I can put a slug in him. Looks like there might be some good meat there."

Charlie shakes his head and drags the hissing gator towards his small truck.

"No sweat, man," he says. "If this was a seven-footer, I'd maybe say yeah. We toss this one back into the Glades. Put more meat on him."

The gator rides away in the animal control truck. The cop writes it up as some kind of a prank.

"Coulda been college kids," he tells the woman in the red two-piece. "Hey, nobody got bit."

"What century are you in?" she asks. "You see any college kids in this neighborhood? All I see are retired people and drugged-out losers. Any self-respecting college kids are on South Beach or down in Cozumel."

The cop shrugs, wishes everyone a good day, and takes off in his cruiser.

"What can I do for you guys?" Red two-piece asks.

"We came to see Uncle Billy," I say. "Did the gator bite you?"

"I scraped my leg getting out of the pool. He came after me right after I jumped in. I moved fast. You must be the guys from Vegas. Nobody here calls him Uncle Billy."

Her name is Bonnie Teller. She's married to Uncle Billy, or Captain Billy Teller, as he's known locally. We duck into the poolside office, where she puts a bandage on her leg.

"We've had some crap around here lately," she says. "Someone hung a dead chicken on a noose over the entrance a week ago. It's one of those Santeria curses. Goes back to old religions in Cuba. Middle of the night, we get phone calls. The guy just says, 'Sell. Don't get hurt.'"

"The old threat in the middle of the night trick," I say. "Something from a cheap punk."

"So, where's Billy?" Jimmy asks. "He around somewhere?"

"He and Mandingo took the Maroon Key out last night. They're supposed to be back soon. You guys want coffee?" She asks.

"Coffee sounds great," I say.

"Coffee," Jimmy says. "I thought the Maroon Key is a piece of property down in the Keys?"

"Yeah, it's also the name of our boat. It's rigged for sports fishing. Cream, sugar?"

"One of each for me," Jimmy says.

"Two sugars," I say. "Who's Mandingo?"

"He's this Haitian guy. He was working as a bouncer at the Scarlet Tide on South Beach. He had to get rough with some of Cesar Fuentes' pals. Cesar fired him. He was renting from us, so Billy took him on as a helper. He's good at handling the boat."

"These guys that want to buy you out, what's the deal there?" Jimmy asks.

"I try not to get involved," Bonnie says. "I know they're not offering enough. This is all new to me. When I met Billy, I was a social worker. I took care of the poor, got them benefits, housing. I was naive. Came here from a little town in New Hampshire. Nobody there needed any government help."

"They still have places like that?" I ask.

"They did two years ago when I left."

"So, how did you meet Billy?" Jimmy asks.

"I needed a place to stay. Sea Change rent was do-able, and Billy's a great guy. What could I do? I fell for him. After a month, I moved into his apartment. He gave me the heads up on Miami. 'Don't be so innocent,' Billy says. 'You're twenty-three and good looking. This town can eat people like you alive.'"

We nod and sip some coffee.

"Billy gave me a Smith & Wesson .38 for protection," Bonnie says. "I was working at a benefits office in Liberty City. I told him I'd never use it, but I kept the gun in my bag to please him. One day, I got stopped by two Black guys. They wanted what was in my bag. They got it, one in the knee, one in the shoulder. I got in my car and never went back."

"Did the cops show up?" Jimmy asks.

"Can't say. I left in a hurry, crying my eyes out. I can still hear one of them yelling, 'Fuckin' honky bitch.'"

She sips her coffee, shakes her head, and continues.

"If the cops did show, they were probably like the guy who just left. A useless uniform ready to pose at the crime scene for the six o'clock news."

Chapter 4

Yogi Berra said, "You can observe a lot just by watching."

We've been in South Florida for part of the morning, and my list of observations keeps growing. I've got things to tell my wife and little daughter Molly when we talk later on the phone.

"You don't have to go to the beach to bathe in the ocean," I'll say. "The ocean gets delivered outside your door, even if you're miles away. It comes up through your lawn. In fact, going to the beach might be a problem. Beaches are disappearing faster than sand deliveries can keep up. Some people who live in shoreline condos are worried about them crumbling into the sea."

"That's crazy, Nick," Dawn will say. "How do people live like that?"

"Are they living in sandcastles?" Molly might ask. She loved the sandcastles we made in Cabo last winter. She'll wonder how people can fit into them.

I'll say goodnight to Molly and have Dawn turn off the speaker setting. Then, I'll talk about the alligator in the pool, Santeria curses, and social workers who shoot thugs.

I know what Dawn will say.

"Nick, be careful. We love you. And take care of Jimmy, too."

Right now, Jimmy is trying to get info out of Bonnie Teller. We're in her small office sipping cups of Cafe Bustelo. Does she know who's behind the Santeria curses and a gator in the pool?

"The Santeria stuff sounds like it might be from this guy Fuentes," Jimmy says. "You think he might be responsible for the gator in your pool?"

"I don't rule him out," Bonnie says. "Cesar Fuentes would love to see someone eaten by a gator. He'd stand in front of the tv cameras and give a speech about what a tragedy it all was. Henri Boyer is the same. A voodoo curse making a gator show up in someone's pool would fit his thinking. Vinnie Malone ain't the type. He's laid back. He's probably after our stuff because he wants to beat Fuentes and Boyer out of it. He's a poker player. Goes for the high stakes games."

"Why are these three guys after the Sea Change?" I ask. "No offense, but there must be a lot of similar properties for sale. Is there something remarkable about this place that we're not seeing? Or are they after this other property of yours, Maroon Key?"

Bonnie fidgets in her chair. She gets up and picks up the marine radio microphone.

"Sea Change calling Maroon Key. Sea Change calling Maroon Key," she says.

She turns up the audio. Static comes from the speaker. A garbled voice tries to get through and fades.

She tries again.

"Sea Change calling Maroon Key. Sea Change calling Maroon Key."

Static and crackles come back again.

"I don't think that was them," she says. "They're still out of range. They won't be in for hours. You guys need to talk to Billy."

We leave our cell phone numbers with Bonnie and head out.

A half-block down the street, Jimmy gives me a things-are-fishy look.

"She either knows nothing and is embarrassed," Jimmy says, "or she knows too much and doesn't want to say. Something crazy's going on. You look at Sea Change. Nothing remarkable. You mention Maroon Key, and you've just dropped a hand grenade."

We turn onto the main drag and drive through more seawater. People on sidewalks wade through ankle-deep puddles. A slow-moving bus throws a wake over the curb.

"It's surprising Harry Feldstein can't find Maroon Key on the map," I say.

"Any more surprising than the red Camaro following us?" Jimmy asks. "Sometimes, I think we're a magnet for trouble."

I catch a look at our new friends in the side mirror. Through the darkened windshield, I see two orange XXL Tommy Bahama shirts wearing too much gold jewelry on their dark skin.

"Think they carry alligators in their trunk?" I ask.

"These guys never learn," Jimmy says. "If I wanted someone followed, I'd get a guy dressed like an insurance salesman and have him drive a grey Chevy."

Collins Avenue has the Eden Roc and the Fontainebleau hotels. Most people have no trouble pronouncing Eden Roc. But Fontainebleau usually comes out Fountain Blue rather than the more French-sounding *Fahn tin blow*. Both are luxury resorts on the ocean, sitting side-by-side, across from a canal called Indian Creek. There are no Indians in the creek today, only expensive motor yachts. The assumption is if you don't have buckets of money or work for someone who has, you don't belong.

Jimmy turns into the driveway of the Fontainebleau and heads up an incline toward valet parking. Our friends in the red Camaro are three cars back due to over-medicated Floridians cutting them off in traffic.

The valet kid takes our Jeep and peels off. We head for the lobby. Our Camaro friends pull in and get out, eager to stay on our tail. We make the lobby and duck into an art display. Our two over-decorated friends race past and scan the place for us.

I stroll up behind them, narrating in my best *New Yorkese*.

"It's so good to be back at Fountain Blue," I say. "You wouldn't believe the flight from JFK. Oh, look. It's Tubby and Chubby. Our friends from the Camaro branch of Fat People Unanimous."

"What the fuck?" Tubby turns around.

Chubby is slower on the uptake and has walked on a few steps. He soon realizes that he's walking alone and turns around.

"Gentlemen," Jimmy says. "Let's sit and have a chat. I know you've been wondering about us. You followed us from the Sea Change."

Tubby throws up his hands to say okay.

Chubby has a problem with that. He reaches behind his back.

"I wouldn't do that," Jimmy says, pointing a thick Miami Herald he picked up from the lobby table. "This newspaper has a magazine with 17 rounds. I wouldn't want to ruin your shirt."

Chubby brings his hand back in front of him.

"Hey, no problem," he says. "I was scratching my back."

"You da Chicago guys?" Tubby asks.

"You could say that." Jimmy motions to a small table and chairs. "We should talk to see what we have in common."

"Yeah, talk," Tubby says. "That's why we're here."

We briefly watch the flow of vacationers eager to make a show of spending money.

Tubby leans forward and extends his hand toward Nick.

"Sorry we got off on the wrong foot," he says. "The truth is we're worried about Billy. He's made some enemies, and that crazy bitch Bonnie isn't helping him."

"You might be right, there." Jimmy shakes his hand.

"My name is Cecil," Tubby says. He pronounces it *cess-el.* "We got the boat repair place on the Miami River." He hands out business cards.

Chubby offers his hand to me, and I shake with him.

"You can call me *Cease-el*," he says.

"Wait a minute," Jimmy says. "Both you guys are named C-e-c-i-l?"

"We're first cousins," Cess-el says. "Born two days apart. Named after grandpa. He pronounces it both ways. Our mothers figured to avoid confusion and still honor the old guy...."

"Okay," I say. "What can we do for you guys?"

"Billy said two guys were coming to help," Cease-el says. "Billy's worried about sharks, the two-legged kind."

"Any of them named Fuentes, Boyer, or Malone?" I ask.

"You got that right. We were down in the Keys with Billy and Mandingo. That's when we got a taste of how much could be riding on this deal."

I look at Jimmy. He has that what-the-hell look on his face.

"Deal? Why don't you tell us about it?"

Cease-el pulls a red velvet sack from his shirt pocket. He pours a dozen emeralds onto the table.

"I'll show you," he says. "These are out of Maroon Key. You're lookin' at twenty grand."

"Nice," I say.

"This could be chump change," Cease-el says. "We think there's way more."

Chapter 5

So, what sensible move should we make with these two guys?

Are they with us?

Are they against us?

Are they crooks?

“Are you hungry?” Jimmy asks. “It’s time for lunch. How about it?”

We make our way through Fontainebleau to an open-air cafe. It’s one of those very posh places. It has an accent mark over the name, so you know you’ll never pronounce it right. We grab a table under a large umbrella.”

Nice place,” Cease-el says. “Is the treat on you guys? If it ain’t, I know a decent pizza joint. Draft beer, too.”

“Not to worry, Cease-el,” Jimmy says. “We’re using the company credit card, so order up.”

“Fine with me,” Cease-el says. “You don’t have to do the Cease-el and Cess-el bit. That’s strictly for our family. Out in the real world, we go by Chuck and Buddy. I’m Chuck, and he’s Buddy. You can’t run a business driving your customers nuts trying to figure out your name.”

We order beers and take a look at the menu. Maine lobster and salads for Jimmy and Buddy. Chuck and I go for the Norwegian King Crab and vegetable flatbread.

“I was going to order the grilled octopus,” Chuck says. “Then I thought of that octopus that got washed up out of a drain into a parking garage. It was on Channel Seven News last night, swimming in a foot of seawater. Right down the road on Collins. You got people catching seafood in their condo parking space. Who needs a boat anymore?”

The main courses come, and we attack them.

I use the opportunity to further explain to Chuck and Buddy why we're here. I say, "My friend Jimmy knows real estate law. I'm just along to make snide comments and shoot people if they don't laugh."

Buddy nods his head and looks at Chuck. Chuck nods. They both laugh.

"Billy said help was on the way," Buddy says. "We've known him a long time. We work on his boats, and we go fishing with him. We have family members working for us. People we can trust. It gives us space to do things like take off for Bimini or the Keys."

A light sea breeze blows through the open-air restaurant. A flock of brown pelicans coasts past, looking for their lunch in the ocean.

"Could be you guys aren't getting the whole story," Chuck says. "It's true Billy would like to unload the Sea Change. He could use the money. Plus, it's becoming a pain in the ass, kinda like Bonnie. He's happy to get out on the boat with customers. He doesn't have to listen to her."

"What about this mysterious Maroon Key?" Jimmy asks. "What's the story there?"

"How 'bout we tell you over coffee and dessert?" Buddy laughs.

Our waitress soon arrives with mango basil mousse, peanut butter cheesecake, and two Key Lime gelato sandwiches. Coffee gets poured.

Chuck takes a bite from his cheesecake, sips his coffee, and begins.

"Billy keeps a couple of his boats at a small dock down in Marathon. He was going to call his business 'Marathon Key Marine,'" Chuck says. "Turns out someone else had that name. So, he changed the signage to 'Maroon Key Marine.' Could be when that's all the trouble started."

"It seems like name change keeps happening to Billy," I say. "What kind of trouble?"

"Depends on what your definition of the word maroon is," Chuck says. "There's the color maroon. Then there's maroon as in marooned at sea."

"We've heard of those," I say. "They don't sound like trouble to me. If anything, I think the name would attract tourists. It sounds like an adventure."

"True," Chuck says. "It's the other association with the word that drew the attention of people hard to deal with. Maroon was a word applied to runaway slaves in the Caribbean. Many of them set up separate communities. They had weapons and knew more about survival than their white owners. There was a group of Maroons in the Lower Keys back in the early 1800s. They salvaged ships lured by scavengers onto the reefs on the Gulf Stream side of the Keys. One was a ship bound for New Orleans from Haiti with jewels, gold, and rare artifacts. It never made it. Some say that treasure is still out there waiting to be found."

"Like emeralds?" I ask.

Chuck looks at Buddy. Buddy nods.

"Yeah, they could be from the Maroons, or maybe some other kind of maroon," Chuck says. "You heard of the *Atocha?*"

"I've heard that name," Jimmy says. "Give me a clue."

"It's the sunken Spanish treasure ship that they found back in the 1980s," Chuck says.

"It sank in 1622 in a big hurricane," Buddy says. "They found part of the treasure. They're still looking for a major part that was on the manifest. Officially, they list three survivors, two sailors, and a slave. Everyone else drowned, according to official records in Spain."

I look at Jimmy. He's interested.

"So, there could have been more survivors," I say. "People marooned with treasure from the ship."

"Yeah, maybe they made peace with the Indians who were here. They could have intermarried and hidden their treasure on one of the Keys," Chuck says.

"But Billy never started the business with that in mind," Buddy says. "It was for people who wanted a taste of the Keys back in the mangrove areas. There's a lot to see back there: good fishing, snorkeling, exotic birds, and shelling. Keys back there aren't accessible by road. You have to go by boat. The boats are shallow draft cruisers with inboard engines. There's also a Zodiac inflatable with a ten-horse for each cruiser."

"Sounds like it could be fun," I say.

"Yeah, Billy sells it as part of a package," Chuck says. "They stay at Sea Change for a few days, then they drive down to Marathon to the marina. The boats are easy to handle. They come supplied with food and drink. Most people come back with an all-over sunburn, some shells, and some good memories."

"I bet you'll tell us about a couple that had a different experience," Jimmy says.

Chuck takes another bite of dessert and smiles.

"They were different. A couple weeks back, a sharp-looking woman in her forties shows up at the Sea Change. She's got her twenty-five-year-old boyfriend, Ronnie, with her. His driver's license says Alabama. Hers says New York. Her platinum card is sound, so Billy figures what the hell. They behave except for her screaming, 'Oh, oh Ronnie,' and laughing like she's out of her head four times a day."

"Next guess," Jimmy says. "Billy sets them up with the boat deal down in the Keys."

Chuck nods, sips more coffee, and continues.

"They take the boat on a Wednesday and head for the keys north of the main chain. Sunday, Billy gets a call. The woman, Valerie Masters, is at the hospital down there. She's suffering from sunburn, insect bites, and bruises. She paddled her way back to Marathon in the Zodiac. Her 'lover' Ronnie is missing. He took off in the cruiser and left her in the inflatable with no gas."

"We go down there with Billy and Mandingo," Buddy says, picking up the story. "We figure it's a lover's quarrel. He got pissed and took off. She's not pressing charges. So, Billy figures we get the boat back, and everything will be fine. We head out in the other cruiser he has down there. Now we got two Zodiacs to search with once we get to the area where she tells us they were."

"It's shallow draft down there," Chuck says. "You're lucky if you have four feet of water under your boat. Sometimes you find a deep hole where there's lobster. Mostly, there's a lot of shoaling over. The Intracoastal Waterway used to run through that area all the way to Key West. Finally, the government gave up on maintaining it. They couldn't keep an eight-foot-deep channel. Now, the best channels through the area are marked with beer cans on a stick."

"And you got red mangrove trees," Buddy says. "They get to be twenty feet high. Everything else is flat. It's hard to see what's around the next bend, or even if there is one."

"Shit, we spent half the day looking for the cruiser," Chuck says. "It's hot, no breeze. About two o'clock, I hear Buddy yelling from one of the Zodiacs. He's found it, run up into the mangrove, grounded in half a foot of water."

"Any sign of Ronnie?" I ask.

"No Ronnie," Chuck says. "He left traces behind, though. There was blood on a gaff hook and bloody footprints on the deck. More blood was on the rail where he got off the boat. Other than that, no Ronnie."

"Just a minute," Jimmy says. "Ronnie cuts his foot on the gaff and decides to get off the boat? Where the hell could he go? How far could he get?"

"Not far," Chuck says. "With blood in the water, he's gonna draw sharks. Even without blood, getting through that mess is a long shot. He's miles away from civilization."

"We got on the hailer, shouting Ronnie's name," Buddy says. "For hours, we searched. No Ronnie. It was getting toward dusk. We decided to pull the cruiser out of where it was stuck to go back to Marathon. It was a real bitch. The boat was stuck in tree branches and sand. Finally, we got the cruiser and the two Zodiacs to pull together. We managed to get the boat unstuck. There was loose sand moving through the water, slapping up on the dry sand of where the mangrove stood. That's when we saw specks of bright green sprinkled in the sand."

"The emeralds," Jimmy says.

"Yeah, forty-eight total," Chuck says. "We marked the spot with a yellow float. We came back the next day. All we found was an old busted-up wooden crate. It had little mollusks growing on it. It could have floated up overnight from anywhere."

"When you got back to Marathon, did you file any report?" I ask.

"No," Buddy says. "We cleaned up the boat and figured it was a domestic between Valerie and Ronnie. Maybe she was lying. Maybe he came back with her. She wasn't anxious to talk."

"Yeah," Chuck says. "They had marine radio on the boat, but Billy never got notified by the Marine Patrol that anyone asked for help. Maybe Ronnie called friends who came and got him."

"After that, things got strange," Buddy says. "For months, the Sea Change's been on the market without any serious interest by anyone. Suddenly three guys are sniffing around."

"Let me guess," I say. "Fuentes, Boyer, and Malone."

Chuck and Buddy nod.

"So, who tipped them off?" I ask. "Did Ronnie alert them, or was Valerie Masters the one?"

"Hey," Buddy says. "Could've been that bitch, Bonnie.

Chapter 6

The company Visa card covers the five-hundred-dollar tab for lunch. After promising to stay in touch with Chuck and Buddy, we head to the Sea Change. Maybe Billy and Mandingo have made it back. We figure we're not on Bonnie's call list.

I drive the Jeep away from the Fontainebleau. Jimmy Cox, the human tote board, is riding shotgun. He's juggling the chances on what Chuck and Buddy told us at lunch.

"It's even odds," Jimmy says, "that Ronnie has made off with a piece of what was buried among the red mangroves. It's also even odds that Ronnie has succumbed to a large shark."

"Fifty-fifty on Ronnie," I say. "Did Valerie Masters also dip into the treasure?"

"Three to one, she helped herself," Jimmy says. "Let's say they each grab a dozen emeralds and come to blows over the last shiny green rock in the sand."

"If Valerie is three to one on grabbing jewels," I ask, "did Ronnie get whacked by Valerie with the gaff? Maybe it wasn't his foot that bled. Maybe his head?"

"Yeah," Jimmy says. "Maybe he didn't make it to dry land. Maybe he made it to a shark."

"Which one of these characters spilled the beans to Fuentes, Boyer, and Malone?" I ask.

"Cuban-American fascist, Haitian voodoo thug, and American dope runner," Jimmy says. "Let's say that both Ronnie and Valerie grabbed some loot and managed to survive. They each tell their favorite bad guy about it. I don't think they're going to tell two favorite bad guys or all three. All three bad guys hate each other."

"So, someone else blabbed," I say. "Three blabbers, three fortune hunters."

"Yeah, I got a feeling about Bonnie," Jimmy says as we drive up Collins Avenue. "She knows more than she lets on. That was the bum's rush she gave us back at the Sea Change."

"So, Billy spills the story on the emeralds to Bonnie?" I ask.

"Sounds right," Jimmy says. "We need to know more about Billy. What's at stake? Is this a favor? Or does Jacky have a piece of the action down here?"

The pond of seawater covering half the road is an excellent place to pull over to call the boss. Though the sign says, "No Parking," it doesn't seem like a cop will wade over to ticket us.

Jacky answers on the first ring.

"You guys getting your feet wet on the Uncle Billy situation?" He asks.

We both manage a loud laugh for the boss.

Jimmy recaps our day. He reels off king tides, an alligator in the pool, gun-happy Bonnie, and missing Billy. Jacky responds with, "Hmm," "Oh," "That's interesting," and "Goddamn it."

Then we get to the Chuck and Buddy tale. The emeralds on some far-off Key starring Valerie and Ronnie gets a different response.

"This isn't just some real estate transaction, is it?"

"No," Jimmy says. "Do we have a piece of the action here, or should we cut and go home?"

"No," Jacky says. "We hold the title on the Sea Change. In fact, we're owners of the boats. Billy's been trying to make a go of things. I wanted him to make money off the fishing charters. If someone wanted to buy the Sea Change at a reasonable price, we'd sell before the place drowned. Billy could walk away with a nice piece of the profits, and we'd get the lion's share."

"Where does Bonnie fit into this?" I ask. "Does she have ownership in anything?"

"No," Jacky says. "Neither Billy nor Bonnie have any ownership. Billy's manager of Sea Change. He owned it once, but that was before we bailed him out. Some developers could build a mid-rise condo where the Sea

Change sits. Even with the town going underwater, there's still those who will take a chance on turning a profit."

"Yeah," Jimmy says. "Harry Feldstein was saying just that. He says once he cashes in, he's off to Puerto Vallarta with Colette."

"Harry's smart," Jacky says. "He'll do it. Listen, do some more digging. Find out more about the players. Let me know if you need help."

Before we can answer, the line is dead.

"How are we figuring this one out?" Jimmy asks. "Should we make appointments with the three treasure rivals to see their offer on the Sea Change? That's not what they're after."

"No," I say. "They think Billy owns the Sea Change. If they offer enough, he'll take the money. If they add more for directions to where the emeralds are, Billy walks with more. The problem is Billy doesn't own anything. The treasure hunters have to deal with Chicago."

We get to the Sea Change. Inside the office, Bonnie sits in her red two-piece swimsuit with her bare feet up on the counter. She's talking to someone on the speakerphone.

"Is that the price for the week?" the voice from the speaker asks.

"The week," Bonnie says. "Think it over and let us know."

"I will," the voice says and rings off.

"Billy called," Bonnie says. "They got a charter in Bimini. They're going after Marlin. Here's his phone number. He's hard to get hold of sometimes. Keep trying."

She hands Jimmy a card with the number.

The office phone rings again. Bonnie lights a cigarette and presses the answer button on the speakerphone.

"Sea Change. May I help you?"

"This is Detective Anna Clark with the Monroe County Sheriff's Office in Key West. We're looking for information on the late Ronald Nolan. We found your card in his apartment. Has he been a guest at your establishment?"

Bonnie slides her bright red toenails off the countertop and sits up straight.

"Uh, I'd have to look that up and get back to you. Can I have your number?"

Jimmy grabs two cards off the desk and writes the number on each. He hands one to Bonnie and pockets the other.

"I called once before last week. Was it you I talked to?" Detective Clark asks.

"Uh, no," Bonnie says. "That might have been Melinda. People say we sound alike."

"Well, I'd appreciate your help with this. Call me with anything you find."

The dial tone sounds loud through the speakerphone. Bonnie presses the button with her red-painted fingernail to turn it off. For half a minute, it's quiet. The silence is broken by people splashing and laughing in the pool outside the office.

Bonnie turns to look at us and lights another cigarette. She forgets about the one burning in the souvenir gator and palm tree ashtray.

"We get calls like that," she says. "Lots of dead beats come through town. They rack up debts and get in trouble with the cops. We don't like to get involved with cops."

"Nor do we," Jimmy says. "Here's what you're gonna do, Melinda. Dig out receipts and anything else you have on Valerie Masters and Ronnie Nolan. We want copies of everything."

"Melinda?" Bonnie puffs on her cigarette.

She tries to compose herself. She looks at her red leather shoulder bag. It's hanging on a hook, out of reach. I figure that's where her gun is, the .38 Smith & Wesson she says Billy gave her. The one she says she uses to shoot street thugs.

"Uh-uh." I shake my head. "No funny stuff, Melinda."

"Melinda? I'm not Melinda," Bonnie says. "Like I told that cop, we sound alike."

"Let's say that you'll do until Melinda shows up," Jimmy says.

"Why should I do what you want me to do?"

"Because." Jimmy slams his hand on the counter. "We're not asking you. We're telling you."

Chapter 7

"We know about the green rocks," Jimmy says to Bonnie. "And we know about Valerie and Ronnie, so don't play like we're stupid. As far as reaching for that red shoulder bag you've been eyeing, I'm saying forget it. Six-to-one says there's a Smith & Wesson .38 onboard that you'd love to have in your hand."

Bonnie takes a drag from her cigarette and looks at the bag, then back toward us.

"A girl has a right to protect herself," she says. "I don't know you guys. You say you're from Vegas. I've met guys from Vegas. They're sleaze bags. They're after money and pussy, and they don't care how they get it."

"Nice try," Jimmy says. "Did you rehearse that along with the Innocent Girl from New Hampshire act? The one who has no trouble pumping lead into soul brothers?"

"Not so innocent," Bonnie says. "This town screws you royal. You come for the perfect tan and parties on the beach. One day, you realize you're carrying a gun to buy a loaf of bread. You're not alone. The guy behind the counter is packing heat, too."

"Yeah, touching," Jimmy says. "Any way you slice this, you're withholding evidence. That cop who called sounds like she's got a dead Ronnie Nolan on her hands. You want me to call her back and tell her you might be involved?"

"Hey, wait a minute," Bonnie says.

"Wait a minute for what?" Jimmy says. "That fat-assed cop that was here earlier? The one you gave shit to over that gator. He'd love to deliver your ass to Key West. If they bring a search warrant, what else will they find here?"

Bonnie reaches for another cigarette.

Jimmy's doing fine with the bad cop act. It's time for the concerned Nick to play good cop.

"Jimmy," I say. "Bonnie thinks that Billy is the owner of the Sea Change and the boats. She doesn't know Chicago owns everything, even the chair she's sitting in. Give her a break, Jimmy. She needs time to absorb reality."

Bonnie sits without speaking for a moment. Her eyes dart between Jimmy and me.

"You're saying that all this belongs to someone else? Billy told me he owned it. I saw tax papers. The business license...."

"Yeah, maybe you saw that," Jimmy says. "You didn't see how everything was over-leveraged to Chicago. It's all far into the red."

"The boats, too?" Bonnie asks.

Jimmy nods.

"We're not here to give you grief," he says. "If there's a way to straighten things out, we'd like to find it. We need your cooperation. As far as the rocks you and Billy have, that's a separate issue. You found them; you keep them."

"You've been talking with the Townsends?" she asks.

"We have," Jimmy says. "They showed us their emeralds."

"The guys sat right here, the night they got back from Maroon Key," Bonnie says. "They'd been trying to find Ronnie Nolan and the boat he stole. Billy, Mandingo, and the two Townsends. They had the jewels in a small bait bucket. They spilled them out right here on the counter. I about died. They're so damn beautiful. Stuff you dream about."

"We saw the Townsends' emeralds," Jimmy says. "They are beautiful."

"Yeah, I know they're pissed at me," Bonnie says. "I don't know what got into me. The guys agreed to a four-way split. I thought that we should have a bigger share, Billy and me. It was our boats they used. At least I thought they were our boats."

"I could see your point if it had started out as an agreement to hunt for treasure," Jimmy says. "Some contracts have people getting two- or three-percent of the haul. The captain gets more than some guy scraping barnacles."

Bonnie gets up from her chair and reaches into a file cabinet.

"Let me see what I can find on Ronnie and Valerie," she says. "I'll dig out mail we have from Fuentes, Boyer, and Malone. They sent letters. I'll make you copies."

"This could be so simple," Jimmy says as we drive away from the Sea Change. "We connect with all three of these guys who are interested in Sea Change and the Maroon Key Marine business. The highest bidder gets it all, and everyone else walks. Billy gets a nice piece of the pie, and he and Bonnie can take the jewels and go off somewhere."

"Yeah," I say. "Everyone will forget about eighty grand in emeralds Billy and the boys found in the Keys. Think about it. Something triggered interest in what they think Billy's holding. Did Ronnie and Valerie find treasure on their trip through the Keys? Is that what they fought over?"

My questions hang in the air as we drive through a foot-high puddle of seawater.

"Or, maybe they didn't fight," Jimmy says. "Maybe Valerie hauls Ronnie off to Key West with a sample of the loot. They leave the cruiser in the mangrove to mark the spot, figuring they'll get back to get more treasure. The Zodiac with an extra can of fuel could take them there with no sweat. Maybe they line up some help. The help turns on them when they get back to the mangrove. Ronnie gets the gaff, and Valerie gets whacked around before escaping to the Zodiac. That's how she got the bruises. Somewhere in route, she runs out of gas and has to paddle the rest of the way to the Marina."

"Okay," I say. "What else?"

"What do I know about Valerie and Ronnie?" Jimmy says. "I don't have their financials or their blood types, but maybe I have enough. She's wealthy enough to pay for a ten-day tryst with Ronnie the stud, who's half her age. According to the registration papers from the Sea Change, Valerie lists her address as New York City. We may have to go up there to get the real lowdown. Ronnie's license says Alabama, but maybe he's been in the beach and bar scene in South Florida for a while. He didn't just show up outside Sea Change with a sign that said, 'Gigolo for Rent.'"

"True," I say.

"If Ronnie runs true to form, "Jimmy says, "he steals off his marks. He takes their watch, hocks it, and runs up their credit cards. He probably hangs with skunks of a similar stripe, his so-called friends."

"You don't think Ronnie's friends would turn on him and Valerie?" I ask.

"Only in a New York minute," Jimmy says.

"The friends come back to the cruiser anchored in the mangroves," I say. "Maybe they're in a small skiff. It could be late, or they don't have the equipment to hunt for emeralds. So, to mark the spot, they run the cruiser into the mangroves. They get Ronnie and haul his ass off. Valerie grabs the Zodiac and takes off in the dark. Ronnie's friends think they'll return the next day. Only they get delayed. When they return, Billy and the boys have retrieved the boat."

"I like it so far," Jimmy says. "When Billy and the guys find the cruiser, they pull it out of the mangrove. That's when they find the emeralds. But when they go back, they find an old crate washed up with barnacles on it. No more emeralds. What happened?"

"Remember how they got the cruiser out of the mangrove," I say. "There were three boats with motors on full throttle pushing water and sand around. When the cruiser came free, they found the emeralds washed up on the sand. The motors pushed them from somewhere under the boats. Prop wash put the jewels on the beach."

"But there were emeralds on the beach when Ronnie and Valerie first showed up," Jimmy says.

"They anchored near the mangrove," I say. "Some new boaters try to motor off with the anchor still holding. You can run the motor like mad. All you'll do is churn up sand."

"And maybe treasure from a wrecked Spanish galleon or a ship out of Haiti," Jimmy says. "The theory works for me. Now, all we got to do is fill in with the facts."

Chapter 8

Back at the Fontainebleau, we take an afternoon swim in the pool to clear our heads. Then it's upstairs to our suite to hash out our next move. Room service delivers food and coffee. There's a lot to think about, and many facts are missing.

"Uncle Billy, for one," Jimmy says. "Isn't Billy the reason that we're here? Think about it. Someone comes to bail your ass out, and what do you do? Take off for Bimini?"

I look out to our balcony and east into the dark blue Atlantic. Somewhere out there is Bimini and Uncle Billy, from what we've been led to believe.

"How many times have we tried that number that Bonnie gave us?" I ask.

"At least six times," Jimmy says. "No answer. Yet, he's supposedly called Bonnie on that cell phone earlier today."

Jimmy picks up a business card from the coffee table.

"I'm calling the Townsends," he says, punching numbers into his phone.

I nod as we wait for the phone to be answered.

"Hello, Chuck, Jimmy Cox, with a question. We got a cell phone number to contact Billy. We're having trouble getting anyone to answer it. Could it be we've got the wrong number?"

Jimmy recites the number to Chuck and clicks the phone setting to speaker.

"I remember that phone," Chuck says. "We used that number to call Billy a few times. We were out fishing the Gulf Stream off Pompano a few weeks back. Bonnie must have called him a dozen times. He got pissed. Plus, we weren't catching fish. Finally, he threw the phone off the stern. He said a hammerhead shark could answer Bonnie's next call."

"Did he get another phone?" Jimmy asks.

"Not that I know," Chuck says. "He's always borrowing someone else's."

"What about Mandingo? He have a phone?"

"Maybe a burner, but he never gave us a number," Chuck says. "Mandingo ain't exactly legal. He's strictly cash. Seems like a decent guy. He gets along with Buddy and me. He's done some spot welding for us at our business, but it's always work for cash, off the books."

I look at Jimmy. He's shaking his head.

"I'm taking a guess," Chuck says. "I bet it was Bonnie that gave you that number."

"Yeah," Jimmy says.

"It figures," Chuck says. "You know the night we brought the emeralds back from the Keys, she made a play for the whole batch. Bonnie thought we were yokels. 'We should keep them all together,' she says. 'I'll put them in a safe deposit box at the bank until we can have the collection appraised.' We said a quick 'nuts to that.' Me and Buddy took off with our share. I don't know if she grabbed the emeralds from Billy and Mandingo."

"It was a four-way split," Jimmy says. "Did each of you get like what you showed us?"

"Yeah, that was mine. I had it appraised for twenty to twenty-two thousand. Buddy's came out to about five hundred more."

"Then the total was well over eighty big ones," Jimmy says.

"Yeah, I'm guessing Billy isn't back in from Boca yet?" Chuck asks.

"I thought he was headed to Bimini," Jimmy says. "Bonnie said he picked up another charter there. Marlin fishing."

"Bonnie says a lot of things," Chuck says. "Billy took the boat to Boca for a high-tech company get-together. They bring everyone down for a week of fishing, drinking, and whoring. Billy was one of eight boats there for a couple days. He should have been back yesterday. The Maroon Key is due in here for a bottom job and a tune-up."

"It doesn't seem right that he's not back," Jimmy says.

"Yeah, to me neither," Chuck says. "Billy wanted the Maroon Key to be in top shape to go down to the Keys and take another shot at getting more treasure. He knew that his nephew in Chicago was sending help. He figured we'd have three large boats and the two Zodiacs. Plenty of room for equipment and supplies."

"I wonder if he ran into some trouble," Jimmy says.

"Yeah, could be," Chuck says. "Maybe he found a hot-blooded bimbo up there. If he gets in touch, let us know. We'll do the same."

"Will do," Jimmy says and rings off.

A half-hour later, we're back at the Sea Change. The courtyard at night looks exotic if you don't look closely at the chipped paint and rusty railings. Colored lights and a couple of flaming tiki torches cast a tropical glow off the pool. Off to one side, three people sit at a table. I remember them from earlier when the animal control guy dragged the gator out of the pool area. The two women had shuffleboard sticks in their hands. The guy was the one with the red fire ax.

We head toward the office and see the door is wide open. We stop as the guy approaches.

"Say, fellas," the red fire ax guy says. "You don't know where Bonnie is, do you? She left the phone ringer connected to the speaker over the pool. Every time it rings, it sounds like a fire alarm. A few minutes ago, it must've rung twenty times. I finally went in to take a message."

"Bonnie's nowhere around?" Jimmy asks.

"No, at first, I figured that she might be in their apartment. I went to knock. No one there, and the door was hanging wide open."

"When did you last see her?" I ask.

"Shortly after you guys left her office, she took off. Tossed a big duffle bag into the trunk of her red Mustang. At first, I thought she was going to do laundry. But that didn't make sense. There's washers and dryers here."

"You answered the phone," Jimmy says. "Any message?"

"Yeah, the guy asked if I was Billy. I told him I was just a guy who got tired of hearing the phone ring. Then he wanted to know if Bonnie was around. I said she was out. Could I take a message? Yeah, he says. Tell her that Vinnie called."

"Anything else?" Jimmy asks.

"He said he'd be seeing her later."

The red fire ax guy's name turns out to be Walter White. I ask him if he's seen *Breaking Bad*.

“Only watched the whole series about five times,” he says. “It’s pretty far-fetched. Those Hollywood guys can make up good stories.”

“We’re vice presidents from the home office of the Sea Change,” Jimmy says, making up a good story of his own. “We’re here for renovation work. Thanks for taking the message.”

“No problem.”

Walter White leaves, and we enter the office.

It looks like when we left earlier in the day, except the red leather bag with Bonnie’s gun is missing. A check of the cash drawer reveals empty slots except for the coin compartments. There are empty hangers in Bonnie’s side of the closet in the apartment and empty drawers. We figure whatever’s missing belonged to her.

“The Bonnie bird is on the wing,” Jimmy says. “How do you feel about us becoming the new managers of the Sea Change?”

“And move from the Fontainebleau?” I ask. “You must be nuts.”

Chapter 9

We sit in the messy Sea Change office, drinking beers from Uncle Billy's rusty fridge.

"What did we do to earn this?" Jimmy asks. "Jacky made it sound like a piece of cake: 'Go down to Florida and take care of a real estate deal. You guys will get to go fishing for marlin.'"

"Yeah, sure," I say. "Now we're fishing for Uncle Billy, or whatever's left of him."

"How are we supposed to take care of this joint and figure out the rest of this mess?" Jimmy asks. "Throwing out the guests and shutting the place down doesn't seem good. Someone still has to keep an eye on the Sea Change."

We look around the office. It's loaded with dusty souvenir ashtrays and postcards from forty years back. It's the most visible part of our colossal mess.

"We could call Jacky," Jimmy says. "But you know what will happen. He'll send the Papaleo brothers down here from Chicago. That's all we need. Those two bozos would love to stagger in here and load the place up with hookers."

"Yeah, well, we need someone. We should be able to choose our own bozos," I say.

My cell phone rings.

It's Harry Feldstein.

I put the phone on speaker.

"My missus is telling me that I gave you guys the bum's rush earlier today," Harry says. "Colette thought you guys were gonna stick around so we could take you to lunch or go out for dinner. When she got back from her tennis lesson, you guys were gone already."

Before I can reply, Colette cuts into the conversation.

"Let me talk to the boys, Harry," she says. "The boys flew from Las Vegas to straighten out with Billy and that bimbo he got involved with. The least we could do is help with the advice. How are we doing that when you let them get away without hearing from Colette, eh?"

For a moment, it seems like the call is between Colette and Harry. We're listening in on a wiretap. Between Harry's Chicagoese and Colette's Frenglish, the exchange becomes hotdog *escargot.*

"Yeah, I wanted them to stay, Colette. The boys were busy doing a thing, you know, for Jacky. *Capisce?* You want I should spell it out for you so the phone company can call the IRS or those assholes at the FBI?"

"Oh, Harry, *je ne sais quoi.* You think I am someone with the loose mouth? *Je ne sais pas pourquoi* the boys don't receive help in this? Then we are friends of the fair weather, *n'est-ce pas?*"

Harry insists he and Colette are not friends of the fair weather.

"Jesus, Colette, let's talk to the guys, see if they can use our help."

We give Harry and Colette a thumbnail sketch of the Sea Change in our best Chicagoese.

Bonnie left with a self-determined and self-bestowed severance package. Billy is overdue at sea. We don't fancy running the joint while working out everything else. Plus, there could be more than a little something in this deal for those who help. *Capisce?*

They *capisce.*

Fifteen minutes later, Harry and Colette have *capisced* their way into the Sea Change.

"The office, it is, *je ne sais quoi,* a pen for a pig," Colette announces as she walks in. "Did that trollop Bonnie leave it like this?"

"The only thing she cleaned out was the cash register," Jimmy says.

"*Merde,*" Colette says. "This Bonnie bimbo is criminal, yes?"

"She is criminal, yes," I say.

I look at Jimmy. He grins.

Harry grabs a beer from the fridge. He looks at his wife, smiles, and shrugs.

Before Colette can tear apart Bonnie anymore, the office door opens. It's Walter White.

"I don't know if this means anything now that you're taking over for your main office," he says. "The day I checked in, a week ago, Bonnie was telling that guy with the big boat to take off and never come back. Maybe he owed some dock rent."

"Big boat?" Jimmy asks.

"Yeah, it said 'Maroon Key' on the back. A big black guy untied the lines and jumped on. An older guy with a beard drove the boat. The older guy had tattoos on his arms."

"That sounds like Billy," Harry says. "Always wears an old Miami Dolphins ball cap."

"That's the guy," Walter White says. "Check your records. Could be a business deduction there."

"Tres bien," Colette says, rising from behind the counter. "I am Colette Feldstein. I will be managing Sea Change with my assistant manager Harry."

"Wonderful," White says. "No emergency, but if you could send clean towels to unit eight...."

"No problem," Colette says. "I'll have Harry bring some down *toute de suite.*"

"Great, happy to meet you, Colette." White turns and leaves.

"Hey," Harry says once the door shuts. "We didn't come here to take over this joint. We wanted to help you guys."

"No sweat," Jimmy says. "We need you to run this joint while we find if Billy's still breathing. There could be trouble. Some characters are pushing themselves into the situation."

"You mean like the hip-hop break dancers that tried to rob my payroll in Chicago?" Harry asks. "I still have the 9 mm. Beretta. I've got the leaded baseball bat, too."

I remember the headline from the *Sun-Times.* **"Robbery Victim Fights Back, Three Thugs Shot Dead, One in Coma."** A quote from the story had Harry saying, "What was I going to do, wait for the Chicago cops? Getting robbed once in a day was enough."

"We want you to know, Harry," Jimmy says. "There's a lot more to this deal than selling the Sea Change and a few boats. We found new info on that Maroon Key stuff down in the Keys."

"I knew there was something big down there," Harry says. "If there's any action, I want in."

"Sans doute, it has something to do with this?" Colette asks, holding up a green stone. "Just now, I found this on the floor."

Chapter 10

"*Emeraude?*" Colette says, holding up the green gem from the dusty floor of the Sea Change office.

"Pretty sure that's what it is," Jimmy says. "We didn't want to get specific on the phone. We can tell you what we know now that you're here."

"You mean there's more than one emerald?" Harry asks. "We're interested. This Bonnie runs off with all the cash from the register. Did she take emeralds with her, too?"

I'm about to tell the whole story as we know it when the office phone rings.

Jimmy hits the speaker button and says, "Sea Change, may I help you?"

"This is Detective Alberto Cortez from the Miami-Dade Police Department. We have a problem regarding one of the boats registered at your business."

"This is Jimmy Cox," Jimmy says. "I'm the corporate representative for Sea Change. How can I help you?"

"You have a sportfishing boat called the Maroon Key. I can give you the registration number...."

"Not necessary," Jimmy says. "That sounds like our boat. What's up?"

"The vessel was found adrift in Government Cut, just off South Beach. It's been towed to the Coast Guard Station. There were two deceased males on board, victims of gunshot wounds. We need to talk to anyone who knows the boat and anyone who can identify the two bodies."

We get the directions to the boat and say we'll be there in a half-hour.

"Shit," Harry says after we hang up. "Billy and Mandingo. I could ID them. I don't think you guys have met them."

He's right. We'll drive Harry and Colette down to the boat.

"Harry, before we leave, I want to say something," Colette says.

"What, you're worried about us getting involved?"

"No," Colette says. "Take the fresh towels down to that nice man in unit eight, *n'est-ce pas?*"

The half-hour we promised Detective Cortez turns into an hour in nighttime traffic through South Beach. Everyone's out enjoying clubs and restaurants. Hookers are out working the street. Performers on one street corner sing Jimmy Buffett songs. A block down, a group of conga drummers play to the crowd. People step around puddles of seawater in the streets.

"South Florida is drowning," Harry says.

"California's on fire," Jimmy says.

"And Vegas is slowly dying of thirst," I say.

"At least we are pooling the car tonight," Colette says. "We all could be driving alone, no?"

We make our way along MacArthur Causeway to the Terminal Island turnoff. It's not hard to find Detective Cortez and the Maroon Key. Two cop cars and other vehicles are parked next to the boat. Evidence techs are examining the vessel.

"You Cortez?" I ask.

"Yeah, what can I do for you?" He's a husky cop who looks like he's never missed a meal but still has a lot of muscle.

"You called the Sea Change," Harry says. "You wanted to know if we knew about the boat or could identify the victims."

"Are you Jimmy Cox?"

"No, I'm Harry Feldstein. Cox and Nick here are from the home office in Chicago. They've never met anyone down here who might be the victims you want an ID on. I think I might know both of them. My wife has met one of them."

"You're local?"

"Yeah, we live at Coral Surf Beach and Tennis Club. I've been out on this boat before, fishing for marlin in the Gulf Stream."

"We got a report earlier in the evening that the boat was at Miami Beach Marina," Cortez says. "There was a loud argument onboard. Security told them to settle down. Someone left the boat shortly after and got into a taxi. When security next checked the dock, they found the boat with its motor on, idling away from the dock. The dock lines had been cut. The tide took the boat into Government Cut. The Coast Guard was notified. They towed it here and called us when they saw the bodies and all the blood."

"Who wants to look at the victims for a positive ID?" Cortez asks. "Step over to the gurneys."

"I don't know if I can bear to see Billy dead from a gunshot," Colette says.

"Then stay here," Harry says. "I'll go look."

"I'll tag along," Jimmy says.

I make it a trio, even though I wouldn't know Billy or Mandingo from a lamppost.

Cortez nods at the attendant standing between the gurneys. He unzips the body bag down to the victim's waist. He's taken one to the head and one to the chest. There's a lot of blood.

"That ain't Billy or Mandingo," Harry says. "This guy's a ninety-pound weakling on heroin."

"I would've said a hundred," Cortez says. "You're probably right about the heroin."

The victim is appropriately laid out in a greasy and blood-stained T-shirt proclaiming, "University of Miami Track Team."

"That shirt should say, 'Tracks Team,'" Jimmy says. "Look at the needle marks on his arms."

We focus on the second gurney. A nod from Cortez and the bag is unzipped.

"This guy ain't Billy either," Harry says. "Is that lipstick and rouge on his face?"

"I couldn't say," Cortez says. "I'm guessing he's not the other guy you mentioned?"

"No," Harry says. "I've never seen either of these two. They weren't carrying any ID?"

"No, we'll try for a match on prints or DNA if it comes to it," Cortez says. "Tell me about your boat. How did these guys get hold of it?"

Jimmy tells Cortez that the boat pulled away from the Sea Change a week ago. That's the last time anyone we know has seen Billy or Mandingo.

"We figured they were out fishing," Jimmy says. "That's what Billy's wife Bonnie told us earlier today when we first got here from Vegas."

"This Bonnie?" Cortez asks. "Why isn't she down here? She ain't worried about this Billy?"

"You could say she's in the wind," Jimmy says. "She unloaded the company cash register early today and took off. She's part of the reason we're down here. Things at the Sea Change are up for grabs. Our boss in Chicago is thinking of dumping the property."

"Can't say I blame him," Cortez says. "You can file a 'Missing Persons' on this Billy and the other one if you want. Here's a card. Your boat'll be tied up while we investigate. You may want to tell your boss about that."

We give Cortez our business cards. Harry writes his number on the back of mine, and soon we're making our way back through the good timers clogging the streets of South Beach.

"How the hell did those two pieces of shit end up dead on the Maroon Key?" Harry asks.

"Good question," Jimmy says. "Maybe a better one is who killed them?"

"Yeah," I say. "I wonder if the same people killed Billy, too."

Chapter 11

All the way back to the Sea Change, I wonder about the mess we left at the Coast Guard Station. How does the Maroon Key end up idling down Government Cut with two stiffs onboard? Both shot one to the head and one to the chest. These aren't your high rollers who didn't pay large gambling chits. No. The two victims are a junky and an overly made-up drag queen from some bargain-basement gay bar.

Somehow, they got on the boat, got into a heated argument with someone, and got themselves shot. Whoever shot the two losers got away. The Maroon Key, its dock lines cut, idled away from the marina into Government Cut.

"Who the hell cuts dock lines?" Jimmy asks as we drive up Collins Avenue. "You toss them off from the dock cleat."

"How the hell did the Maroon Key get down there to that marina?" Harry asks. "Billy wouldn't take it there. He hates those phonies in South Beach."

There are conflicting stories about Billy. Bonnie's version has him in the Bahamas going after marlin. Chuck Townsend says Billy and Mandingo took the Maroon Key to Boca for a tech convention. Walter White says Billy took off on the Maroon Key a week ago after an argument with Bonnie.

We decide to go back to the Sea Change and lock up. Colette says she'll tape her cell number to the window. There may be inquiries before she and Harry come back mid-morning.

All is quiet except for the sound of a couple late-night talk shows coming from two of the apartments. The office is a mess, but not much different than when we left it. One thing is new, the flashing red light on the phone indicates someone has left a message. Colette hits the answer button and presses the speaker.

"Yeah, Cesar Fuentes calling for Billy. There's been a few developments, my friend. As you know, I'm interested in making you a nice offer. Don't want you to get hurt on the deal, so we should talk about Sea Change and Maroon Key. Especially Maroon Key. I'll be at the Scarlet Tide tomorrow afternoon. You can reach me there. I urge you to show."

"That's his South Beach bar," Harry says. "It's part tourist trap, part halfway house for Raiford Prison alums. There's a fifty-fifty chance you won't get out the door without someone trying to sell you drugs. There's been a few busts, but the charges usually get dropped. Our boy Fuentes gets special treatment from local cops and judges."

"A crooked politician bar owner?" Jimmy says. "What is this world of ours coming to?"

"Is fun to make jokes, yes?" Colette says. "We need to put in order the mess of Billy and this Bonnie trollop, no?"

"She's right," Jimmy says. "This place should at least be worth whatever Jacky has invested in it. As far as I can see, it's an ongoing business. People in eight units are paying to stay here, and this Fuentes at least wants to talk about an offer."

"I know a guy that does locksmithing," Harry says. "He's reasonable. I could get him in here tomorrow. We need to protect Jacky's investment. We'll stop at our bank in the morning and get enough cash to run the register. Hell, we couldn't give change right now for the Coke machine."

"You are wrong on that, Harry," Colette says. "In the cash tray, left behind from the Bonnie thief are maybe three dollars in the change. And under that are some numbers on a cash register receipt."

She hands it to me. It looks like someone's worried about taking a big loss, and I mean big. The top line reads, "$24,669,543," followed by the line underneath, "-81,695,045."

"Someone is taking a huge hit on something," Jimmy says after a cursory glance at the figures. "Somewhere in the neighborhood of fifty-seven million bucks. This place can't be worth that much. I know Jacky wouldn't go in that deep. Not on a place like this."

We lock up. Harry and Colette head to their condo. Jimmy and I head for the Fontainebleau.

"Is your head swimming?" Jimmy asks as we work our way along Collins Avenue.

"It's ass-backward," I say. "But going on what we know, someone put the Maroon Key into that marina. And someone shot those two upstanding citizens. Were they shot to silence them?"

"Probably," Jimmy says. "You don't want those two around to tell tales."

"What kind of tales?"

"They weren't charter customers of dear old Uncle Billy," Jimmy says. "Maybe they went up to Boca, stole the Maroon Key, and brought it down here. For all we know, Billy and Mandingo are gator bait in some swamp up there."

"So, 'Tracks Team' and 'Drag Queen' are told to take the boat out and sink it somewhere? Maybe they have a small dinghy to get back to shore? Maybe the dinghy gets loose. They head for South Beach because that's close to their employers, where they think they can get some help?"

"Yeah," Jimmy says. "Those two showing up with a stolen boat means something has to be done to cover up. The first thing is to pump two into each of the two cut-rate pirates. Hell, that's cheaper than paying them. Maybe before that can happen, there's an argument between the two. Should they call their contact or leave the boat and run away? That's when security gets involved, probably asking them if they're registered at the marina. Do they have identification? You know the drill."

"Yeah, security leaves," I say. "Our shooter arrives and pops them each twice. He takes their identification and starts the engine on the boat, putting the throttle at idle speed and setting the rudder to get it out of the marina. He jumps off. The boat tugs on the dock lines, so they're impossible to toss off the cleats."

"No matter," Jimmy says. "A sharp razor or a stiletto does the trick. The Maroon Key eases itself out into Government Cut."

"Okay, wise guy," I say as we pull into the driveway at the Fontainebleau. "We've figured that part out. What about the rest of it?"

"If you mean the part about who paid for the hit? What happened to Uncle Billy and Mandingo? How do Bonnie, Fuentes, the Haitian Voodoo guy, and Vinnie Malone figure into all this? That might take a bit longer. We should sleep on it."

Chapter 12

"I always knew Uncle Billy would be a problem," Jacky says after hearing our report on our first day in South Florida.

From background sounds on his end, I know that he's sitting on his balcony, looking down at Lake Shore Drive and Lake Michigan.

"There's a downside to this deal if we don't protect what's ours," he says. "On the other hand, there's a definite upside to it if the thing about the emeralds pans out."

I look across the glass table at Jimmy. The burner phone set to "speaker" sits next to the large coffee carafe that room service has delivered. A hundred yards or so, just over the railing, is the bright blue Atlantic. It's an excellent morning for being on Miami Beach if you don't have to play for the visiting team in a game featuring Voodoo, alligators, and bullets.

"I don't know the players in this game," Jacky says. "Billy could have let it go how he's connected, or maybe he didn't. One thing I do know is we don't get anywhere by letting some cheesy punks push us around."

Jimmy rolls his eyes at me and shakes his head.

"What are your thoughts?" I ask.

"I'm giving them to you," Jacky says. "Hold onto your shirts."

"Maybe we need to look around more," Jimmy says. "You know, see what develops."

"I can see what's developing," Jacky says. "You two think you can ward off the whole group of crazies down there by yourselves? Think again. Sure, Harry's tough, and Colette, God bless her. She's a smart cookie. I'm sending down some help."

I look at Jimmy. He's tossed both hands into the air and sunk into his chair. I know what he's dreading. The Papaleo brothers turning a bad hand into a total bust.

But Jacky is unpredictable.

"You know Bruno and his girlfriend Angie could be what we need down there," Jacky says.

I start to talk when Jimmy cuts in. Jacky wants to send the company arsonist and a crooked Blackjack dealer to Miami Beach to help straighten things out. I don't know whether to grin or laugh out loud.

"Yeah, we could make that work," Jimmy says. He silently mouths, *"It's not the Papaleo brothers."*

"It'll give you guys a little support," Jacky says.

"It's nice to have things in place if we have to do a proper pull-out," Jimmy says.

"Yeah, that too," Jacky says. "I'm not thinking of a retreat, though. I want to win this game."

I take out the receipt slip Colette found in the Sea Change cash register drawer.

"We found a receipt at the Sea Change with some numbers on it. It looks like someone has invested twenty-four million and change in something, but more than eighty-one million is owed against that. You know anything about that?"

"No, that doesn't sound like anything we're in," Jacky says. "Sea Change isn't worth twenty-four million, and no way there's eighty-one million in liabilities. We hold all the paper on Sea Change. We just pay normal bills. As far as Billy is concerned, he's out of the picture. He's an interesting character but not much of a businessman."

"When Bruno and Angie get here, we'll put them up at Sea Change," Jimmy says. "That can take some pressure off Harry and Colette."

"Bruno needs to look over the place in case we have to make a big renovation," Jacky says. "He just did a renovation in Houston. He's sitting on his fat butt. I think they went to tour the Space Center. Look for them to show up tomorrow."

Jacky clicks off.

"I get the impression that the boss has better things to do," Jimmy says.

I pour coffee from the large carafe and grab another slice of Cuban bread smothered in butter.

"He doesn't know how deep this thing is," I say. "Neither does anyone else. We've seen emeralds, or at least people tell us they're emeralds. The only green stone we have is the one Colette found on the floor of the Sea Change office. Harry said they could get that checked out this morning by a retired jeweler in their building."

"And so far, no one has a line on who these two guys might be," Jimmy says.

He holds up his cellphone. It has a photo of the dead junky from last night. He changes it to reveal the face of the cut-rate queen with a bullet hole in his forehead."

"Jesus," I say. "Who said you could take pictures of the two stiffs?"

"Hey, nobody said I couldn't. Maybe we could show these around. Maybe the Townsend boys might know these guys."

"We could run it past them later," I say. "Part of our first full day as executives in the Florida hotel business."

We're about to get up from our chairs overlooking the Atlantic when the phone rings.

"Mr. Jimmy Cox?" a voice asks.

"Right here."

"This is Detective Cortez, following up from last night. We're still going over the boat registered to your business. You shouldn't expect it back for a few days. Do you have any idea how those two guys got hold of it, or who might have shot them?"

Jimmy rolls his eyes.

"Uh, we're at a disadvantage, Detective Cortez. We got into town yesterday and found the Sea Change abandoned. The couple we had with us last night has agreed to help. I don't think they know much about the boat. They knew Billy and Bonnie Teller, the couple that ran our business, on a casual basis."

"And Billy and this Bonnie are still missing?"

"Yeah, still missing," Jimmy says. "We're going to file a report on him later today. We might be filing charges on her. She emptied the cash drawer when she took off from the Sea Change."

"Lot of that going on these days," Cortez says. "We ran prints of both our victims found on your boat. Do the names Albert Hastings or Jonathan Gerber mean anything?"

"Not to us," Jimmy says. "Like I said, we just got here."

"You might want to check your hotel registration records and see if they turn up. Hastings is the junky. Gerber is the queen."

"We're heading over there now," Jimmy says. "We'll let you know."

"One more thing," Cortez says. "This company you guys represent, what's the name, and where is it?"

"It's Second Base Dugout, Limited," Jimmy says. "It's based in Chicago. It's on the business cards we gave you."

"My mistake. Your company runs hotels?"

"Yeah," Jimmy says. "We're also in wholesale liquor and movies. We run the Galloping Dominos Casino in Las Vegas."

"Sounds like you guys are connected."

"Let's say we're one big happy family," Jimmy says.

"I wouldn't doubt that one bit," Cortez says. "Have a nice day."

He clicks off.

"This guy is fishing," Jimmy says. "He might be useful down the line."

Chapter 13

Morning at the Sea Change shows some positives. Harry is touching up the trim on the building with red paint he found in the tool closet. Another man trims the hibiscus hedge.

"That's Raul," Harry says as we approach. "He works at our condo. I gave him fifty bucks to do some landscaping. Already it's paid off. A couple from Illinois cruised by looking for a place to stay for a week. Colette took care of them. They're in unit nine."

Harry walks with us to the office, where Colette is shuffling through papers.

"I made a list of customers of Sea Change," she says. "Many people are from nice towns in the North. Some are from Quebec. We have the emails, but it looks like no one ever sent them anything to invite them back. I can do this with a message, friendly, no?"

"Tell them that you're the new manager," Jimmy says. "Maybe write something in French? Give them a couple days free?"

"Yes, we just talked with Jacky a few minutes ago," Colette says. "He's sending Angie and Bruno for help, yes?"

"Yeah, save an apartment for them," Jimmy says. "You know them from before?"

"Hell, yes," Harry says. "Bruno did work for us in Chicago. He got rid of a bar and a drugstore we had on the Southside before the you-know-whos destroyed the neighborhood."

"Harry," Colette says. "Do not talk that way about the Black people. Shame on you."

"Who said anything about the Blacks, Colette? I'm talking about street gangs. You forget about the Ebony Draculas or the Midnight Vampires?"

"What can a poor woman do with someone like Harry?" Colette asks, turning toward Jimmy and me. "Anyhow, Angie and Bruno will be good to have. Angie was teaching me the Three-card Monte. We did it one afternoon at the Lincoln Park Zoo and made some mad money."

"Speaking of money," Jimmy says. "Did you have a chance to show the emerald to your retired jeweler friend?"

"Yeah," Harry says. "Somewhere around fifteen hundred simoleons. Good stuff, he says. If we got a quantity of them, David could help move them. He's retired but still active. *Capisce?*"

We *capisce*.

"Did that copper get any clue as to who the two stiffs are?" Harry asks.

"Yeah, here's a couple names." Jimmy hands Colette a sheet of Fontainebleau stationery with the names of our two vics on them.

"Cortez thinks they might have stayed at Sea Change. See what you can find. Maybe we'll keep that info to ourselves. He's already sniffing around Second Base Dugout."

"I know the type," Harry says. "They come on like J. Edgar Hoover. What they really want is a taste of the goodies. He didn't get that thick gold necklace and that Rolex he was wearing for helping old ladies cross the street."

Colette thumbs through the guest register for signs of Hastings and Gerber.

"I don't see either one," she says. "I get the impression cash customers never got a receipt. It is *je ne sais quoi* someone with the hand in the cookies, yes?"

"Yeah, who would know?" Jimmy asks. "If Billy tried to spend most of his time away from here, guess who's been taking all the cash customers for her private trust fund?"

"No wonder the joint's been running in the red," Harry says.

Out in the courtyard, Walter White is in the pool, splashing around with the two women he was sitting with last night. I wonder if they got the Bonnie discount for paying cash.

Jimmy notices my gaze at the pool.

"Forget about it," he says. "We got bigger fish to fry. Let's not upset our guests."

He's right. We head out to see the Townsend boys at their Miami River boat repair. Maybe they know the two stiffs that died aboard the Maroon Key.

Our route takes us past the Coast Guard station. The Maroon Key is still tied along the dock where we last saw it. "Police Line Do Not Cross" tape is draped over the boat and part of the walkway. A lone Miami Dade cop car sits next to it.

"You know they're going over it with a fine-tooth comb," Jimmy says. "If there's any dope on board, it could be a problem."

"We could stick the drag queen and the junky on that," I say. "What if they find emeralds?"

"I can only speak about Chicago and Vegas," Jimmy says. "The cops in those towns would never turn in emeralds found at a double homicide."

"Yeah, why complicate their lives with more evidence?" I ask.

"Be fair, Nick," Jimmy says. "They have to pay for their vacation homes in Tahoe and Lake Geneva."

We roll through a traffic mess in downtown Miami, trying to find Northwest South River Drive. If that isn't confusing enough, there's a Southwest North River Drive on the other side of the river. Of course, the address where the Townsend boys have their boat repair place turns out to be on the other side of the river.

I dial one of their cell phone numbers and get Chuck.

"Hey, we're on the other side of the river," I say. "We got some info to share with you guys. We're working our way over to you, okay?"

"Sure. We're checking this Chris Craft," he says. "It needs an engine overhaul. See you in a few minutes."

It takes more than a few minutes to find a bridge to cross the river. We make our way up the road along the river and find the entrance to Townsend Boat Repair.

"There's beers and Cokes in the office," Chuck says. "Help yourselves. Our cousin Mary will help you. We're just going up the river for a minute to check this thing out."

The classic wooden runabout belches and sputters as it leaves the dock. Buddy sticks his head up from the engine compartment and gives us a wave.

"Back soon."

We wave and head for the cold drinks.

"I'm Mary," a woman behind the counter says. "I handle the office. The boys will be back in a minute."

Behind her is a blackboard. The names of customers and their boats are listed along with cost estimates on the repair and parts. Colorful posters and photos of people enjoying the water are plastered throughout the office.

Jimmy reaches into the ice chest and gets two beers.

"A good day for a cold drink," Mary says.

"It is," I say. "Thank you."

I follow Jimmy outside. I'm about to sit down on an old wooden chair to watch the boat's journey up the river when it happens.

The engine on the wooden boat sputters and stops about a hundred yards up the river. Buddy reaches into the engine compartment.

Chuck yells something at Buddy.

The Chris Craft explodes.

The noise is deafening.

The heat rushes toward us and slams me to the gravel.

My ears ring.

I drop the beer.

Jimmy is on the ground behind a large concrete planter.

I'm stunned.

I yell at Jimmy. I can't hear my own voice.

What happened? Where's the boat?

It becomes apparent as my ears stop ringing.

What's left of the Chris Craft is on fire, floating toward the far shore. Pieces of wood float beside it. Boat cushions are scattered on the water, some of them smoldering.

"A fucking bomb," Jimmy says, getting to his feet.

I look again at the wreckage making its way toward the far shore. The bodies of Chuck and Buddy float near the bank.

I turn toward the office. The windows are shattered.

Mary is inside screaming, "What happened?"

I look at my arm. It's bleeding.

"Your face is bleeding, too," Jimmy says. "Help is on the way."

In the distance, I hear sirens.

Chapter 14

"There's a first aid kit in the office," Jimmy says as he hustles me through the office doorway.

Mary stands behind the counter. There's busted glass all over the floor.

"That explosion wasn't the boys. That wasn't the boat, was it?" She looks at Jimmy, then me. "What happened?"

"You better sit down," Jimmy says to her. "There's been a bad accident."

"Jesus." She rushes through the doorway out to the boat dock.

Jimmy grabs the first aid kit from the wall. He pushes me into an old rattan chair with a cracked, red seat cushion.

"You've got a cut on your arm and cuts on your face," he says. "Looks like you tried to shave with a lawnmower. I'm betting you're gonna live."

"Hope you're not playing long shots," I say.

"Shut up, Nick," he says, proving he has the bedside manner of a shark. "We've got to get you presentable. We don't want you officially involved, like taking an ambulance ride."

He wipes my face with alcohol pads and bandages my arm. I manage to see my reflection in an old mirror hanging on the door to the john. It does look like I had a bad shave. He hides the cut on my arm under a large bandage.

"Hey, I think I'm good to go," I say.

"Not so fast," Jimmy says. He has his phone in his hand, and he's taking pictures of the office blackboard that has info on the boats that are being fixed.

"I think we've got it."

I give him my best shrug and reach for two beers out of the cooler chest.

"Might as well have one," I say. "There's a hell of a show outside."

"Damn, I thought we could get out of here before the uniforms arrived," Jimmy says.

One look at what's happening outside says it all. A Marine Patrol powerboat is idling through the debris. A fire truck is on the far bank. An ambulance sits close to the bank where the two bodies are floating.

Two Miami Dade cop cars pull up on our side.

"What happened?" A tall Black cop asks. Mary's standing on the dock, wringing her hands, looking at the mess in the river. Palm fronds from suddenly naked trees are scattered all over. The tops of the trees are on fire.

"Something exploded. I think my cousins are dead," she says. Tears stream down her face. She grabs the cop by the arm. Her knees buckle.

"Take it easy," the cop says. "We need to get you to sit down."

Another cop runs up with a white plastic chair and puts it in place. They get Mary to sit.

"The boat exploded. Is that what happened?" the second cop asks.

Mary is crying uncontrollably, grabbing onto the cop's arm.

"Probably fumes in the bilge," Black Cop says. "Could have been a propane build-up or gasoline fumes. I always turn on the bilge blower before I start my engines."

"Yeah, that would do it," the second cop says.

The Black cop turns and looks at Jimmy and me.

"You guys see it happen?"

"I heard it," Jimmy says. "Had my back turned. It blew out the windows in the office."

"Yeah, probably propane," Black Cop says, looking toward the debris and the bodies.

We raise our beer cans and take a swig.

"You smell what I'm smelling?" Jimmy asks from behind his beer can.

"Yeah, tar."

"See anyone tarring a roof?"

"It ain't propane or gasoline, is it? I ask. "I think it might be our old friend, C4."

"Speaking of old friends, look who just arrived in an unmarked cop car," Jimmy says. "Detective Cortez. He must specialize in boating homicides."

We ease into the office as Cortez heads for the two cops trying to calm Mary.

"What's the story here? Who's this lady?" Cortez asks.

Cortez, the two cops, and Mary all talk at once.

"Probably a good time for another beer," Jimmy says. "Sit down, take a deep breath, and relax. Here's something to read."

He reaches across Mary's desk and hands me a file folder marked "Pending Work Orders."

"Someone got that C4 onto that boat," he says. "Was it the guy who brought the boat in? Or maybe it was someone else who has a boat in here for service."

The folder has papers on six boats. I think about using my incredible memory to put all the pertinent facts into my brain. But then I hear the voice of my beautiful wife, Dawn, coming from the recesses of my memory.

"Nick, I sent you to the store for milk and bread," I hear her saying. "You come back with Ben & Jerry's, pretzels, and beer. We need to write things down for you."

Luckily, the forms have multiple copies, including a red marked "Additional Copy." It's an easy way to save my thinking power for other things. In seconds, I've disappeared the copies into my pocket.

I toss the folder back onto Mary's desk just before Detective Cortez comes into the office.

"Give me a good reason why I shouldn't be surprised to see you here," he says. "It's been less than twenty-four hours between boats and multiple cadavers. You guys want to tell me about it?"

I look at Jimmy. I'm waiting for him to say something about being on the "Double Murder Boat Tour" or another smart-ass remark. But then he doesn't. He plays it straight, or as straight as Jimmy knows how to.

"We wanted to make arrangements with the Townsend boys to bring the Maroon Key in here for a tune-up and a bottom job," Jimmy says. "They've done work on our boat before. As soon as your people got done playing Junior G-men, we wanted the Townsends to bring it here."

"Yeah, it might be a few days, like I told you earlier," Cortez says. "You know, it's interesting that you two guys hit town, and two days later, we've got four stiffs on our hands."

"Yeah, remarkable," Jimmy says.

"Just sayin'," Cortez says.

"Just sayin', my ass," Jimmy says. "How fucking dumb do you think we are? You think we'd shoot the junky and the drag queen on our own boat and leave it floating around the Coast Guard station?"

"My apologies," Cortez says. "You're right; it doesn't make sense. Mary, the lady outside, says that you two had lunch with the Townsends the other day at the Fontainebleau. Do you want to tell me about that? Anything I should know?"

"Yeah, they stiffed us on the check," Jimmy says. "We came over here today to set fire to their boat. Clever, eh? Now we've got nobody to repair Maroon Key, our floating crime scene."

"Jesus, Jimmy," I say, assuming the role of good cop. "Detective Cortez is only trying to help. He thinks maybe Buddy and Chuck said something to us that could help solve these crimes."

Jimmy wipes sweat from his face and looks at Cortez. The sweat is actually from the outside of his beer can.

"I'm sorry, Detective Cortez," Jimmy says. "They did mention they were having trouble with a Haitian named Henri Boyer. He was trying to muscle into their business."

"Yeah, I know Boyer," Cortez says. "He used to be *Tonton Macoute*. He was hot shit in Haiti, not so hot here. His restaurants fail inspection. His massage parlor girls are walking plagues."

"The Townsends talked about a Voodoo curse," Jimmy says. "Boyer's the one they mentioned."

"Voodoo's bullshit," Cortez says. "Thanks for the tip. We'll take a close look at Mr. Haitian tough guy. Maybe he's the one that put the slugs into the junky and the drag queen."

Cortez turns and heads for the door.

"Glad to help," Jimmy says. "Stay in touch, Detective Cortez."

Chapter 15

We pull away from Townsend Boat Works after getting word that both Buddy and Chuck Townsend are dead from the Chris Craft bombing.

It's a bitter pill to realize the two Cecils are now dead.

"It's a real pisser," Jimmy says. "I liked those guys. They seemed like they'd fit in with our crew. Another thing. They knew the way back to where they found the emeralds with Billy and Mandingo. I'm betting all four of these guys are deceased."

"Well, actually," I start to say.

"Don't bother, Nick," Jimmy says. "I know what you'll say. You'll say, 'Three of them might be deceased. Only one of them is de-Cess-ed.'"

I let Jimmy have his moment of triumph before replying.

"Our chances of finding the lost treasure just washed down the drain."

"Normally, yes," Jimmy says. "But in South Florida, things are just as apt to wash up the drain. Have you forgotten Valerie Masters and the late 'Oh, oh Ronnie' Nolan?"

"Right," I say. "Val and her pal are the reason the emeralds were found in the first place. If we find Valerie or info that Ronnie left behind, we have a chance at the jewels."

Jimmy nods.

Traffic moving toward Miami Beach is at a standstill.

Hunger overtakes us. It's late in the day, and we haven't had lunch.

Calle Ocho, the heart of Cuban Miami, is close by. We park in front of Alfredo's Café.

"You guys been here before?" Connie, our waitress, asks. She's an attractive woman of about thirty.

"First time," Jimmy says.

"Yeah, I usually remember the good-looking guys," she says.

"That's us," Jimmy says.

"You guys know we got snow coming tomorrow." She winks.

"No way," Jimmy says.

"Snow cones," she says. "Good for all this heat. The boss has a machine coming tomorrow. He thinks he'll strike it rich."

"That's better," I say. "Snow cones, I can take. I got a five-year-old daughter who loves the pineapple-flavored ones."

I show Connie a photo of Molly.

"Beautiful child," Connie says. "You must have a beautiful wife."

"He does," Jimmy says. "What if the poor kid had his schnoz?"

"*Hay, que horror,*" Connie says with a wink and a smile.

"Funny. What do you have that's better than snow cones?" I ask. "We're hungry. What do you recommend?"

"*Medianoche* sandwich," Connie says. "It's made with roast pork, ham, Swiss cheese, pickle, and egg bread. You're going to love it. It gets put in a sandwich press and toasted."

"Sounds better than the snow cone," Jimmy says.

"Make it two," I say.

The *medianoche* is everything Connie promised. As we pay the check, I ask if she knows Cesar Fuentes.

"He comes around when he needs our votes." She winks. "The boss gives him a few bucks, and we don't see him until the next election. Just as well. He's kind of a bullshitter, always talking about some big project that'll save Miami. It ain't going to happen. Many *viejos* sit around here wishing for Havana of the fifties. That's not going to happen, either. I tell people to enjoy South Florida while it's here."

We drive across the causeway to Miami Beach and the Scarlet Tide, Cesar's bar. He's expecting Billy to show up to talk about a deal for the Sea Change and Maroon Key. His message on the answering machine at Sea Change left the impression that Billy was still functioning and not missing in action.

There are two ways you could take this. Number one: Cesar really thinks Billy will show up in the flesh. Number two: Cesar already knows that Billy has been erased from the picture, and he's covering his ass by leaving the message.

"You've got to like old Cesar," Jimmy says. "He leaves that message where he says he doesn't want Billy to get hurt on the deal. Isn't that like saying, 'This is a nice place you got here. It'd be a shame if something bad happened to it?'"

"Yeah, the old protection racket. So, what does Cesar do if Billy waltzes into the Scarlet Tide and orders a beer?" I ask. "Would shitting a brick be out of place in ultra-hip South Beach?"

"Let's look at it this way," Jimmy says. "Bonnie's run off with the Sea Change's cash and probably the emeralds Billy and Mandingo had for safekeeping. From what Walter White said, Vinnie' Shrimp Boat-Drug Peddler' Malone planned to meet her. That leaves two other interested parties, Cesar and Henri Boyer. Somebody in this mess popped the junky and the drag queen aboard the Maroon Key. None of these people are interested in owning the Sea Change. They're after emeralds and whatever else is on some backwater Key."

"So, Bonnie is the source for Malone," I say. "Somehow, she learned from Billy or Mandingo where to look for the treasure. So, how did Cesar and Henri get wind of the treasure? If Valerie Masters told one of them, that leaves the other getting their info from Ronnie Nolan, who's listed as deceased by the Monroe County Sheriff's Department."

"Yeah," Jimmy says. "That all seems plausible, but something is missing. Remember, they're all still looking for a deal with Billy."

"So, they know the area where the treasure is, but no one knows the exact spot."

"Something like that," Jimmy says. "Cesar or Henri put the gator into the pool at Sea Change. Kind of a stimulant to getting things to the serious stage. Malone wouldn't do it. His girlfriend could have gotten hurt with that stunt. We were right to sic Detective Cortez onto Boyer. It'll keep him guessing for a while. It's never fun to have the authorities on your back, especially when you're running filthy restaurants and massage parlors with free STDs."

Parking is a bitch on South Beach. We circle the block that the Scarlet Tide is on for the third time. Ahead, a Cadillac sits in the last legal place. Its brake lights go on, then off. Again they go on.

"Maybe he's getting ready to leave," Jimmy says. "Pull up next to him, and I'll ask."

Jimmy opens his window as we come beside the Caddy. The old guy behind the wheel looks up in surprise.

Jimmy looks back at me and winks. He turns back to the Caddy.

"Excuse me, sir," Jimmy says. "Are you planning to move your car when your niece gets done fixing your zipper?"

The Caddy starts immediately. The "niece" gets out of the car and wobbles on her six-inch red spike heels. She rearranges her cut-off t-shirt and a black bikini bottom that shows off the tramp stamp above her ass and wiggles down the street. The Caddy moves in the opposite direction.

"Shame, Jimmy," I say. "Breaking up a loving couple so you could have their parking place."

"It was bound to fail," Jimmy says. "She was after his money. He was just using her for sex."

Chapter 16

The Scarlet Tide makes a good impression as you enter. Larger-than-life paintings of a beautiful red-headed woman decorate several walls. Another wall has large photos of boats and beaches on perfect tropical days. The interior reminds you of a trendy club or art gallery.

But then you start to notice that you're getting bullshit instead of substance. It's like the large casinos in Vegas with fountain shows and canals. Water? Hey, we got plenty. The hot, dry desert out there? Lake Mead disappearing? Never mind that. Why should you worry?

Water is also the issue at the Scarlet Tide. There's been too much of it. The red carpeting seems frayed around the walls. Or maybe it's rot caused by a mixture of seawater and way too many soakings of disinfectant. The smell of booze fills the air, but it doesn't cover the smell of decay and chemicals.

It's early evening. The place is busy. Beach bums wearing T-shirts and cut-offs mix with tourists wearing resort wear purchased for their trip to Miami. I notice a few price tags still attached to the Tommy Bahamas. I pick up a conversation through the loud music as we head to the bar.

"Miriam and Alex were here last year," a sun-burned blonde says to her escort. "They said it was a snap to connect."

"Blow?" Tommy Bahama Man takes a drink from his Dos Equis bottle.

"Just takes dinero," Sun-burned Blonde says.

"No problemo, Babe."

"This is where they did that fashion shoot for the Scarlet Fuentes label. The one in ELLE, I think," Sun-burned Blonde says.

"Yeah, you look good in that stuff."

We leave Sunburned Blonde and Tommy Bahama Man to continue searching for a dope dealer. Behind the bar, a fat guy in a pink pastel suit and purple shirt checks receipts with the barmaid. Can Pastel Suit be Fuentes?

"No, Cesar's not available," Pastel Suit says. "You got a complaint I can help you with?"

"Yeah, can you tell us how we can get hold of Henri Boyer or Vinnie Malone?" Jimmy asks.

"What do you mean? Those guys aren't welcome here. If they come around, I'll have security throw their asses out."

"That's too bad," Jimmy says. "We were supposed to meet Cesar to discuss the Sea Change and Maroon Key sale. We're part of the outfit that helps Billy Teller with the heavy lifting. Maybe Boyer and Malone are more interested."

"Wait a minute," Pastel Suit says. "I'll see if he wants to chat with you."

He heads to the end of the bar and pushes through a heavy wooden door.

"Norman is a bitch," Joanne, the barmaid, says. "He'll be back after his fag fit. Want a beer?"

The Dos Equis is cold and tastes like it should.

"You get much water in here on the king tide?" Jimmy asks.

"Enough to wet the carpeting," Joanne says. "It acts like a sponge. The bottoms of the chairs and tables get wet. It's not like it's a surprise anymore. 'Yellow Submarine' gets played a lot on the jukebox. That's us. That's South Florida. It's worse down in the Keys."

Jimmy tosses out a curveball that even I'm not expecting.

"Yeah, we heard you got wet in here. A guy we met down in the Keys was telling us. Ronnie Nolan. I think he hangs out here."

"Haven't seen him in a while," Joanne says. "He's always with some rich broad. I don't know what they see in him. He gets a little out of control at times."

"Yeah, that's what we thought," Jimmy says. "He was pretty drunk when we met him."

Norman is back.

"Follow me, gentlemen. Mr. Fuentes will see you in his private office."

If the barroom crowd looks like an ad for resort wear, Cesar Fuentes looks like he just stepped out of *Golf Digest*. His green Izod shirt tops a pair of red slacks. He's lean and no doubt mean. His smile suggests a cunning shark. Behind him is a wall with large renderings of the same red-headed woman on paintings in the bar. The smell of expensive cigars and cologne almost covers the odor of mold in the office.

"I understand you're here on behalf of Billy Teller," he says as he rises from the chair behind his desk. "I thought I'd be seeing Billy."

His handshake is firm, and he looks you in the eye, but there's a short shift from your face as his eyes check out the rest of you. I figure he's wondering what kind of heat we're carrying. Pastel Norman probably has a gun in his pink suit. Cesar, no doubt, has one within reach.

"Billy's unavailable," Jimmy says. "He's done a remarkable job managing things down here for the home office in Chicago. My associate and I are handling negotiations."

We hand Cesar our business cards.

"I see." Cesar displays his Shark World dental array. "I was hoping that if a deal for the properties were to be made, Billy's expertise might be included as part of the deal. You see, it's easy to get hurt if you don't know the ins and outs of dealing with the South Florida community."

"Yeah, things can get pretty explosive down here," Jimmy says.

"Yes." Cesar smiles. "I heard there was a boating accident earlier today on the Miami River. Such a shame."

"Boaters should always check the bilge before starting their engines," Jimmy says. "The smell of exploded C4 can ruin your picnic-on-the-water lunch."

"Maybe it wasn't an accident," Cesar says. "There are violent people in South Florida willing to stop at nothing to get their way. We're big on security here. We're planning not to get hurt."

"Yes, our people are thinking the same," I say, handing Cesar my card. "Chicago likes security."

"We wanted to tell you our accountants are working on a price based on the current market," Jimmy says. "There have been some adjustments. We'll be getting back to you in a few days."

"Of course," Cesar says. "I'm always glad to listen to new proposals. Don't make a deal before you let me see if I can make a better offer. I know there are others interested. I think their problems are where they get their money. Drug and sex trafficking are unreliable sources of funding."

"Not the best of types for the country club," Jimmy says. "I can't help but notice your pictures of the beautiful woman with red hair. Someone close to you?"

"Yes, my wife, Scarlet. A talented young woman. I'll tell you about her sometime. Next time bring Billy if you can. Norman will show you out."

We make our way through the Scarlet Tide's crowded barroom. Sun-burned Blonde and Tommy Bahama Man have a third at their table, a guy wearing sunglasses and a silk shirt. His head swivels from left to right and then back as he talks to our drug-seeking couple.

Out on the street, Jimmy asks, "Was that guy with the two tourists looking around for narcs? Or was he trying to size up the next customers before someone else sold them dope?"

"Don't know," I say. "You'd think a place as nice as the Scarlet Tide would have an up system for drug peddlers."

"Hell," Jimmy says, "They could even offer test drives and financing."

I'm about to answer when I notice Joanne, the barmaid standing in front of the Scarlet Tide. She's taking a cigarette break. The roar of the angry ocean attacking the darkened beach across the road seems to move closer.

"Did Stormin' Norman get you guys in to see Cesar the Great?" Joanne asks.

"Yeah, we had our two minutes of fame," Jimmy says. "Hey, what's with all the pictures of the red-head."

"Scarlet," Joanne says. "Another lost soul. She was married to Cesar for a couple years. Her designs got big write-ups in fashion magazines and made a ton of money. It all came to a sudden end about a year ago. She and Cesar were diving off Key Largo when she got attacked by a shark. They say it was bloody and over quick."

"Cesar saw it happen?" Jimmy asks.

"Yeah, he was there. Stormin' Norman, too. It shook Cesar up pretty bad. After that, all the pictures of Scarlet started going up on the walls."

"He must have been heartbroken," I say.

"Yeah, the five-million-dollar policy on her helped to soothe his feelings. He's a hard guy to figure out. I asked Stormin' Norman once about what makes Cesar tick. He said the only thing he knew for sure is that Cesar always wants more."

Chapter 17

Back at the Fontainebleau, we try to sort out the bloodletting. Jimmy has the photos from Townsend Boat Works displayed on his laptop. The six invoices of current Townsend customers are spread out on the coffee table. Somewhere in this mess could be the answer to who put the bomb on the Chris Craft that killed Chuck and Buddy.

"We're starting to see the players up close," Jimmy says. "Someone wants Billy, Mandingo, and the Townsends out of the way. A double shooting on the Maroon Key and the bombing on the Miami River aren't coincidences."

"True," I say. "But remember, whoever did the shooting didn't get Billy and Mandingo. They got the junky and the drag queen."

Jimmy stands and stretches as he thinks.

"Okay, try this. Someone knows the Maroon Key is going in for service at Townsend Boat Works. Maybe they also know that Billy's got that gig at the Boca tech convention. Someone decides to do away with Billy and Mandingo somewhere between Boca and the Boat Works."

"Yeah, but Billy and Mandingo don't look like the junky or the drag queen," I say. "The shooter would have to be blind to make them the targets."

"Or maybe someone tells the shooter that Billy and Mandingo were seen leaving Boca on the Maroon Key," Jimmy says. "Now the boat shows up at the South Beach Marina. Whoever's in charge tells the shooter to kill the guys on board."

I stand to walk around.

Jimmy sits down.

We need to think.

A breath of ocean air on the balcony gets me back in rhythm.

“There are three teams against us,” Jimmy says. “Fuentes heads one. Vinnie Malone and Bonnie Teller head another. Then there’s the voodoo massage parlor king, Henri Boyer.”

“Jesus, it’s got everything,” I say. “Sex, drugs, rock ’n roll.”

“Murder, money, treasure,” Jimmy says. “We should write this shit down and sell it to Hollywood.”

“After we find the treasure,” I say.

“And before we get killed over it.”

“So, you were saying about these three teams?”

“Yeah. Fuentes says he wants Billy for his business expertise,” Jimmy says. “We know that’s crap. Billy’s expertise is in being a fuck up. Fuentes wants Billy to tell where the treasure is.”

“Someone else has a good idea of where it might be,” I say. “Bonnie Teller’s coaching Vinnie Malone on that. She probably pried enough out of Billy and Mandingo to figure out the area where the emeralds were found.”

“We know that Ronnie Nolan probably told Fuentes about it,” Jimmy says. “Maybe they’re the ones that offed Ronnie and tried to do away with Valerie Masters.”

“So, that leaves Valerie to hook up with Henri Boyer?” I ask.

“Yeah, we know Boyer didn’t get interested in the Sea Change or Maroon Key on his own,” Jimmy says. “Someone had to tip him off about the jewels. If Ronnie is Fuentes’ boy and Bonnie is kissing up to Malone, that leaves Valerie to tell Boyer.”

“So, who’s doing all the killing?”

“If we know the why, we might be able to figure out the who,” Jimmy says. “If Fuentes can be believed, he thinks that Billy is still alive. Someone who wanted Billy out of the way hired the two creeps to do the dirty work. You’ve seen the Maroon Key. It’s big. It wouldn’t be hard for the junky and the drag queen to hide below deck. Pictures of the boat in the Sea Change office show a small skiff secured to the bow. We didn’t see that skiff at the Coast Guard station. It’s missing.”

I reach into the bag of potato chips we picked up at 7-11. Salt, grease, and crunchy carbs help me think. A cold beer helps to wash it all down. It clears the palate and the mind.

"Okay, Jimmy. You want me to play fill-in-the-blanks."

"Take your best shot," he says, grabbing for what's left of the munchies.

"If Fuentes is still operating on Billy's being alive, he didn't kill anybody in Boca. He also didn't order a hit on the two guys on the Maroon Key. Whoever did any of that wanted Billy and Mandingo out of the way. The same goes for the Townsend bombing. With all four of them out of the way, the only people we know who have been to where the emeralds were found are Valerie Masters and Ronnie Nolan."

"But Ronnie's dead," Jimmy says. "Before he died, he could have spilled some of what he knew to Fuentes."

"Yeah, but maybe not enough," I say. "Maybe Ronnie shopped it around, dangled the bait in front of Boyer, too. Boyer figures he knows enough to figure out where to hunt for the treasure, so it's goodbye, Ronnie."

"And while he's at it, goodbye Billy, Mandingo, and the Townsend boys," Jimmy says. "No competition. He figures he can scare Bonnie away from doing anything about the emeralds with sharks in the pool and chickens in nooses. Doesn't know she's thrown in with Malone."

"On the other hand," I say. "Maybe Malone and Bonnie hire the junky and the drag queen to off Billy and Mandingo. They're supposed to kill them and toss them over the side out at sea. I'm betting a couple anchors are missing. Enough to hold a couple bodies to the bottom for a while."

"Things go fine," Jimmy says. "But then the dinghy lashed to the bow gets loose. Our two hitmen can't sink the Maroon Key and get to shore. They panic and bring the boat to Miami Beach, figuring they'll ditch it there. Maybe beach it and burn it on one of the causeways. Except someone recognizes the boat. Suddenly, their little scheme comes to an end. They know too much."

"Maybe there's a clue in these red sheets," I say.

I pick up the invoices we took from Townsend Boat Works.

The Florida registration numbers are listed with the names and contact info of the people who brought the boats in for service.

I read them off to Jimmy as he looks at a photo he took of the blackboard at Townsend.

"They all check with what you said," Jimmy says. "We should have Glover track these down through government databases. We might get info on who planted the C4."

I nod. Detective Jake Glover of South Vegas PD can plug into the mysteries of the cyber world. If we get a good history of the boats, we might turn up things about the owners.

"There's one other thing listed on the blackboard in my photo that you don't have an invoice for," Jimmy says.

"What's that?"

"Under the list of the six boats. Take a look for yourself.

He spins the laptop around.

In the bottom corner of the blackboard is the figure, "24.669543."

Underneath it is the figure, "-81.695045."

I pull out the cash register tape we found in the drawer at Sea Change. On it are the exact figures. I'm about to say something to Jimmy when my phone rings.

"Uh, is this Nick?" The voice sounds familiar.

"Yeah, what's up?"

"This is Walter. You know, Walter White from your Sea Change resort."

"Yeah, Walter." I turn on the speaker setting.

"That Bonnie woman came back and tried to get into the office tonight. She was trying different keys, and none of them worked. I poked my head out because of her swearing and jiggling the keys in the lock. She saw me and asked if someone had changed the locks. She said she left an important piece of paper in the cash register."

"What did you tell her?"

"I told her to come back in the morning when the office was open. She was making so much noise that my wife couldn't sleep."

"What happened then?"

"She started swearing really loud at me like I was somehow to blame. I told her to knock it off, or I'd be calling the cops."

"Did she leave, then?"

"Only after she kicked the office door a couple times. That's when I called the cops. I told them some drunk was getting loud near the pool. People couldn't sleep."

"Did they send a squad car?"

"Yeah. A couple of cops flashed their lights around. I told them the woman had taken off already. They sat around in the squad car a few minutes and took off."

We thank Walter and wish him a pleasant rest of the night.

"What do you think?" Jimmy asks.

I show him the receipt with the numbers on it.

"We need to figure out what these figures mean," I say. "Could be the stuff dreams are made of."

Chapter 18

Our day in Miami Beach begins with the blood-red sun rising above the blue Atlantic. The air is fresh. Brown pelicans coast by in ragged formation, looking for breakfast.

An early morning newscast does its best to destroy that beauty by informing South Florida beachgoers that they're swimming in shit. An environmental group says that recent breakdowns in sewer pipes have allowed the fecal matter to settle in the sand just inside the surf line. People are standing in shit while they show off their expensive beachwear and work on their tans.

I tell this to my wife on my call to Vegas.

"Jesus, Nick," Dawn says. "That says a lot about our culture."

Our daughter Molly is listening. She can't believe what I've just said.

"Daddy, you're always telling a funny story." She has the giggles. "I'm going to tell Nancy and Eliza what you said. People are swimming in poo-poo." Nancy Nakamoto and Eliza Perez are her friends from school.

"What else have I said that's so funny?" I ask.

"Well, you said about an octopus coming up through a pipe in a parking garage. I can see him chasing people around. That's funny. You said that Uncle Harry and Aunt Colette are worried about their building falling over. Are there big sticks holding it up? That's funny. And big puddles of the ocean are coming up in people's backyards. It sounds like you're in a cartoon, Daddy."

"Yeah, it feels like Wile E. Coyote," I say.

Dawn tells Molly to get ready for school.

"It's just you and me now," Dawn says. "How bad is it?"

I tell about the shooting of the two scumbags aboard the Maroon Key and the bombing of the Townsend boys on the Miami River. Then I talk about Fuentes and how his fashion designer wife, Scarlet, became shark bait.

"Is this shit worth it?" Dawn asks. "Every time Jacky sends you on one of his missions, it has danger attached."

"I know, Babe. Once we get a full look at all the players, maybe we'll tell Jacky to settle for a good price, and we can bug out."

"I love you, Nick, with all my heart. You know you're my soulmate. But I know when you're bullshitting, too. You and Jimmy can't wait to stick your noses into something that might explode."

"Yeah, well..."

"Go ahead. I'm not telling you to stop. I am taking out more insurance on you. Our daughter's going to Harvard when she's ready if Harvard is still standing."

"Yeah," I say. "If any of us are still standing."

We talk a while more. Dawn mentions new exhibits in the museum she runs at the Galloping Dominos Casino. It started as a place featuring artifacts from the Middle East. Lately, it's begun to showcase items from Aztec and Mayan cultures.

"The visitor count is way up," she says. "I think it's because people have respect for their old cultures. There's a feeling that much of the past is being lost."

"Yeah, much of the present, too," I say.

We do our kiss-kiss, and I love you. It's time for both of us to start our days. I can hear Jimmy on the phone with Cassandra in Vegas in the next room.

"Nah, of course, it's safe," he tells his wife. "The bad guys aren't after us. They're after each other. We'll find out what it's all worth, and we'll make a deal. Nick and I have it figured out."

I can't hear Cassandra's response, but I remember a few choice ones from her that I managed to overhear through the years. My favorite is, "If Nick pissed in his pants, you two would be trying to sue the beer company and the tailor."

"We're being careful," Jimmy says. "I don't think Jacky wants us down here for long. He's tired of Billy running the biz into the red. A decent offer, and we're on our way home."

Room service comes with breakfast. I tell the guy to set it up on the balcony. I'll wait 'til after Jimmy eats to tell him about the shit all the beachgoers are standing in.

Halfway through the strawberry-topped waffles and sausages, we get a call from Harry. He and Colette are at the Sea Change getting ready for the arrival of Bruno and Angie. We mention Bonnie Teller's late-night visit and how she tried to kick down the office door at Sea Change to get a piece of paper.

"Yeah, I heard a bit about that from Walter," Harry says. "That must be the slip that Colette found in the cash drawer. What do you make of it?"

"Those same figures were on the customer blackboard at Townsend Boat Works," Jimmy says.

"I saw what happened," Harry says. "That's terrible for that family. I went with those guys on the Maroon Key with Billy a couple of times. They were fun."

"We were there when it blew," Jimmy says. "We were supposed to meet the Townsends."

"You saw it blow up?"

"Yeah," Jimmy says. "We wanted some info before meeting Fuentes, Malone, or Boyer."

"Maybe whoever it was, was after you two guys, too," Harry says.

I look at Jimmy. He frowns.

"Let's hope they aren't," Jimmy says.

"Amen to that," I say.

"Hey," Harry says, "One of the reasons I called, Henri Boyer wants to come over to meet with you guys. He called a few minutes ago. Should I call him back for some time this afternoon?"

"Yeah," I say. "What time are Bruno and Angie getting in?"

They called from the airport," Harry says. "They just got their rental car. Maybe half an hour."

"We're on our way to you," Jimmy says to Harry.

We ring off.

"We're on our way after taking care of a few details," I say. "There's the matter of running our cast of South Florida friends through our clearinghouse in South Vegas."

Detective Jake Glover answers on the first ring.

"The phone says it's you, Nick," Glover says. "That means that Jimmy is probably sitting nearby. What kind of a mess are you two in?"

We recount the last few days we've spent in sinking South Florida. Every time we mention an incident, Glover reacts.

"Jesus. A junky and a drag queen shot on your boat."

"Jesus. Two guys blown up on the Miami River."

"Jesus. Voodoo, sharks, shit in the water."

"If you say, 'Jesus' anymore, we're enrolling you in catechism classes," Jimmy says.

"I get it," Glover says. "What do you want? As if I didn't know."

We tell him we're emailing a list of names and boat registrations to be checked out.

"I would ask how soon you need the info," Glover says. "But knowing you two like I do, your answer to that would be, 'yesterday, if not before.' Send the list. I'll do what I can."

"That sounds like a plan," I say.

"It shouldn't take too long. Later today, I'll have something. Hey, you might be headed down to the Keys and Key West. I'll give you a tip. Captain Elmo's Saloon."

"Sounds like a good watering hole," Jimmy says. "I take it you've been there?"

"Several times. I go for the Hemingway Look-Alike Contest. I finished fourth one time, got on the front page of the *Key West Citizen*."

"But you don't look anything like Hemingway," I say.

"That don't matter. It's attitude what counts. One of the judges said that I looked like an expert on bullfighting."

"Bullfighting or bullshitting?" Jimmy asks.

"Same difference," Glover says. "The other guys weren't so hot either. Anyway, I got to know Captain Elmo. I do favors for him, checking out people. A lot of the local hotshots and politicians hang out at his place. He knows where some of the bodies are buried. *Capisce?*"

We both *capisce.*

"You get down there. Check him out. Tell him Jake Glover sends his very best."

We say goodbye to Glover and head for the door.

"You don't suppose that Captain Elmo knows anything about Ronnie Nolan?" Jimmy asks.

"Maybe Valerie Masters, too," I say.

Chapter 19

"I'm glad you waited for me to get done eating before you told me what people are standing in when they visit the beach," Jimmy says. "It's shocking. It's funny, too. But then, after you think about it, maybe the joke's on us. All of us."

He steers the Jeep down the Fontainebleau driveway onto Collins Avenue. Harry has called us back from the Sea Change. He says Henri Boyer, the Voodoo massage parlor king, will meet us at two in the office.

"You mean we're all standing in shit of some kind, and we don't even realize it?" I ask.

"You listen to bullshitters like Fuentes talk about pushing back the tide and turning seawater into freshwater, but then their efforts end up with people standing in shit and paying for the privilege...."

"Adding insult to injury," I say.

"Adding epidemic, maybe," Jimmy says. "You wouldn't let your kid go play on Miami Beach."

"Not in a million years," I say.

Palm trees line Collins Avenue. It's a sunny day, the kind you see on travel posters. We should be worrying about sunblock. Instead, we're wondering where the next bullet or bomb might be landing. We're standing in shit, looking for treasure.

Jimmy breaks the silence.

"Uncle Billy's dead, I figure. He and Mandingo, you can kiss their asses goodbye. I give it a ninety percent certainty."

"Make it a hundred," I say. "Whatever's left of Billy and Mandingo might be joining the shit storm on Miami Beach on an incoming tide."

Laughter comes out of the Sea Change office as we approach. The booming voice of Bruno de Rosa, the company "renovation expert," holds down the deep end of the ensemble. The soprano laughs of Colette, and Bruno's main squeeze Angie, fit nicely with the tenor counterpart of Harry Feldstein and his inimitable, "Ah, go on, Bruno. You're full of shit. How can you expect us to believe that?"

Bruno's response is also funny and rings with truth.

"Believe what you want, Harry. If I said that in front of a grand jury, some of our friends would get three to five."

"They wouldn't be friends then," Jimmy says as we enter.

Angie jumps to her feet and gives Jimmy a hug.

Bruno gives him a punch on the arm. After I get the same treatment from our newly arrived helpers, we talk over where things stand for our crew in South Florida.

"Jacky filled us in on some of it," Bruno says. "The rest of your story fits what I already know about Billy. He's kind of a loose goose, you know?"

"Nick and I never met him," Jimmy says. "Harry and Colette have been filling us in."

Bruno nods.

"I got him out of that jam in Nashville. They busted him with a couple bales of pot."

"How'd that go down?" I ask. "You set fire to the courthouse? Blow up the jail?"

"Nah, one of those country singers, some babe that Jacky knew, was doing the judge. Turns out his honor had a problem. He owned a rib place in Memphis that was doing okay until the local soul bros found out the judge owned it. They didn't like how he treated Blacks when they came before his bench. Next, there's picketing in front of the place and business ain't too good."

"I get it," Jimmy says. "Someone advises the judge to take out more insurance on the place. Never know. Could be a fire."

"They figured it must have been a slow leak in the propane tank near some overheated electrical circuit," Bruno says.

"So, that's how Billy walked," I say.

"The deal benefited everyone," Bruno says. "The judge collected, Billy walked, and the blacks in Memphis got rid of a place they hated."

"Jesus, they could use you on the Supreme Court," Jimmy says.

I'm about to make a snide comment of my own when Detective Cortez enters.

"What's this, a meeting of the minds running the Sea Change?"

"Detective Cortez, how can we help you?" Jimmy asks.

Cortez looks around the room. A red-haired guy in a golf shirt and slacks stands behind him. Red wears an expensive Rolex on his wrist and his badge on his belt. I figure he's the gun-in-the-ankle-holster type.

"Detective Cohen thought we should make a personal appearance," Cortez says.

"Welcome to the luxury of the Sea Change," Jimmy says.

"Do I see a familiar face in the room?" Cortez asks. "It wouldn't be Bruno, uh what was the last name? Was it de Rosa? Yeah. Shouldn't you be doing time somewhere for arson?"

"Not me," Bruno says. "I'm in the renovation business. You got me mixed up with someone else."

"You weren't a person of interest in the Fazio's Restaurant fire down here a few years back?"

"Someone saw me walking a poodle near the fire. They got confused."

"Confused or convinced not to testify?"

"You're the detective," Bruno says. "You figure it out. I'm here to see what we can do with this property. It needs extensive renovation. Maybe I can get you a part-time job hanging wallboard."

"Maybe you can tell me what you know about the bombing at Townsend Boat Works."

"That's yesterday's news," Bruno says. "I just got in this morning. You want to see our tickets?"

Cortez looks around the office at our assembled crew.

"I take it none of you are Bonnie Teller?" He asks.

"No, she never came back," Jimmy says. "She emptied the cash drawer and took off. Bonnie's not what you could call stable. She told us that she wounded a couple of soul brothers in Liberty City sometime back. If you find her, you could pin that on her."

"You know how many *shvartzer* shootings we have in Liberty City?" Detective Cohen asks. "Maybe we should pin all of them on this Bonnie. Then we could catch a break and go home at a decent hour for a change."

"Cohen is right," Cortez says. "The last thing I want to do is chase around Liberty City looking for victims."

"Yeah, we get it," I say. "What do you want Bonnie for? We never filed a complaint on her emptying the cash drawer."

"We got a line on two guys up in Delray Beach," Cortez says. "Could be her husband and that guy he used on the boat. They scared the hell out of a couple strolling along the beach. Made them drop their strawberry ice cream cones."

"Scared them, how?" Jimmy asks.

"What was left of the guys washed in on the tide," Cortez says. "They were handcuffed together. The sharks took some chunks. Does anyone want to do us a favor and make a positive ID?"

"I could do it," Harry says. "I knew both of them."

"I knew Billy, too," Bruno says. "I'll take a ride with Harry. Tell us where we need to go."

Cortez hands the address to Harry and turns toward Jimmy.

"We went to see Henri Boyer about the boat blowing up. He wasn't at his office. The secretary said he was due back from Haiti next week."

"Sounds like a hard guy to pin down," Jimmy says.

"Yeah," Cortez says as he turns to leave. "He's a real class act."

Chapter 20

Henri Boyer arrives at the Sea Change about two minutes after Cortez and Cohen leave. Funny how fast someone can get from Haiti to the Sea Change when emeralds are involved. He's accompanied by a bald-headed priest named Jacques Dupres, who wears the collar, black shirt, and crucifix suspended from his neck.

"I hope you don't mind," Boyer says. "Father Jacques is an important leader in the South Florida Haitian community. I think having him with will help explain our interests in this matter with Sea Change and Maroon Key."

I look at Boyer. He reminds me of Bunk Moreland, the fat cop on "The Wire." On the other hand, Father Jacques looks like a victim of lunch theft by Boyer.

"We know about Billy and his friends finding gems on some far-off Key," Boyer says. "That's really not what we're interested in. Our concerns are about something more historic. It goes back to what many of us Haitians consider to be the initial onslaught of the Europeans on our American ancestors. The rape and enslavement of an innocent people."

I look at Jimmy. He's nodding at Boyer to continue. Instead, Father Jacques speaks.

"We're looking for the skull of a Taino woman who was the companion slave of Christopher Columbus when he lived in Haiti. It is said that she bore him a son, but she died in childbirth."

"And what makes you think we might have access to it?" Jimmy asks.

"I understand your suspicions," Boyer says. "The attempts at tarnishing my reputation are widespread among the political establishment in South Florida. Commissioner Fuentes is a leading detractor of my Haitian community and me."

"What's Fuentes got against you?" I ask.

Boyer looks around the office and out at the courtyard by the pool. He leans toward us as if he's about to let us in on a cosmic secret. Instead, he plays the race card.

"Cubans like Fuentes got here by flying from Havana with suitcases full of other people's money," Boyer says. "Most of our Haitian community arrived half-drowned with only the clothes on their backs. Fuentes and his kind don't like us because we're black. When we become successful, his kind insists that we're crooks. He'll tell people that my restaurants don't pass inspections. That's because we don't want to pay off his inspectors. He doesn't tell you about Channel Seven taping his boys asking for bribes. The state's attorney was supposed to act on that, but guess what? She's a Cuban, too."

"Okay," Jimmy says. "Did Channel Seven tape the inspectors at your massage parlors, too?"

Boyer shakes his head and looks at Father Jacques.

"You see the walls we run into?" he asks.

Father Jacques shakes his head.

For a minute, there's silence. Then Boyer continues.

"Health clubs, not massage parlors. Fuentes and his Cuban garbage purveyors would like you to believe that I'm running a sex slave racket and serving arsenic at my restaurants."

"Spare the sob story," Jimmy says. "you've got a notion we can deliver this skull to you. Where'd you get that idea?"

Boyer pats Father Jacques on the arm and smiles.

"One of your workers, Mandingo, is a member of my church," Father Jacques says. "He helps out when he can at our run-down building. Mandingo used to work security for Senor Fuentes at the Scarlet Tide. He didn't like how Fuentes let drug dealers peddle narcotics in the bar. He tried to tell Fuentes what was going on, and Fuentes fired him."

"Yeah," Jimmy says. "That's how he ended up working for us at the Sea Change. Billy hired him on. So, how do we get from Mandingo getting bounced from the Scarlet Tide to this Columbus skull you think we might have a handle on?"

"Mandingo wants to help the church," Father Jacques says. "He told me about the emeralds they found and how one of your employees had them in a safe deposit box. Someone else in the party who found the emeralds had them appraised and found they might be worth fifteen hundred dollars each. Mandingo wanted to donate half his share to us."

"Nice," Jimmy says. "You could buy gold candlesticks."

"Except, that's not who we are," Father Jacques says. "We run a legal program to get immigration problems straightened out. You probably know that Mandingo is without proper papers. He also has a family back in Haiti. He'd like to bring them here."

"That still doesn't answer my question about the skull," Jimmy says.

Boyer reaches into a red leather folder and places a drawing on the countertop. It looks old, like maybe a couple hundred years old.

"This is what we're looking for," he says. "It left Haiti in the early eighteen-hundreds. There were a lot of upheavals back then. Factions killed people over control of the country. The Columbus skull was part of a prized collection of artifacts going back to when the Europeans arrived. When things got too hot in Port-au-Prince, Maurice Levant, leader of one faction, seized part of the collection and tried to ship it to New Orleans."

We stare down at the drawing. The top of a skull is there. It's decorated with a frog carved into it. Emeralds are around the frog. There appears to be a line of gold on the edge of the carving. Next to the frog is "*Xpo-Ferens*," carved into the skull. Jimmy takes a picture with his iPhone.

"It's a coqui frog," Father Jacques says. "It was the Taino symbol for a woman. That's a fine line of gold around it. Probably no more than an ounce. It's what's next to it that gives it its importance. That's how Christopher Columbus signed his name. '*Xpo Ferens*'. It's part Greek and part Latin."

"The collection left Haiti, bound for New Orleans," Boyer says. "It never arrived. The ship ran aground on rocks off the Keys. The two survivors ended up in Key West. The historical records say it was a storm that shoved the ship aground and tore it up."

I look at Jimmy. He's mulling it over.

"That's a large territory down there in the Keys," Jimmy says. "What leads you to believe that the skull was in with the jewels that Billy and his crew found?"

"When Maurice Levant shipped the seized collection, it was packed in with his collection of emeralds and gold bars," Boyer says. "The gold bars had his personal seal impressed into the metal. Several years ago, one of the smaller bars washed up on one of the Keys near Marathon, not far off from where emeralds were found by Billy and his crew. A piece of wood from an old chest was also found. It was engraved with the name of Maurice Levant. It was from the shipwreck. He had sent several chests. Some had personal effects with the gold and the emeralds. The one with the seized collection had just emeralds and gold bars."

"You want us to hand over the skull to you if we ever find it?" Jimmy asks. "I hate to be crass, gentlemen, but what's in it for us?"

Father Jacques looks at Boyer. Boyer slowly nods.

"We know of a collector who would pay ten million dollars for the skull," Father Jacques says. "We would gladly split the money with your organization, fifty-fifty."

"What's to prevent us from finding our own collector and grabbing the ten mil?"

"There are people who want artifacts seized by Levant to go back into the original collection," Boyer says. "They will be outraged if any of us found the Columbus skull and sold it to the wrong party. To them, it not only has historical significance, but it has a mystical presence as well."

"Sounds like a threat," I say.

"Call it a promise," Boyer says. "We can find the skull, sell it to the right party, and walk with blessings. You can keep the rest of the treasure and get another five million. Please think it over. With Billy and Mandingo, it should be easy for you."

"We'll let you know," Jimmy says.

The two Haitians stand up and head out the door.

As the door shuts, my cell phone rings.

It's Bruno calling from Delray Beach.

"What's left of Billy and that other guy wouldn't make good cat food," Bruno says. "Harry and I agree. They're both DOA."

Chapter 21

That brings the body count to six since we arrived in "The Sun and Fun Capital." Make that seven if you want to count the skull of the Taino woman who departed the planet some five hundred years back. If we find her Christopher Columbus autographed remains, we can claim five million bucks. That's according to Haitian big-wig Henri Boyer and his most holy sidekick Father Jacques Dupres.

Where to begin sorting out this mess?

"Maybe it's sorting itself out," Jimmy says. "Maybe attrition is the answer. Whoever's left on the board at the end of the game is usually the winner."

"Yeah," I say. "Big board. Big game. Five out of the six people that saw the emeralds wash up on the Keys are dead. Dear old Valerie Masters is the only one left. She's probably up in New York. I don't think she's working with Boyer and Father Jacques. Do you think she's in with Fuentes? She could have connected with him if she hung around the Scarlet Tide with the late, great 'Oh, oh, Ronnie' Nolan."

"Maybe it's this way," Jimmy says. "Fuentes and his crew, Vinnie Malone and his crew, and the Boyer/Father Jacques contingents have all heard about the emeralds and whatever else they might find. It could be this skull isn't bullshit. Maybe they heard it from Ronnie Nolan before he died. Or they could have heard the story from Valerie or Bonnie. You follow?"

I nod.

"The big question is this: why don't these people go and find the treasure?"

I do the noncommittal shrug. It gives Jimmy the dramatic pause he loves before he does his "District Attorney Nails the Crook Act."

"The answer is that none of them know where it is. They only have an idea based on the vague descriptions from the people who were down there.

Had they been patient, they could have followed Billy, Mandingo, and the Townsend boys to the loot."

"One of the parties knows more than the others," I say. "The one that's killing the guys that were down there knows more about where the emeralds were found. They figured they could find it on their own. That's why the bombing. That's why the shooting of the drag queen and the junky. And that's why they killed Billy and Mandingo."

"If you eliminate the other searchers, you can go down at your leisure and do the search," Jimmy says.

I'm about to answer when the office door opens.

It's hard to tell which part of her gets through the doorway first. The extra-long fake eyelashes? The silicone boob job? Maybe the oversized red wig?

"Can you guys set me up with a room for a working gal?" She slides onto a stool in front of the counter. "Usually, I deal with Bonnie. Sherry's my name. We go way back."

"Bonnie took a few days off," Jimmy says. "We're filling in."

"Cool," Sherry says. "I slip her a C-note each day for the room. She stuffs it in her bra."

"Maybe you didn't notice, but neither of us is wearing a bra," Jimmy says. "Besides, that doesn't sound like Bonnie. She doesn't work that cheap."

"What are we talking? A deuce?" Sherry tosses her hands in the air. "Come on, Bonnie and me, we used to be street sisters. Like I say, we go way back."

"How far back?" Jimmy asks. "Maybe you can tell us about Bonnie and the soul brother shooting in Liberty City."

"Uh, I think you might mean Coconut Grove?" She takes out a cigarette and lights up.

"Could be," Jimmy says. "We're new in town. We just got in from Vegas. You ever work the strip out there?"

"Outcalls, sure," Sherry says. "I worked the brothels out in Pahrump, but that got morbid in a hurry. Too many old cowboys taking their last ride on Sherry. So, what about it? A deuce?"

"You haven't told us about the soul brother shooting," Jimmy says.

Sherry glances around the room.

"Let's put it this way," she says. "Maybe someone like Bonnie and a certain red-head get picked up at a bar in the Grove by the local version of say Denzel Washington. Old Denzel wants to make it with two white women at his cottage. It's tucked behind one of the big houses."

"So, does this Denzel character have a friend?" Jimmy asks.

"No, he's got that superman attitude. He don't need a friend. He's got a bottle of Viagra, and he wants to dominate two white women. He's willing to drop six big ones for the privilege."

"Sounds like a fun guy," Jimmy says.

"A buck's a buck, and a girl's gotta eat," Sherry says. "Usually, these guys just want you to compliment them on their equipment and bullshit about how Black men are the best studs."

"But this guy was different?" I ask.

"It started okay with him taking turns on us, switching every few strokes," Sherry says. "Then, it was spankings. A little of that's okay, but then he brought out the whip. I thought he was kidding until I caught a lash on my ass."

"What happened then?" Jimmy asks.

"I screamed. Then it got worse. He brought out a straight razor. Bonnie freaked. She reached for her bag and brought out a gun. 'Oh, you want to play,' he says. He moves toward us, waving the razor like he's ready to slice and dice. I'll never forget that. Two shots. So damn loud. One to his chest. One to his head, and Bonnie saying, 'Not today, motherfucker. Not today.'"

"Jesus, that could have ruined your whole evening," Jimmy says.

"No shit. We got the hell out of there fast," Sherry says. "I thought the cops would be there any minute, but no one showed up. We caught a cab down the street. The Herald ran the story the next day. Said the dead guy was some kind of a shrink."

"That's a hell of a story," I say.

"Yeah, well, if you know Bonnie...."

"We do," Jimmy says. "We'd love to help you, but we can't let you stay here. If you turn around and look at the guy by the pool...."

"Yeah. Who's he?" Sherry asks.

“Name’s Walter White,” Jimmy says. “He’s a special agent out of Washington investigating prostitution and drugs. He’s staying here for a while. He’s been all over our books, and he’s been asking a lot of questions about Bonnie. That’s why she’s taken off for a few days. He’s already busted a couple of working gals, trying to get them to turn on some of the pimps and dealers.”

“I know the type,” Sherry says as she heads for the door. “He looks like a real dick. They love to quote Bible verses when they cuff you and slam your ass into their squad car.”

“Sorry, we couldn’t help,” Jimmy says.

“No, we’re cool,” Sherry says. “Thanks for the heads up. Here’s my card. You guys want some pussy? Give me a call.”

As she leaves, I grab two beers from the rusty fridge and hand one to Jimmy.

“One to his chest. One to his head,” Jimmy says. “That sound familiar?”

Yeah,” I say. “The junky and the drag queen got the same exit plan, and whoever killed them knew enough about the Maroon Key to idle it away from the dock into Government Cut.”

Chapter 22

"Columbus was a real son of a bitch," my wife says on our evening call from Las Vegas.

She would know. Her degrees from USC in cultural studies put her way ahead of me when it comes to the ancient world. On the other hand, I got one of my "degrees" organizing Teamsters and shutting down trucking firms. The only thing ancient in that battle was the attitudes of management. They thought employees should work for peanuts and live off the shells for their retirement.

"If you're wondering if Columbus could have had a sex slave, he probably had a dozen," Dawn says. "Would he have autographed their skulls? How would Jimmy put it, 'I'll lay you eight to five he did.' Why are you asking?"

It takes more than a few minutes to describe the situation. Bombings, shootings, and shark attacks take time. A shrink trying to slice up two hookers draws some attention, as does the appearance of Henri Boyer and Father Jacques Dupres at the Sea Change. What really gets her focus is the ten-million-dollar skull.

"Who would be after that, Nick?" Dawn asks. "Who would pay that kind of money for something like that?"

"I was hoping maybe you knew?" I ask.

"A large museum? Maybe a private collector with money to burn? Or maybe it would have some political or mystical purpose for whoever had it. It could be something to do with Voodoo. Then some don't want the cruelty of Columbus to get out into the open. They want to cover up the antics of their hero, Christopher. On the other hand, maybe it's just bullshit."

We kick around the idea for a while but come to no conclusion.

"I'll do some checking," she says. "I'll ask around. I know a woman who took pre-and post-Columbian contact courses. Her doctorate came out of that field."

We kiss-kiss goodbye.

I no sooner hang up when my phone buzzes again. It's Detective Jake Glover of the South Vegas PD. The only degree he has is the third degree.

"I checked out the names you guys gave me. I'm sending over a file attached to an email."

"Any surprises?" I ask.

"You mean other than the fact that you and Jimmy are still running around loose?"

"I'll take that as a compliment."

Glover clears his throat and takes a drink of something. It's probably a shot of Southern Comfort with a splash of Coke. I use the break to sip on my beer. If he's guessing my drink, he'll say something like, "Panther Piss in the can from 7-11."

"Yeah, you got a few jokers in the deck," Glover says. "This Ronnie Nolan gets busted for larceny about every three months. The charges get dropped by sympathetic stooges in the judiciary. Read what I sent. It gets interesting. Ronnie's got some connections."

"Had some connections," I say. "The latest word is Ronnie's last connection is to a slab in Key West. From what we heard, he died from knife wounds, or maybe a shark attack."

"The shark must have been carrying," Glover says. "According to the ME in Monroe County, Ronnie took one to the head and one to the heart."

"There's a lot of that going around here lately. You don't suppose there's some kind of a virus, do you?"

"South Florida is a virus," Glover says. "You want to hear about Valerie Masters, or should I go back to watching the Warriors beat the Celtics?"

"Give me the inside scoop on dear old Valerie. Is she famous for something? Notorious?"

"Obviously, you're not acquainted with great literature," Glover says through another sip. "Valerie is a widely respected author. Doesn't the book *Boy Toy Joy* ring a bell with you? What about *Care and Feeding of Your Boy Toy,* or *Getting Your Boy Toy to Behave*?"

"What?" I ask. "She's the author of that crap?"

"The best-selling author," Glover says. "She'd be way ahead of the game if it hadn't been for her unfortunate bouts of domestic violence."

"Okay, I get it. Some of Valerie's toy boys turned on her and beat the shit out of her."

"Nice try," Glover says. "We should have bet a few bucks on that one. You got it exactly ass-backward. Sweet Valerie comes complete with a bitchy attitude and an ornery composure. She's had to make cash settlements on some of the toys, so they'll shut up and go away. The five-figure amounts help them soothe their hurt feelings and bruised bodies."

"Think she could have done Ronnie Nolan?"

"Not likely. She's domestic abuse. No guns. Strictly things you find around the house— booze bottles, frying pans. She allegedly hit one of the boy toys with an electric fan and whipped him with the cord. That was at her house in Coral Gables. She lives large. Every time she gets busted for beating up one of the boy toys, her book sales go up."

"Sounds like an all-American success story," I say.

"I'm surprised I didn't hear some snide remark from your partner," Glover says. "He fall asleep on us?"

"No, we're at the Sea Change. Jimmy went down to the utility shed to figure out the circuit breakers in this joint. We keep losing power at night. Somehow the pool pump is on the same circuit as the lighting for the sign out front. He thinks a law degree confers electrical engineering expertise."

"He might be shocked when he finds out it doesn't."

"Jesus..."

"I know, pretty bad, pretty bad."

"You find any other dirt on anybody on the list I gave you?"

"Still looking into some of them," Glover says through another sip of whiskey. "You've got a list of all the boats at Townsend Boat Works and owners' names and addresses. Nothing there stood out, but you should look at it. There may be a connection from somebody on your end. Harry Feldstein might know some of the names."

"Good idea. I'll check it out with him."

"Good. I got to get back to the game. I'm betting the Celtics can beat the point spread."

We ring off.

I look around the office. It's in better shape than when we first saw it a few days back. The red leather bag with Bonnie's .38 is gone. The countertop where she rested her red toenails is clean. Some improvement. A little, at least.

I go back to my laptop to look at the file Glover has sent. Nothing stands out. A bunch of names. People, addresses, and boats. The stuff on Ronnie Nolan and Valerie Masters is better. There's even a picture of Valerie on the cover of a writer's magazine. According to a Miami-Dade police report, she's five feet two, with eyes of blue. America's sweetheart. Detective Glover has done an excellent job.

I hear the office door open. I'm about to ask Jimmy to grab some beers for us out of the rusty fridge. Except when I look up, it isn't Jimmy. It's a walking slime ball holding a Sig Sauer P229 pistol, complete with a suppressor, aimed at me.

"Here's the way it's gonna be, motherfucker," he says. "You got a paper with some numbers on it. Bonnie left it in the cash drawer. You're gonna give it to me. Ya got it, motherfucker?"

"Yeah?" I ask. "What if I don't got it, motherfucker?"

"You making fun of the way I talk, motherfucker?" he asks.

Before I can reply, a bullet whizzes past my head into the wooden cabinet behind me.

"I'm not fucking around," Slime Ball says. "Gimme the paper Bonnie wants, or the next one goes through your head."

Chapter 23

Slime Ball's Sig Sauer pistol pointed at me keeps looking larger. His vocabulary stays small. To prove it, he repeats himself.

"I'm not fucking around," he says. "Gimme the paper Bonnie wants, or the next one goes through your head."

Outside the dimly lit Sea Change office, the pool lights flicker. I think of lightning in one of those Frankenstein movies. Slime Ball could play the lead role.

How do I talk my way out of this one? Where's the cavalry when the hero needs it?

"Uh, sure thing," I say, stalling for time. "That paper's around here somewhere. One of the girls was cleaning things and straightening out files. I'll find it."

Can I turn, duck behind the counter, and grab my Glock before Slime fires his cannon at poor old Nick?

I glance around for possible cover behind the wooden counter. It looks like plywood. A half-inch thick. It won't do shit to stop what Slime is firing.

Would thick metal do it? The only metal is the red fire extinguisher sitting in its white plastic base. It might stop a bullet from entering my head.

But what about the rest of me? Slime doesn't seem like the marksman type. He's more the type that would waste a whole clip to kill a canary.

"Quit bullshitting," Slime Ball says. "Bonnie says she left it in the cash register."

To reinforce Slime's version of logical thinking, he sends another bullet whizzing past my ear. He's fighting the shakes. He's high on something and dancing around like he should have taken a piss an hour ago.

If I duck right and roll toward the fire extinguisher, can I get the Glock out of the back of my pants before Slime gets off a clip?

The pool lights flicker again like lightning in a horror movie. They back-light Slime making him more the monster than he probably deserves. He's just a cokehead with a cannon in his hands.

"The cash register, motherfucker," he says. "She put it in the fucking cash register."

"Okay, okay," I say. "Let me see if I can open it. We're having trouble with the electric."

"No shit, this place is a dump."

I hit the button to open the drawer, knowing that the precious paper isn't there. Will I get a second chance? Or will Slime unload a clip on me?

The drawer slides out.

A loud buzz echoes through the office.

The pool lights flash. Everything at the Sea Change goes dark.

"What the fuck?" Slime says.

I duck and roll to the floor in the dark.

Slime fires three shots at where I just stood. They destroy the cash register.

I'm on the floor. I reach for my Glock, only it isn't there.

It's somewhere loose on the floor from my duck and roll, but I can't make it out in the dark.

"You're one dead motherfucker," Slime says.

He comes around the counter fast like he wants to kill someone.

Me.

I kick my legs out. Slime goes down hard.

We're on the floor together, grabbing and punching.

He bites my hand. I poke his eyes.

I know I have to kill him.

He's the seven-foot rattlesnake in my bathtub.

The giant black scorpion from my worst nightmare.

He reaches, feeling for his gun on the floor.

Maybe he'll grab my Glock.

I grab something metal. It's the red fire extinguisher.

I swing it at Slime's head and connect with enough force to stun him.

He turns toward me. I can just make out a gun in his hand.

I slam the base of the extinguisher onto his head.

He falls back to the floor. The gun fires. The bullet ricochets off the fire extinguisher.

"Motherfucker." Slime moans.

"Motherfucker, my ass," I say.

Again, I slam the end of the extinguisher onto his head. He's down but not out.

But he's going out. I slam the extinguisher again. Now I'm on my knees over his body, yelling.

"Motherfucker. Motherfucker. Die, motherfucker."

I slam again.

I'm killing the rattlesnake.

I slam again.

The black scorpion.

I slam again.

The lights in the office come back on.

Slime's eyes are closed. There's blood all over the fire extinguisher and the floor.

The Sig Sauer with the suppressor slips out of Slime's left hand. His right hand still holds my Glock. But he isn't going to shoot anyone.

Ever.

The office door opens.

It's Jimmy.

"What the hell, Nick?"

I'm laughing and crying at the same time.

"Look at my hands," I say. "They're bloody. They're bloody."

"Jesus," Jimmy says. "What the hell happened?"

I hear "Jesus" echoing through the room.

It takes a minute to register who all's saying, "Jesus."

It's Bruno and Harry back from Delray Beach.

"Nick needs a drink," Jimmy says. "We all could use one."

"There's a bottle in my room," Bruno says. "I'll get some cleaning materials, too."

"I know where they're stored," Harry says. "I'll get the first aid kit from the car."

A few minutes later, after a few hot towels, some bandages, and a few shots of Jack on ice served in plastic glasses, I'm ready to talk.

"Who the hell is this guy?" Bruno asks, staring down at what's left of Slime Ball.

I tell my story to the three nodding heads.

"Maybe I shouldn't have left to try to fix the circuit breakers," Jimmy says.

"No, you could have stayed and got us both killed," I say. "Your circuit breaker experiments saved my life."

"You know what this means, don't you?" Harry asks. "It's that goddamn Bonnie and that asshole Vinnie Malone. We can't let this one slide."

"Damn right," Bruno says. "Nobody hurts us and gets a free pass."

Jimmy has Slime Ball's wallet.

"Four hundred bucks, a gram of coke, and pictures of his car, a red Dodge Charger with a naked broads license holder on the front. The back has the understated metal chain license holder."

"His name ain't really Slime Ball, is it?" Harry asks.

"No," Jimmy says. "You're looking at what's left of Myron Moran of Dania, Florida."

"Myron Moran, or Moron Moran?" Harry asks.

"Not much difference," Bruno says. "We saw his car parked when we pulled in."

"Yeah," Harry says. "Well, we can't leave him here. I don't want Colette and Angie to see this. Besides, it would be bad for business to have a stiff stinking up the place."

Chapter 24

The four of us sit in the Sea Change office, staring down at what's left of Myron Moran, aka "Slime Ball." He's no longer adding blood to the puddle on the floor, and my pulse is no longer running the marathon in a New York minute. The smell of spent gunpowder exits the room through the rattling exhaust fan above the back door.

"We need to get rid of this guy," Bruno says. "But where?"

"Hey, I've seen this guy before," Harry says. He's holding Slime Ball's driver's license.

"So, what? Is he somehow famous?" Bruno asks.

"In a way. He and Vinnie Malone were involved in a big dust-up at the Scarlet Tide. It made the news, a front-page scandal. Cesar Fuentes tried to stop Malone and his buddy here from entering Scarlet Fuentes's last fashion show. Cesar told Malone that he didn't want him near his wife. Supposedly, Malone wised off, saying, 'What's it to you, Cesar? You don't care about her needs. You only want to do lines of coke with Norman in your Jacuzzi.'"

"I bet that went over well," Jimmy says.

"There was a fight. Slime Ball here punched one of Fuentes' lackeys in the jaw and busted it. Malone got tossed into a table full of champagne glasses. They say that Scarlet ran over to see if Malone was hurt, crying, 'Vinnie, Vinnie.' The cops showed up, and Cesar tried to get everything hushed up. He didn't want to press charges. He wanted it to just go away. Too bad. The press was there to cover a fashion opening. They got a bonus. Instead of being a feature for the weekend edition, it was front-page news, the lead story on the tv news that night."

"So, Vinnie Malone was doing Cesar's wife?" Jimmy asks. "Is this his pattern? Like now, he's doing Billy's wife?"

"He doesn't consult me before he drops his pants," Harry says. "If I were betting, I'd say yes."

"I'd go with that," Jimmy says.

"Anyway, word got around about Malone and Scarlet being lovers and that Cesar Fuentes was *un maricon*. The Cuban community ate it all up. They love stories about scandalous love affairs and rich guys turning out to be queers. That all ended when Scarlet died in the shark attack. Cesar got back the sympathy of the community and five million bucks to boot."

Jimmy's got one of those grins. He looks like the cat that just found a way to do in the canary and put the blame on the poodle.

"I know what we can do with our friend Slime Ball," he says.

"Better do something," Harry says. "The sun will be up in about four hours. Hard to dispose of a stiff in the daylight unless you're feeding gators in the Everglades."

"I was thinking of someplace a little closer," Jimmy says. "We need to get to work, get Slime Ball into his car, clean up. I think this will work."

It doesn't take long for us to arrive at our destination. Traffic is light as we head south. The streets are dark. Most businesses are shut up tight for the night. The street sweeping machines make their way along Collins Avenue. An occasional cop car sits by the curb. Homeless people use the quiet to sleep against the walls of shops. The loudest sound comes from the ocean attacking the beach.

Jimmy's plan works without a hitch. In minutes, our caravan heads back north on Collins. A couple cop cars speed past us, going south. Flashing lights and sirens. The quiet night is over. I get on a burner phone and start my list of calls to the news media.

"Hello," I say. "This is Detective Cohen. I just wanted to straighten out a few facts about tonight's shooting at the Scarlet Tide on South Beach...."

Morning is getting close to noon when we finally wake up in our suite at the Fontainebleau. A hard night deserves a good rest, followed by waffles and sausages delivered by room service.

"Click on the tv news," Jimmy says. "Let's see how our show is doing."

"...Jennifer Roberts is live outside the Scarlet Tide on South Beach," the announcer says.

Police tape surrounds Slime Ball's car and drapes itself around the corners of the Scarlet Tide.

"A fatal shooting at the famous Scarlet Tide on South Beach, Bob," Jennifer says. "Miami-Dade law enforcement is on the scene, investigating how it happened early this morning. According to a source in the detective bureau, dead is Myron Moran of Dania, with a gunshot to the head and one to the chest. Moran, police speculate, was trying to break into the club using a tire iron. Notice the busted window on the front of the club. Someone inside the club shot Moran using a Sig Sauer pistol with a silencer. The gun was found just inside that busted window."

"Is there a suspect in custody, Jennifer?" Announcer Bob asks.

"Not at this time, Bob. His car was parked in front of the club. Police found cocaine on Moran. Moran was involved in a fistfight at the Scarlet Tide last year when he and alleged drug smuggler Vinnie Malone tried to crash a fashion opening at the club. Speculation led some to believe that Vinnie Malone was having an affair with Dade Commissioner Cesar Fuentes' wife, Scarlet. The well-known fashion designer died shortly after that incident in a shark attack in the Upper Keys."

"Any reaction, Jennifer, from Commissioner Fuentes or Vinnie Malone?"

"According to a police source, Commissioner Fuentes has no idea who might have been in the club at the early hour of four am. Everything was locked-up. We called Vinnie Malone. He says that Myron Moran was a guy he didn't know very well, a casual acquaintance he'd run into at various clubs. What was he doing trying to break into the Scarlet Tide? Malone couldn't say."

Announcer Bob comes back into view.

"Thank you, Jennifer. We'll have more on that story this evening. There are still no leads in the case of a fishing captain and his first mate, who washed up dead in Delray Beach. Authorities are investigating. There may be a drug connection in that one. Oscar Talbot has more."

Oscar stands near a group of palm trees near the ocean.

"The bodies of Captain Billy Teller and his first mate, an undocumented Haitian going by the name of Mandingo, washed up here, on Delray Beach yesterday. The two men were handcuffed together. Both received gunshots to the head and to the chest. Police say they were then tossed into the ocean, possibly tied down with weights. The two were identified yesterday by acquaintances. The DEA says the investigation continues."

Before Bob can thank Oscar, Jimmy clicks off the set.

"Looks like we did okay with it," Jimmy says.

"Yeah, great shot of the naked bimbo license plate holders on Slime Ball's car."

"How'd you like the waffles?" Jimmy asks. "Everything okay?"

"Yeah. I'm glad we did what we did with Slime Ball and Fuentes."

"What else?"

"I keep thinking about Slime Ball's bullet ricocheting off the fire extinguisher."

"I know." Jimmy shakes his head and looks out toward the ocean.

"That could have been the end of me," I say. "It was that close. We might be getting too old for this kind of crap."

"Or maybe we're getting too smart." Jimmy looks back at me and hands me a napkin from the serving cart. "It looks like your allergies might be kicking up again."

I wipe my eyes and look up to thank him, but he's already gone to get ready for the day.

Chapter 25

"It's like this," Harry says. "You look at comparable canal front properties in this neighborhood. A place the size of the Sea Change goes for more as an empty lot than it does as what we might charitably call 'a boutique fixer-upper'"

We're sitting in the Sea Change office, inhaling the not-so-subtle smell of bleach and other disinfectants. They're the leftovers from cleaning up remnants of Slime Ball's demise.

Jimmy looks at Harry and then glances at me for my reaction.

"Are you saying that we could lose money by selling this place as is?" Jimmy asks.

"Developers don't want to buy something they have to tear down," Harry says. "They want a clean slate. If they buy and have to demolish, it creates a mess of permits and assholes coming out of the woodwork trying to preserve a historic site. They don't want the headache."

"You calling this dump a historic site?" Jimmy asks. "Nothing ever happened here that anyone wants to own up to."

Harry shrugs.

"If somehow, we make the building go away, aren't we looking for trouble from an arson investigation?" I ask. "Detective Cortez has already spotted Bruno on the scene. It would take an idiot not to tie him into the deed."

Bruno waves and smiles from the beat-up red Naugahyde chair next to the souvenir postcard rack.

"I'm betting Cortez is negotiable," Harry says. "He didn't get that big gold chain from the Police Athletic League. We could give him something to make him happy. He's sniffing around. I'm not sure he's doing this because he's a good cop. He might be hungry."

"You got proof on this vacant property price instead of one with a place like this on it?" Jimmy asks.

"Sure, across the canal. You got six floors of luxury units with a pool and their own small boat docks. That empty lot sold quickly for a million more than this joint has asked. I could show you more, but that one's the nearest example."

"We should run this through Jacky," Jimmy says.

"I teased him with it earlier today," Harry says. "I said you guys had been kicking around the possibility. I'm not taking any credit. I just said you two were smart and should be listened to. Of course, if he says go ahead, I want my taste."

"Of course," Jimmy says. "We'll all get if this works."

"We got to head out," Bruno says. "We promised the girls we'd do lunch at the Eden Roc."

"Supposed to be good food, nice view," Harry says. "We'll catch you two later."

They leave. I look at Jimmy.

"Is this idea of Harry's a little far out?"

"No more than the rest of what's happened since we arrived," Jimmy says.

I look down at the spot where Slime Ball bled out. Anyone who looked close could pick out the bullet holes in the wall from his Sig Sauer. There's another bullet hole in the ceiling beam from the slug that bounced off the fire extinguisher. I'm about to say something to Jimmy when two familiar faces enter the office.

"Jesus," Detective Cortez says. "What's with all the bleach? You two kill someone and have to cover your tracks?"

"It's our new manager, Colette," Jimmy says. "She thinks that the smell of bleach will drive away all the vermin. I think she got carried away."

"It'll drive away the two-legged variety," Cohen says.

"What can we do for you gents?" I ask.

Cortez slides his butt onto one of the stools in front of the counter.

"A few loose ends, you could say."

I look at Cohen. He's still standing, casting his eyes around the room. If he's looking for anything out of order, he's in the right place. The whole joint is hinky. I hope he doesn't have a nose for spent lead.

"What kind of loose ends?" Jimmy asks.

"For starters," Cortez says. "You can come get your boat. We're done with it. It's still got half a tank of fuel. You'll need new dock lines. The Coast Guard tied it off with a red plastic line."

"I'm betting the anchor is missing," Jimmy says. "There's supposed to be a small skiff, too. Any of your cops fond of dinghies?"

"Our people aren't like that," Cohen says, staring up at the ceiling.

"No, we're hard-working cops." Cortez winks. "We've been thinking, though, about how you boys hit the town, and next thing the body count goes up. You got the drag queen, the doper shot dead on your boat, the Townsend boys were blown to hell, and then your captain and first mate show up dead on Delray Beach."

"It's funny that good police work hasn't kept anyone safe around here," Jimmy says. "Maybe you boys need to work harder. Next, you'll be trying to blame us for that goof that bought the farm last night at the Scarlet Tide."

"It's that asshole that worked for Vinnie Malone," Cortez says. "He bought it trying to bust in through the plate glass window at the Tide."

"Maybe he was in a hurry to buy drugs," I say.

"Sure, wise guy," Cohen says. "I got a bone to pick with you. Some guy called it into one of the news stations right after it went down. Said he was me. I wanted to make sure they got the facts right on the shooting. I heard the tape of the phone tip. It could have been you."

"You sure? Whenever I call in an anonymous tip, I try to sound like Sylvester the Cat. Did the caller say, 'thufferin' thuccotash?'"

"Very funny," Cohen says.

"It was probably some other Cohen on the force," I say. "Don't they give out a ten-dollar reward for the tip of the week?"

"I think it's twenty."

"Tell you what," I say. "We'll go down to that station together, and I'll tell them it was me. Then you and I can split the twenty bucks. Now that's the kind of community police work that pays off."

"Yeah, very funny," Cohen says. "Hey, what's with the hole in your ceiling beam? That a bullet hole?"

"We're thinking termites," Jimmy says. "We're scheduling some work to be done on the building. We can't have the place collapsing on people."

"How about I get on the counter? Dig into that hole to see what's in there?" Cohen says.

"How about you quit acting like the Jewish Gestapo and getting a search warrant," Jimmy says. "You know, we could help you guys big time, but not if you're going to treat us like dirt. Or maybe you like stumbling around from one unsolved case to another."

"Hey...," Cohen starts to say.

"Wait," Cortez says. "Let's hear them out."

"I just want to say what I think," Jimmy says. "Before we become allies."

Cortez nods.

"I'm betting the doper and the drag queen were shot with a .38. That sound right?"

Cortez nods again.

"Regarding Billy and his sidekick Mandingo, I'll ride the same horse, a .38."

"Okay," Cortez says. "Good so far. What else you got for me?"

"How about a year ago in Coconut Grove, a black guy dies in his cottage after taking one to the head and one to the chest? That one was a .38, too."

"That sounds familiar," Cortez says. "Tell me a few details."

"Among the toys found around his naked body were a whip and a straight razor."

"Jesus," Cohen says. "That sounds like that psychiatrist."

"Coleman Jennings," Cortez says. "Dr. Feelgood. How far does all of this lead?"

"Depends on how far you want to go," Jimmy says. "All those slugs came out of the same gun, held by the same shooter. It starts with a hooker named Sherry. It should go all the way to taking out a major drug smuggler with charges of conspiracy to commit murders. Maybe you don't want it? It could also take out one of the smuggler's major retailers on South Beach. Once all the rats start ratting on each other, no telling where it will go."

One look at Cortez and Cohen tells me they're ready to bet the farm. They need a slight push.

"Jimmy," I say. "You might be putting too much pressure on our guests. Maybe Drug Enforcement is a better fit?"

"No, we want it," Cortez says. "What do you want in exchange?"

Chapter 26

Pizza with beers in a darkened restaurant is a great way to talk with Detectives Cortez and Cohen. We listen as they open up about what it takes and takes out of you to be a cop in Miami.

"They'll tell you you're working a shift, but they never tell you that your hours are more a suggestion than a rule," Cohen says. "If you do everything by the book, you're fucked."

"People hear the word 'cops,' and they think of that goof on *Blue Bloods*-chasing perps over rooftops and tossing bums over the hood of a car," Cortez says. "They don't realize one of our major concerns is having enough disposable gloves. We have to handle the geniuses this great society has left in the gutter."

"It's one thing for a guy to walk on a DUI because he's got an in with the judge or the prosecutor," Cohen says. "When they get a wrist slap on murder one, it cuts deep. You know the truth. You have to live with it."

"You send some guy to prison on a minor drug charge," Cortez says. "Is that doing any good? He'll come out resentful and ready to commit a major crime with his new friends. What the hell does that do to make things better for the public?"

"We know you guys aren't angels," Cohen says. "You ever do any time?"

"Only for drunk and disorderly," Jimmy says. "Way back in the days when we were young and chasing tail around in Chicago bars. Most of it was Nick's fault."

"We've settled down since then," I say. "I still keep a muzzle and a leash handy for Jimmy. We're usually in Vegas, helping to manage the Galloping Dominos Casino. We live across the fairway from each other on a golf course. We're both married to smarter women than us and much better looking. Jimmy's labradoodle, Zorro, is teaching my five-year-old daughter to do backflips into our pool."

"What really brought you down here?" Cohen asks.

"Billy Teller," Jimmy says. "He's a total fuck up, or he was. He's a shirt-tail relative of our boss. Billy's the kind of guy that gets busted in Nashville for pot in his trunk because he's too cheap to fix his brake lights."

"There's a whole spawn of those guys down here," Cohen says. "They come down I-95 from dumps up north. Rather than drive off into the ocean, they stop in Miami, snort some coke and wonder why the world isn't handing them free money."

"Anyway, Billy's run the Sea Change into the ground," Jimmy says. "We're here to accept a decent offer on the property and leave town. There's another investment down in the Keys, a small marina, that we have to clean up after Billy, and then we get to head home."

"The Sea Change is pretty run down," Cortez says. "That could be a problem. You got plans to make it more attractive to a buyer?"

"We're trying to bring back the wooden floors in the place to see if that helps," Jimmy says. "Old pictures of the place show beautiful oak underneath the varnish that's been ground down over the years. We'll try sanding and putting down linseed oil to see how that goes. We'll hire locals to do it, maybe some of the jobless that are down on their luck. The idea is to see if we're better off demolishing the place or keeping it."

"Linseed oil can be tricky," Cohen says. "It's been known to self-combust if rags are tossed into a box and left to generate heat."

"Do you think that could be a problem?" Jimmy asks.

"Not in my book." Cortez smiles. "You might be better off with a vacant lot."

Everyone laughs. Our waiter brings another pitcher of beer.

"Anyway," Jimmy says. "We're shutting down the place, shipping our guests over to the Eden Roc for the remainders of their scheduled stays. No sense getting a bad name while trying to clean up Billy Teller's mess."

"Sounds like a good plan," Cortez says. "I'm thinking it will all go well. Now let's discuss our end of the bargain."

"I should start with the story that got everyone excited about buying the Sea Change," Jimmy says. "Supposedly, two clients of the Sea Change went down to Marathon and rented a boat from Billy. They went to one of the Keys in the flats north of the main road. The story goes that they found jewels there. The two had an argument and left separately, one in the boat, the other in a Zodiac. Whether they found anything is questionable. No one saw jewels, but that didn't prevent Billy, Mandingo, and the Townsend boys from going down to check it out."

"Did they buy a treasure hunter guide to the Keys?" Cohen asks. "There's a bunch of phonies peddling all kinds of scams down there."

"Don't know about that," Jimmy says. "They did come back with a story that they found jewels down there. They let the word out, and people like Malone and Fuentes got interested. Could they buy the Sea Change and hire Billy to be their guide to all that hidden wealth?"

"So, Billy runs a scam in an attempt to unload the Sea Change?" Cohen asks.

"He ain't exactly new to this," Jimmy says. "He used to unload fake jewelry back on Maxwell Street in Chicago. He probably flashed some of the cheap glitz around here as part of the so-called treasure he found."

"Cute," Cortez says. "Who do you think clipped him?"

"Cherchez la femme," Jimmy says. "Billy's wife, Bonnie, has been warming up Vinnie Malone's bed. She's the one who emptied our cash register and took off. She came back later to grab more from the office. The problem was we had changed the locks. One of our guests got into a shouting match with her and called the cops. She took off running."

"So, why so sure that this Bonnie shot her husband and this Mandingo guy?" Cortez asks.

Jimmy looks at me and nods.

"Let's talk for a minute about Coleman Jennings," I say. "The black shrink takes one to the head and one to the chest from a .38. I'm assuming your boys took prints from the crime scene."

"Yeah, but nothing matched up with anyone in the system," Cohen says. "There were prints lifted off some sex toys, and some blood was found on the business end of a whip. Again, no one in the system matched up."

"We pushed it pretty hard," Cortez says. "Jennings was famous, had an image like Obama. People were shocked. He was a frequent critic of politicians like Fuentes."

"Yeah, Fuentes made some comments about black people that got him heat from Jennings," Cohen says. "The Haitians and the Bahamians were down on old Cesar. So were a lot of our home-grown Blacks. The Townsend boys were trying to get State Senator Lincoln Pierce to run against Fuentes."

"That gets me wondering if old Cesar had something to do with the bomb that took out the Townsends," Jimmy says. "I'm not sure we can help you there, but we have something you'll like."

"I think we can give you a working gal to match up to the blood on the whip," I say. "There's a good chance she'll fit some of the prints. She was there when it went down. Lean on her heavy, and you'll get the shooter. She'll give you Bonnie in exchange for getting off easy. The slugs from Billy, Mandingo, and the two on our boat should match up with Bonnie's heavy metal."

Cortez smiles and sips his beer.

"So, if we get that far...?"

"You can get Malone," Jimmy says. "Bonnie knows a lot about his operation. My guess is that Malone did a lot of business with Fuentes before they had the falling out over Scarlet. Interestingly, both Malone and Fuentes bought into the story that Billy and the crew had found a treasure in the Keys. It wouldn't surprise me if you found out that one of them had bombed the Townsend's boat."

"So, word got out that Bonnie knew where this so-called treasure was hidden," Cohen says. "Take out the four guys who know where it might be, and you have a clear shot at it."

"Yeah," Jimmy says. "We figure she shot the drag queen and the junky when they showed up in South Beach asking what to do with the Maroon Key. The best guess is that the two heroes were supposed to sink Billy and Mandingo to the bottom. Maybe scuttle the Maroon Key or set it on fire and take the small skiff to the shore up near Delray. Somehow the skiff got away while they were shoving bodies overboard. They panicked and brought the boat to Miami."

"I like it," Cortez says. "We have a confidential informant who can verify Malone selling to Fuentes. We've been waiting to get more dirt, but multiple murders make it all the sweeter. So, where do we find this star witness?"

Jimmy nods at me.

"Her name is Sherry."

I slide her card to Cortez.

"She does outcalls," I say.

"I'll bet she does." Cortez smiles and winks.

Chapter 27

It doesn't take long for things to start happening.

The morning after our pizza and beer with detectives Cortez and Cohen, we inform our guests at the Sea Change that the rest of their stays will be at the Eden Roc. Management in Chicago has decided to honor them with the upgrade. Major construction and remodeling of the beautiful place they've been staying is about to happen. All are happy about the upgrade.

"Don't suppose the Eden Roc lets gators into its pool?" Walter White asks.

"Only if they have a high credit rating," Jimmy says.

A phone call to Jacky in Chicago to let him know our plans goes better than expected.

"Harry filled me in on what you guys were thinking of doing," Jacky says. "If you've got carte blanche from our new-found friends in law enforcement, it could fly. I know a couple developers who might be interested in the empty site. They like to work from a clean slate."

"That seems do-able, now," Jimmy says.

"It's better still if you can get even with who's responsible for Billy's demise."

"We can do that," Jimmy says.

"Good," Jacky says. "I don't want to mention any names, *capisce*? But nobody walks away after doing dirt to any of us."

Jimmy and I *capisce*.

Our online ad for workers to restore the wooden floors at the Sea Change is getting attention.

Bruno sits in the office, screening applicants over the phone.

"The response is great," he says. "It's just hard to separate the sheep from the goats, especially when we want to hire the goats."

The other problem with Jimmy's "bring back the wonderful oaken floors" campaign is that there may not be oaken floors. It's a line of bullshit he tossed out to Cortez and Cohen. The whole building has cheap linoleum. We're guessing that there's some kind of wood underneath.

Bruno waves his hand at us and motions that we need to hear the phone call he's on. He punches the speaker button.

"Back to you, Don," Bruno says. "You say you worked construction on work release?"

"Yeah, they had me in on a drunk and disorderly. A bad rap all around. They had us building fences and gates out at the cattle farm. Well, we didn't want to work too hard in the heat. Neither did our supervisors. Around ten each morning was a 'coffee break.' They'd bring us a case of beer. Made the work go better. By noon we were thirsty again. Another case of brewskis with the pizza, and we'd bust our asses until two. That's when 'afternoon coffee break' came."

"More beers?" Bruno asks.

"Yeah, yeah, and a bottle of vodka, too. Jesus, could we build gates. Pretty damn straight, too. Two-by-sixes with bolts and nuts, not nails. No fuckin' bull was walking through that."

"How many guys were on your crew?" Bruno asks.

"Just the three of us and the two supervisors. I could give you their phone number, but I don't think the supervisors work there anymore."

"Not important," Bruno says.

"Anyway," Don says. "The three of us got out together, and we stay in touch. We do jobs like what you're talking about. We're good drinking buddies. Semper Fi, number one. Goddamn right."

"You think you and your buddies would have any trouble ripping up linoleum and sanding floors for a coat of linseed oil?"

"Piece of cake. What's it pay?"

"Three hundred cash a day, plus we supply the sandwiches and the beer. We don't want any unhappy workers."

"When do we start?"

Bruno writes down Don's info and tells him a few more details.

"How many guys you got like that?" Jimmy asks after Bruno gets off the phone.

"Eleven, but maybe only six or seven will show up."

By noon, the hardware store delivers the sanders and other tools along with way too much linseed oil.

As we move things around to the units, it hits home what a dump the Sea Change is. The air conditioners are smoke-stained leftovers. They look like they're about to fall out of the moldy wood-paneled walls. The furniture is Goodwill rejects. The televisions are an embarrassment, and the place smells of piss and cheap cigars.

We stack the furniture in two units near the office, clearing the way for our workforce. We're ready, waiting for word from Cohen and Cortez that things are moving on their end.

The Sea Change office smells of corned beef, pickles, and mustard. Remnants of what the deli delivered are scattered all over the counter. Harry finishes his beer, belches, and tosses the can across the room toward the trash can.

"You only missed the three-pointer by a mile, LeBron," Bruno says.

"I was fouled in the act of shooting," Harry says. "Where the hell are those guys in trying to arrest that hooker? Shouldn't we have heard?"

I look at Jimmy. He looks at his watch and shrugs.

"The waiting is the hardest part. Have another beer."

Seven p.m. rolls around. Nothing from Cortez and Cohen.

"We need you two to take the Maroon Key down to Marathon," Jimmy says. "Nick and I will hold down this part of the plan. I know we'll need a new anchor and some dock lines. There's a marine supply store that Billy used to deal with not too far from here. Think you can handle it?"

"Nothing to it," Harry says. "Be okay if we take Colette and Angie?"

"Sure, why not?" Jimmy looks at his watch again.

"Could be fun," Bruno says. "We'll load up a cooler."

We sip our beers and stare at each other.

I look at the clock above the doorway to the office. It's 7:15. I wonder if time is slowing down or maybe getting ready to back up.

Jimmy starts to say something but is interrupted by the ringing phone.

It's Cortez.

"One of our guys took down the exotic Sherry at a motel just off the interstate," he says. "Prostitution, possession of a gram of coke. Brought her in, fingerprinted her, and what do you know? She matched up to a glass at the Coleman Jennings crime scene. She started to sing that she didn't do it. She was just a gal with hard luck, trying to make a few bucks."

"Of course," Jimmy says. "We're all choir boys, too."

"About then, Cohen starts playing good cop, telling her that maybe she could walk on probation if she cooperates," Cortez says. "All we want is the shooter. Sherry says she doesn't know much about her, but she knows Bonnie hangs out with Vinnie Malone. She's seen the two of them together at clubs on South Beach. She says she would have gone to the cops after the shooting, but she was afraid that Bonnie would find her and kill her."

"Of course," Jimmy says. "What are friends for?"

"We go over to Malone's with a warrant," Cortez says. "We knock on the door. First, Malone says that Bonnie ain't around. Then we hear her inside. That's enough. We bust past Malone. Bonnie stands there, screaming, 'You fucking asshole,' at Malone for letting us in. We cuff her and read her the Miranda. Then we notice Malone reaching into a red leather bag and tossing something off the balcony into the water below."

"I'm guessing it's a Smith & Wesson .38," Jimmy says.

"It was a wet Smith & Wesson .38 when our diver retrieved it," Cortez says. "Looks like multiple counts of murder one for Bonnie. So far, we've got accessory after the fact on Malone along with obstruction of justice. There's a possibility of a conspiracy to commit murder, too."

"Sounds like you've had a busy day," I say.

"Could get a lot busier in the days to come," Cortez says. "Malone might be willing to get a lighter rap for what he knows about Commissioner Fuentes."

"We're glad it's turning out for you," Jimmy says.

"Me, too," Cortez says. "How's your remodel project? Are you getting it together?

"Almost ready. Most of the pieces are in place."

"Good," Cortez says. "Anybody gives you any shit about it, tell them to see me."

Chapter 28

Our early morning drive to the Sea Change has all-news radio reporting the latest:

"A breakthrough in the murder of psychiatrist Coleman Jennings," the announcer says. "Sources say police have two prostitutes in custody. They may have taken part in the killing of the popular Coconut Grove doctor. One of the women lives with an alleged major drug smuggler. All have South Beach nightclub connections. We'll bring you details on this as they become available...."

"Jesus, Nick," Jimmy says. "Don't tell me you did some of those Sylvester the Cat phone tips. Cohen's going to be pissed."

"Not me," I say. "Maybe some reporters have done some digging."

A minute later, my phone rings. It says, "Cohen." I'm ready for him to go ballistic.

"You hear what the news stations are saying this morning?" Cohen says."

"Yeah, but..."

"But nothing," Cohen says. "Isn't it great? We chose a few better reporters and dropped a few hints on them. We want those involved to get scared. Who knows where this could lead? We think that the C4 that blew up the Townsends came from one of those projects of Commissioner Fuentes. We want all the players to be nervous."

"That sounds like a plan," I say. "They get nervous; they'll make mistakes."

"Yeah, isn't it great? Got to run. Talk later."

He rings off.

"Another happy customer," Jimmy says. "We need to get our end done and move on."

We roll up to the Sea Change. Harry and Bruno are talking with a group of men who look like they might be capable of working. Some are drinking coffee and Red Bull while sitting on the tailgates of old pickup trucks.

"We'll show you the job," Bruno says, walking the crew into one of the units. "It's straightforward. Rip up the linoleum, sand the wood, and lay down the linseed oil."

"You want us to take the floor sander and rip right through this shit you got covering it?" One of the barely sober crew asks.

"No way," another guy says. "You got to chisel it. Pry it loose."

Most get the idea that the linoleum has to be ripped up before any sanding can start. One guy gets to work, ripping up a linoleum section with a small crowbar.

"Just as I thought," he says. "It's a medium-grade oak that they used a lot of right after the war. The VA was backing housing for vets. Tons of it came down here. I think we can bring it back."

I look at Jimmy. This guy says there's natural oak flooring at the Sea Change. He's impressed.

"Excuse me, but how do you know all that?" Jimmy asks.

"I've seen a lot of it," he says. "Henry over there tells me that you and your friend here are the main guys honchoing the project. That right?"

"You mean Harry?"

"Harry, Henry, whatever. Give me a minute to talk to you guys."

We step out into the courtyard by the pool.

"I get what you guys are trying to do with this place," he says with a wink. "By the way, my name's Don. I talked yesterday to one of your guys, Barney."

"Bruno," I say.

"Barney, Bruno, whatever."

"So, what do you think we're trying to do here?" I ask.

"It's obvious," Don says. "Look at the crew you have. Most are low grade. Look at what you ordered for the job. Too much linseed oil and heavy-duty equipment. I know where you're headed. Believe me, I've been down this road before."

"You say it's obvious," Jimmy says. "What's so obvious?"

"Okay."

Don takes a cigarette out of a metal case with "Semper Fi" engraved on it. His Zippo has the Marines emblem on it. When he lights his cigarette, I worry that he'll go up in flames from the alcohol on his breath. Somehow, we luck out. Two puffs, and he's ready to say more than "Okay."

"My guess," Don says. "And I'm rarely wrong about these things. You guys got yourself in deeper Shinola than you bargained for. You figure hiring this crew can get you squeezed out of the shitter."

"The shitter?" I ask.

"Yeah, the one with your bank," Don says, winking. "I've seen it before. You've got a heavy loan. It's probably past due, and now you gotta show some tight ass from the bank that this joint has a chance. My crew can help with that. Give us that apartment we were just in. Let us bring it up to a glow. Then let the asshole from the bank see it. Believe me, he'll be impressed. Let the other guys you hired pull linoleum from the other units. We'll come after them and straighten it all up."

"That sounds good," Jimmy says.

"Good? We're fucking pros. We're better than good."

"So, how much more of a bite does better than good go for?" Jimmy asks.

"Better than good is worth another hundred per man each day," Don says.

"You must have read my mind," Jimmy says.

It doesn't take long to see that Don's crew, the half-stewed Leo and Arnold, are good workers. The pieces of linoleum are stacked neatly outside the door to the unit. The floor sander hums along, and soon the natural grain of the oak is exposed to daylight for the first time in decades.

The work in other units is for shit. Pieces of busted linoleum are all over the floor while Run-away floor sanders bounce off the walls. A container of linseed oil spills.

By noon, two of the twelve units are sanded to perfection by Don's crew. Two others are a mess of half-sanded floors and rough piles of linoleum.

"Don't worry," Don says. "My guys will straighten up those units. We'll get the other guys to start applying the linseed oil. They can grab some rags and get it started. We'll keep an eye on them."

Lunch arrives. Large deli sandwiches and cases of cold beer are a big hit with the workers. Some look like they haven't eaten regularly.

The beer disappears during lunch, and Harry goes to get more.

"We don't want the boys to get thirsty," he says.

We want the boys to get drunk enough to forget most of this, I think.

It doesn't take long for more linseed oil containers to fall and spill. Part of the mess gets rubbed into the floors. The rest is wiped up with rags tossed into large cardboard boxes.

Bruno helps the situation by complaining about the leaking oil containers in one of the rooms.

"The whole carton of containers leaking all over," he says. "It's those goddamn delivery people. They just threw it in there. Linseed oil and some kind of thinner."

"Typical," Don says. "They hire illegals to do delivery. I bet they shorted your order, too."

"No short order here," Harry says, handing Don a pint of vodka. "Drink up, my friend."

"Thanks, Henry."

By four o'clock, it's the end of the workday. Harry pays the crew with crisp hundred-dollar bills. In minutes, our team staggers out, promising to return the next day.

"Make sure these guys have left the windows open to ventilate," Don says. "Don't need any major fuck ups."

Four of the units are sanded and oiled. They're beautiful. Two other units are starting to look good.

"It's a shame knowing what will happen to this," Jimmy says. He takes a few photos of the beautiful oak floors.

The rest of the Sea Change is a mess. Half-sanded floors hold piles of busted linoleum. Empty beer cans and vodka bottles sit in the corner of each unit beside boxes of rags with too much linseed oil.

The hot afternoon Florida sun beats down on the Sea Change.

All the windows and doors.

Shut tight.

Just in the case of rain.

Of course.

Chapter 29

I have to search for any news of the Sea Change's burning. You'd think a well-executed plan that left ashes piled around a swimming pool would get headlines.

Think again.

I find our story far down on page four in the local section. "Fire Destroys Derelict Building," the newspaper says. For a minute, I wonder how they found out the guys that did the floor sanding are derelicts.

Our story on Channel Seven News goes, "Also in the news, a fire destroyed a small building on a local canal. Fire Marshal Stan Murphy says improperly-stored paint was the cause of the blaze."

On All News All the Time Radio, we're part of the traffic report. "Fire's out in that blaze on the canal, total loss, no casualties, no delays."

It's all due to our story being upstaged by far bigger news.

"Breakthrough in Coleman Jennings Murder."

"Alleged Drug Smuggler Malone Arrested in Possible Multi-Murder Plot."

"Police Question Commissioner Fuentes in Boat Bombing, Drug Peddling."

There's more. Network news and the scandal tabs can't resist.

"Hooker May Have Killed Husband, Shrink, Three More."

"Scarlet Fuentes Death, Bloody Shark Attack? Or Insurance Killing?"

Another story says police are talking to Fuentes's right-hand man, Norman. They want to know what happened when Scarlet died in the Upper Keys. One rumor says police are offering Norman immunity to tell what he knows about Fuentes and what he saw when Scarlet died.

Even our old friend Myron "Slime Ball" Moran finds resurrection in the news. Did "Slime" get shot trying to collect drug money from Fuentes at the Scarlet Tide? South Florida can't wait to find out.

Excitement doesn't extend to anything involving the Sea Change. It's all matter of fact, with a bit of vig tossed in on the side.

Fire Marshal Stan Murphy stands with us, admiring the neat piles of burnt wood and ash that Sea Change has become. "Looks like your insurance will cover the clean-up," he says. "You can let it out for bids. No telling how long that will take, of course. Or what kind of rednecks and dopers will show up to do the job."

Jimmy gives me the wink that says, "Set the hook."

"Gee," I say. "There must be a better way. We're from out of town. Hate to hang around for that."

"Yeah, Detective Cortez says you guys wanted to leave once you straightened this out."

"Oh, you know Alberto?" I say. "We had dinner and drinks with him and Jerry Cohen the other night. Nice guys."

"Here's the thing," Murphy says, looking around like he's about to tell us who really killed Jimmy Hoffa. "I'm not supposed to do this, but you two guys look like you're okay. I got a cousin who can get this cleaned up today. He'll have it hauled in no time."

Jimmy and I do the "ooh-and-ahh" bit for Murphy, and soon we settle on a price that's too much. We figure it's worth the extra bucks. Not every fire marshal will remove an entire crime scene for you.

Bullet holes?

And the slugs that made them?

No additional charge.

"One minute," Murphy says, stepping aside to make a phone call.

As promised, he's back in a minute.

"Danny will have his crew here in an hour. As far as payment goes...."

"Yeah," Jimmy says, "We'd rather not hang around here waiting for your cousin. How about we pay you, and you can pass it along?"

"Happy to."

"Any objection to cash?" Jimmy asks. "Nick, here, won big in a poker game the other night. You'd be doing us a favor, actually. We don't want to be carrying around that much cash in our Jeep rental. Like you say, there's a lot of rednecks and dopers hanging around. Our boss in Chicago will reimburse us if we can get a receipt of some kind."

"Chicago?" Murphy says. "No problem."

We follow him to his Fire Marshal car.

We leave with a receipt that says, "Murphy Heavy Equipment Engineering, No Job Too Large, No Job Too Small." It's dated and signed by Stanley Murphy himself.

We have another task on our list before we leave for the Keys. Our South Vegas friend, Detective Jake Glover, gave us info on some of the players and where they live.

The only surviving person who saw the emeralds down in the Keys backwater flats is Valerie Masters, the best-selling author of the Boy Toy books. Glover says there's a good chance we can catch her at her South Florida home.

"We should drop in on old Valerie and see what she says about her tryst with Ronnie Nolan," Jimmy says. "We might learn something about the treasure spot they visited."

"Maybe it's something she doesn't want to talk about," I say. "Maybe she got a handful of emeralds out of it. No big deal to a famous author."

"Or maybe she doesn't want to talk about how she sliced up Ronnie," Jimmy says. "We need to talk to that detective down in Key West, Anna Clark. She might have more on Ronnie's demise."

The houses keep getting bigger as we drive through Coral Gables. Soon we come to a large, gated place on at least an acre. A sign in front says, "Masters," in Old English type. The gate is open. We park on the circular drive at the front of the place.

We're almost to the front door when it opens. Out steps a short, dark-haired man wearing white pants and a white shirt. He's barefoot, holding a four-foot-long machete. If it were a foot longer, it would be as tall as him.

"You want to talk?" He asks. "You hold on."

He pushes past us and starts hacking at something next to a red hibiscus bush.

"You son a bitch," he says and hacks some more. "Kill you, goddamn, kill you."

I look at Jimmy.

"Should we boogie?"

Jimmy's about to answer when the man drops his machete and turns toward us.

"So sorry to upset," he says. "Burmese python. Big pain in ass."

Big is an understatement. We look at what he just hacked up.

"Jesus, there's twelve feet of snake here," Jimmy says.

"Yeah, all the time," the man says. "Never was until lately. Assholes bought them as pets. Now they're loose, all over. I kill two, three a week. What can I do for you?"

"We're looking for Valerie Masters," Jimmy says. "We're from the company that owns Maroon Key. We wanted to talk about her experiences with our boats down in the Keys. Is she around?"

"No, she take off, already. My name is Sammy. I take care of house for her."

"Is she coming back?" I ask.

"Not for a while. She has house in Key West."

"She goes down there to get away from the snakes?" Jimmy asks.

"Hah, no. They have snakes. She can handle snake. She taught me. Two or three whack, snake's gone."

Or maybe Ronnie Nolan's gone.

After a late lunch in Coconut Grove, we make our way back through heavy traffic toward the Beach. The plan is to rest up at the Fontainebleau and get an early morning start to drive to the Keys. We swing past the site where the Sea Change stood to see if Danny Murphy's crew has started to clear away the debris. To our surprise, they're finished. The site is clear, and the last truck is headed for the dump.

Danny stands next to a front-end loader, drinking beers with two of his crew. He wears a work shirt with "Danny Murphy" tagged on the front and a cap with "Dixie Forever" scrolled on it. The other two guys are wearing NASCAR hats. They pass a joint around.

"Y'all gotta be the guys from Vegas," Danny says. "How you like what we done?"

"It's perfect," I say, leaning out the window of our Jeep. "Better than what we expected."

"Got to run," Jimmy says as he pulls away.

I hold my tongue for half a block, but Jimmy beats me to it.

"I always say, Nick, you never know what kind of rednecks and dopers will show up to do the job."

His grin is about three miles wide.

Chapter 30

We leave the Fontainebleau's luxury as the sun shows its red face over the Atlantic. Our journey down to the Keys takes us past the towns of Homestead and Florida City, where the land starts to fall away. Water appears in large patches along the road. It's the ocean sneaking in with fingers of rising water to attack what passes for land as we enter the Keys.

The highway goes by different names: Dixie Highway, U.S. One, Federal Highway, and Overseas Highway, depending on who's giving directions. We've left the urban sprawl and sewage-laced beaches of South Florida and entered a different tragedy in the making.

Billboards along the road offer a sampling of sins.

"Help Find Out Who Killed Me" reads one that displays the face of a teenage runaway.

"Gentlemen's Relaxation Parlor, Happiness Guaranteed," reads another, displaying the face and body of maybe another teenage runaway.

"Pride Goeth Before Fall," the next one says. It displays the picture of a preacher with a pompadour.

Still, another proclaims, "Jo-Jo's Gun, Bait, and Tackle. Go for the Kill!"

"Jesus," Jimmy says from behind the wheel. "Everything here is a goddamn morality play."

"It fits in with the thin strip of low-lying land and run-down buildings," I say. "The high point of anyone's day must be about six feet above sea level and subject to the rising tide."

Just beyond the scrub trees to our left is the Atlantic. A few hundred yards to our right is Florida Bay, with hundreds of keys.

"We need a pit stop and some coffee," Jimmy says.

Several miles later, we pull into Brewster's. It's in a sunbaked strip mall where half the stores are empty. A discount shoe store and a nail salon are the only other functioning businesses. Dying palm trees and out-of-control bougainvillea hedges decorate the busted-up parking lot.

There really is a Brewster.

His apron says, "I'm Brewster," in large red type. He's a husky guy in his eighties. From behind the counter, he's busy with a running commentary on fishing. Another man sits on a stool at the counter. He looks up from his bacon and pancakes and nods.

"Yellow Tail come through here on the tide, and damn if we didn't catch a mess of 'em, Junior and me. Junior about shit, it was so good. 'Course, I'd seen that kind of run before. Back in the day, we had big catches."

"You're always pissing and moaning," Pancake Man says. "Next, you'll say, 'Hell, this used to be paradise. Now it's waiting for the big surge.'"

"You tell me, Earl," Brewster says. "Are half the buildings around here not up to code? Not that anybody is payin' rent. The state says half of the stuff around here should be pulled down, and the people living in those shacks should high tail it out of here."

"You gonna lead them north to some trailer park for old farts?"

"Not me," Brewster says. "I came in on the big Labor Day hurricane in '35. I'll leave on another one. Some poor gator will get what's left of me."

We sit at the counter a couple stools down from Earl.

"Still making breakfast, gents," Brewster says. "Coffee for a starter?"

We nod.

"Where's the can?" Jimmy asks. "It's a long way from Miami. My rottweiler here has to go."

"Pretty big rottweiler," Brewster says, looking at me. "It's out in the back, next to the boat dock. Right through the back door."

"I can hold it till Jimmy gets back," I say. "Tell me about those pancakes."

The pancakes are delicious, and the bacon is even better. The conversation is interesting.

"I've seen how the ocean around here changes everything," Brewster says. "It's a combination of rising sea level and stronger storms. You have to be an idiot not to see it or some politician on the take for a bucket full of moolah."

"I noticed out back that the water is almost level with your dock," Jimmy says.

"It's the ocean coming for revenge," Earl says.

"Earl's right," Brewster says. "Hell, you should've been here a few days ago when we had the king tide. It was over the dock. You would have had wet ankles trying to get to the bathroom out there."

"Down here is where they made that Bogart movie, Key Largo," I say. "That place still standing?"

"Someplace in Hollywood, maybe." Brewster pours more coffee and wipes a part of the countertop with his dirty apron. "Couldn't say for sure. Some places could have resembled that at one time. Most of what you see down here is a bunch of hype. You want the real beauty of the Keys? It's out there in the flats. That turquoise-colored water that you can see forever through. That's the real treasure. The stuff on land just supports those going out to where it's still free. Out of the control of the three-piece suits."

"They found some treasure down here back in the eighties, didn't they?" Jimmy asks.

"Yeah, way down past Key West," Brewster says. "You boys hunting for treasure?"

"No, we're down here to close up a small boat operation in Marathon, Maroon Key."

"That the place where that woman claimed her gigolo boyfriend beat her up? I heard about that. She's some kind of goofy writer of women's sex stories."

"That's the place," Jimmy says.

"I found some treasure down around Marathon back when I was a kid," Brewster says. "Found an old Spanish coin on the beach. Thought I'd find more and get rich. It didn't happen. I did find a couple of silver dollars, though. The gamblers used them a lot back when the place was wide-open, rum runners, two-dollar whores. Shit, now it's nail salons and cheap shoe stores."

"Any Burmese pythons around here?" I ask.

"We had a couple. One came down sitting in a rich Yankee's dinghy he was trailing behind his fifty-foot yacht. That was funny. He got excited and pumped a shotgun empty into the snake. 'Course, it also put big holes in the dinghy. Damn thing started to sink. Heard another was found up around the Card Sound Bridge. Think they hacked that one with a machete."

"Got to watch it if you're treasure hunting," Earl says. "Damn snakes might get you. Crocs and gators, sharks."

"Hell, you're full of good news today," Brewster says. "They ain't goin' treasure hunting. They're here to close up that Maroon Key place."

"I heard that," Earl says. "Just sayin' that Maroon Key place has had its share of bad luck. Didn't that sex book lady's lover disappear into the mangroves? He could've met up with a shark."

"And next, you're gonna bring up that old tale about the skull," Brewster says.

"This one of those Halloween stories?" Jimmy asks.

"No, nobody got chain-sawed or nothing," Earl says. "It's what we saw out there. We were on our way back from Content Key. It was turning dark fast like it sometimes does around here. Three of us in the boat, kids, teenagers—fishing and drinking beer. The beer got the best of us, so we stopped the engine and took turns standing up to pee. Quiet as hell, no wind, no wave action. I'm looking down, doing my business. I see something green in the water. First, I figure it's some of the phosphorus sea life common to the Keys. But damn, the more I look at it, I see it ain't moving, and it has the shape of a skull, like if someone drew a skull using little green dots."

"So, what did you do?" I ask.

"I turned to Caleb and Rooster and told them to look. They saw it, too. Then the boat starts to drift with the tide going out. We grabbed paddles and tried to get back to where it was. I didn't want to start the engine and shake up all the sand. We saw more green lights, but they turned out to be marine life."

Brewster pours more coffee and wipes his hands on his apron.

"I ain't sayin' he's nuts," Brewster says. "I've heard other people tell a story like his. You can see a lot of strange things down here. I thought I saw a UFO one time. It was out in the flats one night. I look east, and there's this diamond shape hanging there, getting brighter. Turned out to be the moon coming through a bank of thunderheads. For a couple minutes, I was convinced that I saw something special. Damn, I guess I did. It weren't no UFO, though."

"Things like that can shake you up," Earl says. "I think a lot about what I saw that night. Was it a message from someone dead, wanting to be found? Or was it a warning of some sort to stay away?"

"Ever go back to look for it?" I ask.

"Couple times with our girlfriends. Drank some beers, smoked some weed. Never saw a damn thing except the Marine Patrol telling us to move on. They said, 'There's a big storm coming.'"

"Hell," Brewster says. "Storms? They ain't seen nothing yet."

"Storms in the Keys can come up out of nowhere," Earl says. "We've had hurricane-force winds form right on top of us. A clear evening turns into a life-threatening gale. Terrible if you're out on the water and lightning's hitting your rigging."

Brewster puts our change next to our coffee cups.

"He's right. It's nature showing who's boss. I've seen boats destroyed and people drowned. An hour later, it's so clear you can see the stars."

"We get storms like that," Jimmy says. "Flash floods in the middle of the desert."

Earl asks where we're from.

"Vegas," Jimmy says.

"I heard about those storms," Earl says. "I know you got snakes, too."

"Yeah," Jimmy says. "It's the two-legged variety you got to worry about."

"Same here," Brewster says. "A lot of them wear three-piece suits."

Chapter 31

Back on the road, I check for phone messages.

Henri Boyer sends his love: "Lots of things happening. Too bad about Vinnie and Cesar, eh? Ha-ha. I Heard Sea Change had a fire. Good insurance will make you happy. I hope you're still interested in hunting down the skull. The money is good. Five million. Gimme a call."

Harry checks in: "We just got into Maroon Key. Checking into a nice motel. Everything went well. Boats are in good shape, thanks to Zimmer. He's the guy with the other part of the docks. I think we owe him some money. See you soon."

"Yeah, I figured that," Jimmy says. "It's called a marina, but it's only four piers. Zimmer runs a couple of fishing boats out of his two. Billy was paying him to watch over our end and to set up people who came down to rent boats."

My dear wife is next on our hit parade: "Nick and Jimmy: Cassandra and I talked with Angie and Colette. They told us about how busy you guys are down there. We heard that somehow the Sea Change was lost in a fire. Would you mind explaining to us with all that rising water down there, wouldn't it have been easier to have it lost in a flood?"

Damn, those women are wise," Jimmy says. "Any more messages?"

I press to hear the last one.

"This is Valerie Masters. Sammy told me you boys stopped by my house in Coral Gables. I've got a place just off Duval Street. When you get to Key West, give me a call. We'll get to know each other better and maybe do something nice."

"*Cherchez la femme.*" Jimmy slams his hand on the steering wheel. "She wants us to star in her next Boy Toy book, *Nick and Jimmy's Treasure Hunt.*"

"The femme fatale," I say. "I don't think our wives will sign a release, do you?"

"You want to see a *femme fatale*? Cassandra will come down here and kill the bitch."

"We should at least listen to what she has to say. Maybe she has matching dog collars for us."

The two-lane highway hopscotches its way from one key to the next over bridges that show off views of the beautiful flats in Florida Bay. Turquoise water under bright blue skies with white clouds gives you the message. There's something addictive about the Keys.

Somewhere out there in that water, I start to think. The skull? The emeralds? Killer sharks? Snakes? A sportfishing boat crosses under us as we drive over a bridge. The two guys on board raise their beer cans in a salute. The two women lift their t-shirts, flashing their boobs at us.

"Must mean we're headed in the right direction," Jimmy says.

"You see any alternative route?" I ask.

He doesn't answer. I know he's hashing out something. I am, too.

We put our heads together a couple days ago and figured out what the mysterious numbers found in the Sea Change office and on the blackboard at Townsend Boat Works mean. It comes down to a GPS position in the lower Keys. Do we think this is where the emeralds were discovered? Where Ronnie and Valerie had happiness for a while until they argued about what they found? Could the skull be lined with emeralds? Is that what Earl and his buddies saw?

If we're so sure of what we know, why don't we go and find the treasure? Isn't that what we're here for? Or maybe we're not so sure.

We could just say the hell with it. Go home after selling off the boats and settling up with Zimmer at Maroon Key Marina.

But we won't. I know it. There's something inside us that drives us both. We're outside guys. Not necessarily outdoors guys, but outside the norm. We don't do suits and ties for very long. Nine-to-five doesn't work for us. We'd rather go searching for a skull that doesn't exist than sit in a boardroom watching an expert explain flowcharts.

I think about Brewster. He'll hang on till the big hurricane surges through his café and washes him away. He'd rather drown in seawater than die of boredom in a glorified retirement center.

Along the road are signs that say this is the evacuation route in case of storms. It's the only road leading out of the Keys. It's also the only road toward Key West, assuming you're evacuating from something else.

I call our group in Marathon.

"You guys getting close?" Bruno asks. "We can book you a room. It's nice down here. We met Zimmer. Nice guy all around."

"We're heading down to Key West." I look at Jimmy. He nods. "Okay, if you guys can hang loose? We've got some things to check down there before deciding what to do."

"Sure, we're at the Key Colony Beach Golf and Tennis. Zimmer offered to take us fishing in the Gulf Stream tomorrow. No problem with any of that on this end."

"None on this end, either," I say. "Have a good time. We'll stay in touch."

We roll past Marathon onto the Seven Mile Bridge, the longest in the Keys. On our right is what's left of the old Seven Mile Bridge. There's a permanent wide gap where a draw bridge used to let large boats pass from oceanside to Florida Bay. The new bridge is high enough to allow vessels to pass under at will. A tall shrimp boat does just that. I flash on Vinnie Malone. Fresh seafood onboard? Or drugs?

We roll on.

Big Pine Key has stilt houses on steel and concrete pilings, one of the latest attempts to fight rising seas and killer storms. A quick look at the side roads near the homes reveals large patches where the ocean is above the road grade.

"Water World," Jimmy says.

We enter Key West late in the afternoon. We've phoned ahead for a suite on the oceanfront off Duval Street.

"I'm sorry, the hotel is all booked up," the receptionist says.

"As it should be, Sweetheart," Jimmy says. "This is Johnny Sorrento of Atlas Prime Productions."

"Just a moment, sir."

A pause, and she's back.

"The oceanside suite is ready for you on arrival, Mr. Sorrento. Ask for Marvin. He'll take care of you and your party."

Jimmy thanks her and rings off.

"Johnny Sorrento? Atlas Prime Productions? You working a separate career in porn?"

"I don't know who they are, either," Jimmy says. "Jake Glover told me I should try it for this place."

I wonder if other places are honoring the Johnny Sorrento hustle. They keep a suite ready for dear old Johnny to show up and pay cash off the books, split among employees who know how to handle Johnny.

We pull in under the hotel's main entrance. Jimmy can barely get "Sorrento" out of his mouth before Marvin hustles us to the oceanside suite, billed as a $400 per night stay. A bucket with ice-cold bottles of Beck's is ready for us.

Jimmy blesses Marvin with two C-notes for the night's stay.

"Hope you have an unforgettable time in Key West," Marvin says.

And may you live in interesting times, I think, remembering the Chinese curse.

Dinner at the Hurricane Oceanfront Suites is also on the Johnny Sorrento Plan. Marvin informs our waitress Corinne that we deserve the best of the house, and she shall be rewarded with cash. We're led to a table overlooking Key West Bight, where all the boat traffic below seems to have stopped to watch the sun go down.

Sauvignon Blanc arrives chilled along with shrimp cocktails. Lobster Newburg with all the trimmings, comes next. Key lime pie for dessert with cappuccino tops it all off. The fare should be in the two-hundred-and-fifty-dollar range. Corinne informs us that a C-note will do. Jimmy hands her two. One C-note gets tucked into Corinne's bra below her "Margaritaville" tattoo. The other goes back to the checkout station, where Marvin smiles at everyone entering.

"This town reminds me of someplace," Jimmy says as we walk out of the hotel and head for Duval Street. "I can't quite place it."

"Maybe Disneyland for adults?"

"No mouse ears but plenty of Key West-themed T-shirts," Jimmy says.

We watch people cross Duval Street from one bar to another, working their way down the street. Jimmy Buffett music pours out of the open-door saloons. Ernest Hemingway strides along Duval on the front of colored T-shirts.

We find it just off the corner of one of the side streets: Captain Elmo's Saloon.

It looks like Captain Elmo is selling a lot of Hemingway T-shirts. Many of the people in the bar are wearing them, plus the area over the bar displays a whole batch in different colors. All yours for twenty-five bucks. Then it becomes clear these aren't Hemingway shirts. These are Captain Elmo shirts. Captain Elmo is a thin version of Hemingway with the same beard. I look at a red shirt that someone on a barstool is wearing. Then I look up at the wearer. It's Captain Elmo wearing Captain Elmo.

"You gonna stand there gawking at me, or you gonna come over and introduce yourselves?" he asks. "I don't allow strangers in my bar. You look to me like friends I ain't met yet."

There's a gruffness about him that makes me want to like him. For every snarl, there's a wink.

"This is Jimmy," I say. "I'm Nick. A friend of ours in Vegas said we should look you up."

"Jesus," Captain Elmo says, "I think I paid that debt. You guys aren't kneecap busters, are you?"

"No," Jimmy says. "Our friend is Jake Glover."

"Glover, eh? The only Glover I know thinks he can pass for Hemingway. Damn near convinced the judges. He had a beautiful lady with him last time he was down, a redhead named Maureen. I think she runs a bar in South Vegas."

"Patches," Jimmy says. "It's Jake's second office."

"What brings you guys down here? You on vacation?"

"Maybe we should sit and have a beer," Jimmy says. "It's complicated."

Captain Elmo nods.

"Follow me." He leads us to a booth in a roped-off area in the rear of the bar.

"Jesus, we should at least buy you a drink," I say.

"Lucy." Captain Elmo motions to a nearby waitress. "These are some friends of mine from Vegas--Jimmy and Nick. Bring them a beer, and I'll have that café con leche, dear."

Lucy smiles and goes to get the drinks.

"Say whatever you want to say," Captain Elmo says. "Believe me, forty years in this biz, I've heard it all."

We run through our tale of how we got saddled with problems at the Sea Change, the multiple murders, the drug deals, crooked politicians, and possible long-lost treasure. Captain Elmo takes it in with an occasional wince or a "Jesus." He understands the shorthand that some would call "Chicago-ese."

The Sea Change was "lost in a fire." Billy and Mandingo died from "instant lead poisoning." The Townsend boys encountered "a sudden high-pressure area" in the engine compartment of a small boat.

We pause to sip from our beers.

Captain Elmo holds his hand up to stop us from going further.

"I was wrong," he says. "Forty years in this biz, I haven't heard this one. You got an out-of-control hospitality hostess' terminating the lifetime contracts of a shrink, a fag, a junky, her husband, and their first mate. You also got a best-selling author of chick porn, possibly offing her gigolo lover over a long-lost treasure that might not exist."

Jimmy and I look at each other. Before we can say anything, Captain Elmo continues.

"Then you got Haitians looking for the skull of a sex slave that Christopher Columbus autographed some five hundred years ago."

We nod.

"I left out of my recap the possible fake shark attack killing of a fashion queen for the insurance. I also left out her sleazy husband's political fraud and drug peddling activities. Anything else?" Captain Elmo asks.

I'm about to say something about Earl's sighting of the skull thirty years back when Captain Elmo holds up his hand again.

"From what you're telling me about this Ronnie guy, if he's still hanging around, you should try the Spider Dog Tap. It's a dump out on Stock Island. Two scuzz balls, the Everett Brothers, Lenny, and Mark –they run the place. They would be the types to be Ronnie's pals. They peddle grass and blow to the Jimmy Buffett fans that come down to do Margaritaville. They also have a beat-up dive boat for snorkel trips. A couple of losers."

"They still around?" Jimmy asks.

"Far as I know. They're not the ambitious types. Where the hell would guys like that go?"

"Some of them end up in Vegas," Jimmy says.

"Lucy, bring us another round," Captain Elmo says. "Make mine a double Crown Royal." He looks around the bar and leans on the table. His arms are tattooed, a mermaid on the left, an anchor on the right.

"Life can be a real son of a bitch sometimes," he says. "Let's talk a little more. I want to get to know you guys. Where are you staying?"

We tell him the Hurricane Oceanfront Suites.

"Figures," he says.

"How so?" Jimmy asks.

"Johnny Sorrento. You guys got to know about that. Who told you? Jake Glover, maybe?"

We nod.

"It's how some workers can afford to live here. Rents are sky-high. A lot of the help lives on boats, some anchored out. Some stay in rundown shacks miles out of town on back roads."

"It's the first time we used Johnny Sorrento," Jimmy says. "We don't even know who he is."

"He's a character on an old Perry Mason TV show. A big-time gangster who's innocent of the murder he's being accused of. Of course, Perry gets him off the rap. I can't remember if he offers to go straight. For all I know, he's working as a busboy where you're staying."

"You follow all this old crime show stuff?" Jimmy asks. "We got a friend who writes about these old shows. Clancy Booker."

"Black guy. Drinks JTS Brown bourbon," Captain Elmo says. "He and his partner in crime, Murray Bender, did a show here with old movies and TV shows. Sold quite a few books. In fact, they sat right in this booth one night, telling me stories about old Las Vegas."

The six degrees of separation game goes on. We discover money launderers, horse trainers, members of rock bands, and plastic surgeons we have in common.

"Christ, we're practically related," Captain Elmo says. "What do you think? You want my help?"

Jimmy nods.

Captain Elmo nods back.

"Whatever my help adds up to, I expect a taste of some sort, should you make anything happen." He waves to Lucy. "Bring another round, Sweetheart. We're talking."

"We need to know more about Detective Anna Clark and Valerie Masters," Jimmy says. "They might have the info we might need."

"I know them both. They've been in here from time to time," Captain Elmo says. "One thing you got to know about Key West women. They're not fools. Many of them are opportunists, ready to re-invent themselves on a dime. We had a barmaid who went to work as a secretary to the mayor. She won a seat on the county commission. Now, she's a state senator, married to a federal judge."

"I'm guessing that Anna Clark and Valerie Masters are in that category," I say.

Captain Elmo looks around the room and then turns back to us.

"People who treat them as little women don't last long."

Chapter 32

"People think this town is year-round Fantasy Fest. They come here to live the life they get from Jimmy Buffett songs and books they've read about Key West. They think Hemingway still lives here, some of them. Most have never read Ernest Hemingway. They wouldn't know him from Mickey Spillane. Sometimes, I think I'm driving through a movie set as I come down Duval Street. The shops remind me of movie storefronts, propped up from behind with long two-by-fours."

It's not Captain Elmo speaking. It's Detective Anna Clark. We're sitting in her cubicle at the Monroe County Sheriff's Office, sipping morning coffee.

"So, your company had the Sea Change in Miami Beach," she says. "What can you tell me about the late slippery Ronnie Nolan that I don't already know? Maybe you have something to tell me about dear old bitchy Valerie Masters. I understand that she and Ronnie might have been warming up the beds at your establishment."

Jimmy and I nod.

"They were there and gone before we got into the game," Jimmy says. "We came to South Florida to sell the Sea Change property to get it off our boss's hands. It was suffering from poor management. We thought it would be a simple process of finding the right buyer and settling on a price. We had no idea we'd be getting tangled up with criminals."

Detective Clark looks at Jimmy and smiles.

"Save the choir boy speech. I wasn't born yesterday. I have a good idea of who you two birds are. The stories coming from your hotel are intriguing. Who had the idea that a fucked-up drug dealer like Billy and his homicidal hooker wife was a good combination to run a business?"

"Good point," Jimmy says. "That wasn't us. That was someone way above our pay grade. We're the ones that came in to clean up the situation."

Clark turns to look at me. She smiles and brushes some of her curly brown hair from her face.

"And who are you? The silent partner just along for the ride?"

"No, I'm here for comedy relief."

"I'm fascinated by how you guys get away with it. So innocent. Getting the fire marshal to clean up an arson site was brilliant. That takes some balls."

"We can leave if you prefer."

"Cute," Clark says. "Let's talk instead."

"I don't mind a mutual exchange of information," Jimmy says. "We'll share if you share."

"I'm not sure we're on equal footing here," Clark says. "I've done some digging on you and your organization. Let's just say that your group skates a little too close to the edge to be on equal footing here. I'll go part way, but that's it. I'm not opening my files for you guys."

"That's a real shame," Jimmy says, leaning toward Clark. "We've done some digging, too."

"I'll bet," Clark says. "Bartenders and hookers? They're not the most reliable source of info."

"How are you doing with the nose candy these days?" Jimmy asks.

Clark smiles.

"You've been listening to Captain Elmo? That was twenty years ago when we did coke together at his Super Bowl party. Hell, the sheriff was there. He wasn't the sheriff then. He was a narc. We wanted to see what was so special about it. It was a one-time toot."

"I don't know about this Captain Elmo," Jimmy says. "I know more about Captain Frank Beaudette from the New Orleans P.D."

The smile on Clark's face disappears.

"Oh?" she says.

"Frank's a good guy," Jimmy says. "Some of our people talked with him about the powdered sugar problem you had last year at a cop convention. A little out of control, maybe, but as I say, Frank's a good guy. He was nice enough to let you slide."

She looks around the large room of cubicles to see if anyone's tuned in. They aren't interested in us.

"What do you want to know?" she asks.

"What happened to Ronnie Nolan?" I ask. "The story goes that he was diced and sliced by someone or something out in the flats."

"A little of both," Clark says. "A fisherman found what was left of him floating in a busted-up rowboat near Content Key. There were cut marks on his body from a sharp blade, maybe a knife or a machete. Shark bites on his legs. One foot was bitten off. Don't know how he got into the boat. He'd been dead a couple of days. He didn't smell like orange blossoms. We followed up trying to get the story out of Valerie Masters, but all she'd say was that they argued, and he took off without her in a rented boat. She got back to Marathon with bruises and insect bites. She said she never wanted to see him again. Said he was a flop in the lovemaking category."

"Not according to our source at the Sea Change," Jimmy says. "The word is that she was yelling, 'Oh, oh, Ronnie,' four or five times a day while they stayed there."

"That's Valerie," Clark says. "She had that macho actor, Norbert Kent, down here a few months back. The lovemaking got loud, and so often, the cops were there three or four times a night. They thought she was getting killed. When he left town, she told everyone about his drooping little spaghetti dick."

"We figure Ronnie was a gigolo who worked out of the Scarlet Tide, Cesar Fuentes' place in South Beach," Jimmy says. "He'd pick up rich women there."

"I met Fuentes several times down here," Clark says. "He makes a big deal out of giving our local Cuban-American politicians a couple hundred bucks when they run for office."

"Did he come alone?" Jimmy asks.

"Scarlet was here with him. Everybody loved her. They tolerated him with his anti-Castro and anti-science speeches. Everyone else has tried to move on from that. Fuentes keeps wanting to beat a dead Fidel while we drown in rising seas."

"Did Ronnie ever bring any of his marks down here?"

"As long as his princesses were paying the freight, Ronnie would take them anywhere. Yeah, he'd waltz them around here, help spend their money. Tell them stories about finding the rest of the gold that Mel Fisher found from the *Atocha* back in the eighties."

"Is the Ronnie Nolan case still open?" I ask.

"Technically," Clark says. "Between us kids? Nobody's breaking their ass to find out what happened to Ronnie Nolan. He was a small-time con man who told bullshit stories about hunting for treasure. He's dead and gone. So what? Key West seems to be doing all right without him."

"If we find out anything more on Ronnie, we'll let you know," Jimmy says.

"Great," Clark says. "I can hardly wait."

"I'll bet," Jimmy says.

"You're the second party that's been here about Ronnie in the last few days. A Haitian named Henri Boyer came in to ask about poor Ronnie. He wanted to know if Ronnie had any family. I said a few street hustlers were all I knew about. Boyer had a priest with him. Wanted to give Ronnie a decent burial, a big funeral. I told them they were too late. Ronnie's gone to dust. His ashes are in the ocean floating past that treasure he never found."

Chapter 33

We leave Detective Anna Clark's office with answers leading to more questions.

Why are Henri Boyer and Father Jacques down here asking about the late Ronnie Nolan? Was he the one who told them about finding emeralds in the Lower Keys? Did he tell them about seeing a skull in the water like the one Earl told us about up at Brewster's?

Clark says they found what was left of Ronnie Nolan in a busted-up rowboat near Content Key. He was hacked with a sharp blade and also bitten by a shark. With one foot bitten off, how did he get into the rowboat? Did Valerie Masters do a Burmese python disposal on poor Ronnie?

Maybe Ronnie could make it to Key West after he argued with Valerie. Did he go back out with his pals, the Everett brothers, to find what was in the water? Are they the ones that hacked him up? Did they watch a shark take his foot and then toss him into the old boat?

"Those are some questions," Jimmy says. "Where can a couple clever sleuths go to satisfy their thirst for knowledge?"

"Your choice," I say. "The Spider Dog Tap, run by Ronnie's so-called friends? Or the Key West home of machete expert and best-selling boy toy author Valerie Masters?"

We make our way to Stock Island. It's right next to Key West. We agree that the scuzz bar run by Ronnie's so-called buddies might quench our thirst for clues. If nothing else, it will quench our thirst for a beer.

The Spider Dog Tap looks like a strong wind will take it all the way to Tampa.

Picture an open-air tiki hut with a couple sheets of plywood on sawhorses for a bar. The barstools are white plastic chairs found at Walmart. A guy wearing a yellow golf shirt and faded jeans stands at a gas-powered grill cooking fish. Behind the bar is a guy heavily tattooed in the latest prison style. He's got a three-day growth of scruff on him that matches his oil-stained shirt. He looks like whatever crime you're interested in, he's willing to do it.

"Guaran-fuckin-tee you'll like it," the barkeep says.

He's not talking to us.

A woman wearing cut-offs and a red Margaritaville t-shirt has just handed the barkeep some money. My best guess is it's a folded-up C-note. Another best guess: it's for dope.

"Down the road, Hon, you'll see a red VW bus. Our man is down there, and he knows you're comin'," the barkeep says. "I just rang him up."

"Thanks, Buckshot." The woman wiggles her ass into a Mustang convertible and heads the way Buckshot pointed.

"You guys thirsty, or what?" Buckshot says to us.

"What kind of brew you got?" Jimmy asks.

"All we got is Bud in the cans today. The goddamn delivery driver must be stuck in some dive."

"What do you have when he shows up?" Jimmy asks.

"Bud and Bud Light."

"Bud sounds about right."

Buckshot looks at our Galloping Dominos shirts.

"Been to Vegas, I see."

"Yeah, had a good time there," Jimmy says, leaving a blank canvas for Buckshot to fill.

"I was at that Dominos place," Buckshot says. "Won a hundred-thousand-dollar jackpot couple months ago. I went out and blew it all on whoring and partying with my friends."

"That right?" Jimmy says. "I heard someone hit it big on that Bananaganza game they got there."

"You're looking at him. I got a system. The pit boss shit when I hit the lucky number."

Buckshot reaches into an ice chest and sets the two beers on the bar.

"Grouper sandwiches," he says. "You want any, you got to order from Herman over there. He does the food. I think he's Lenny's brother-in-law."

"Lenny?" I say.

"One of the owners," Buckshot says. "He and Mark took a snorkel party to one of the reefs."

"So, you must be the man in charge?" Jimmy says.

Buckshot's about to say something when his cell phone rings. He steps back from the bar and turns his back to us.

"What? What the hell do you mean? You don't have it? Jesus, do I have to do every damn thing around here? She paid already. Shit, I'm coming down there."

He ends the call and looks toward the grill.

"Herman, watch the bar. I got to go down the road."

Buckshot gets into his rusting yellow Camaro and heads toward where he sent the woman in the cut-off shorts and red Margaritaville top.

Herman walks over, reaches into the cooler, and grabs a beer for himself.

"Crazy place," he says. "I don't know what I'm doing here with this bunch. My wife wanted me to see if I could help out her two brothers, see if I could get the place above water."

"I'd say this whole island is about a foot and a half from going under," Jimmy says. "I'm surprised we're all not wearing life vests."

"This global warming stuff keeps up; the whole nation will be wearing life jackets," Herman says. "Imagine that. You'll be required to wear one, so they won't find your bloated cadaver floating down your street as a health hazard."

"That guy that just left said you could fix us a sandwich," Jimmy says.

"Buckshot? Yeah, I've got some nice grouper and fresh Cuban bread. Happy to do it."

"Buckshot?" Jimmy says. "He some kind of skeet shooting champ."

Herman laughs.

"You could say he was on the receiving end, but it wasn't any skeet shooting champ delivering it. He was shot in the ass, running from a convenience store stick up. Did a three-to-five upstate."

Herman walks over to his grill.

"Bananaganza?" I say. "Where the hell did you make that up from?"

"Just thought I'd throw some chum out on the water, see if Buckshot would bite."

Herman comes back from the grill with two fish sandwiches on paper plates.

"Hope you like them. I think Buckshot won't be back for a while. Ain't hard to figure him out. He'll take that gal back to his old cabin cruiser. It's easy to spot them types. She's just another coke whore. Key West's full of them."

"You have a good understanding of the Keys," Jimmy says. "You been down here long?"

Herman looks around the Spider Dog Tap. Off to one side, a fat man wearing a Miami Dolphins T-shirt sits snoring on one of the plastic chairs. His feet are propped up on another. It's only a matter of time and fundamental physics when his ass will slide off the front of the chair, and he'll topple to the floor.

"Top of the line clientele," Herman says. "Been here two weeks, and I'm ready to go back home to Madison, Wisconsin. Margery, my wife, wanted me to see what I could do to get her brothers on the right track. Tell the truth, I don't think it's possible. I've seen too much bad. Some of the town's okay. We did the Hemingway House. The art galleries are interesting, and the steel drum bands are nice, but her brothers just won't listen. This place with fixing up could be a gold mine. But her brothers don't want to hear any of that. they say they've got something bigger in mind."

"What's that?" Jimmy asks. "They heading for Vegas to play Bananaganza?"

"They might as well," Herman says. "They're telling me they got a line on finding some long-lost treasure. You know what I think?"

There's a pause as Jimmy and I do the noncommittal shrug.

Herman slugs down the rest of his beer and belches.

“Only a couple goddamn fools would waste their time chasing long-lost treasure.”

Chapter 34

I think about Herman's condemnation of fools wasting their time chasing long-lost treasure. Of course, he's referring to the Everett brothers, but I wonder if it's a message that Jimmy and I should heed.

"You hear a lot about sunken treasure in the Keys," Jimmy says. "I know Mel Fisher found the Atocha treasure back in the eighties."

"Yeah, I've seen displays from that one," Herman says. "Mel's people went through archives in Spain, bought expensive equipment, and hired people who knew the ocean."

"And your brothers-in-law?" Jimmy says. "They do any of that?"

"Shit. Take a look around," Herman says. "This joint is three months in arrears. That and a leaky skiff with engine trouble is the best they can do. They had some slick guy down here the last time Margery and I were down. That was two months back. This Ronnie Dolan or Nolan guy was hanging around. I asked what he did for a living. Lenny points to his pecker and says, 'He lets the ladies buy him everything.' So, this time we get down here, they're talkin' about this treasure. I ask how they're going to find it. 'Ronnie's told us a lot about it,' Lenny says."

"Ronnie must be a gigolo," Jimmy says. "What's the treasure, some woman's credit cards?"

Herman laughs, reaches into the ice chest, and pulls out three beers.

"Damn, that's worth a round on the house. I pretty much said the same, only I had him taking her jewelry and cash. I did hear more about their plans. They say they know where to look, but they need some high-tech equipment to pinpoint it. They've got some fancy sonar unit on order, costs about four grand. I have a sneaky suspicion that they hit my wife for that one. I figure they'll end up broke or in jail the way they're going."

"So, is this Ronnie gigolo still around?" I say.

"Don't know and can't say I care. Margery and I have a restaurant just outside Camp Randall Stadium in Madison. I'm anxious to get back to it and take care of our own thing. We get a lot of the football crowd—dyed-in-the-wool Badger fans going back generations."

Jimmy starts talking about betting on football. It's my chance to take a bathroom break.

The "Buoy's" room at the Spider Dog looks better than the rest of the place. It's almost clean and has decent fixtures. The usual graffiti lines the walls. Above the urinal is "Flush it twice. Miami needs the water." Another has the time-worn, "We aim to please. You aim, too, please."

Surrounding the mirror are snapshots of people having fun at the Spider Dog. Most have drinks in their hands. Some are hugging or giving high fives. There are a couple shots of a large skiff with two guys standing next to it. A sign beside it reads, "Spider Dog Dive Trips."

I notice another photo of the two men with another guy standing between them. I've seen this face before. It was on the report Jake Glover emailed to us. It's Ronnie Nolan.

More photos are hanging on a bulletin board next to the "Gulls" room. The same guys stand beside the same boat hanging in the "Buoy's" washroom, along with more pictures of the Spider Dog crowd doing their thing.

I notice another photo next to it.

In the photo, Ronnie has a drink in his hands. He's wearing his gigolo uniform: an expensive Tommy Bahamas shirt, a gold necklace, and a Rolex watch. His aviator sunglasses are resting on top of his head. He stands between two women. One has a mountain of red hair, long eyelashes, and large breasts. The other wears a red two-piece swimsuit. Her nails on the hand that holds a drink aloft are bright red. A red leather bag is draped over her left shoulder.

"Sherry, Ronnie, and Bonnie," I say. "Trifecta."

My iPhone captures pictures of the Everetts and the one with Ronnie, Bonnie, and Sherry.

Chapter 35

We say goodbye to Herman and the Spider Dog Tap on exciting Stock Island. Our thorough investigation has led us to verify that Ronnie Nolan did hang out there with his friends, the Everett brothers, Mark and Lenny. Thanks to the science and art of alcohol-driven photography, we now have visuals for all three. We've also verified that the Spider Dog is not in the best shape, financial or otherwise. I start to wonder if the late Uncle Billy Teller had been their financial advisor.

We've also found that Bonnie Teller of .38 caliber Smith & Wesson fame had some action of her own at the Spider Dog. She was accompanied by her faithless companion, Sherry the Hooker, and surprise, "Oh, oh Ronnie," Nolan.

"Jesus, talk about birds of a feather," Jimmy says. "Did these people all break out of the same nuthouse?"

That's what they call a rhetorical question. I decide to toss a few more birds into the list of nuthouse escapees in the spirit of cooperation.

"Okay, we now know that the Everett brothers are part of the hunt for the treasure. We know that Henri Boyer and Father Jacques Dupres are looking for it. Hell, even the two of us have been offered the job."

"Vinnie Malone and Cesar Fuentes would like to be in the hunt, but they're locked up. So are Bonnie and Sherry. Last I heard, they were all in without a chance for bail. Does that leave Valerie Masters as another party interested in the goodies?" Jimmy asks.

"We need to find out."

"There's something else that's bugging me," Jimmy says. "The two different stories on how Ronnie met his end. Jake Glover says the word from the Monroe County Medical Examiner is that Ronnie took a bullet to the head and one to the chest. Detective Anna Clark says he was hacked up with a blade and lost a foot to a shark. Then somehow, he got into a rowboat where he became fly bait."

"I've been wondering, too," I say. "Are these two looking at the same stiff? Could it be they're high on dope? Maybe they just don't give a damn. Anna Clark certainly doesn't care that Ronnie Nolan got killed. I think she's happy that he's gone. If he's gone."

"If is right," Jimmy says. "This guy Herman seems to know how screwed up things are at the Spider Dog with his wife's brothers. But he doesn't mention Ronnie getting chopped up or shot. He tells it like old Ronnie's still alive, hustling some babe for money. You'd think a story like Ronnie's fateful trip would be getting a lot of play. All we've heard has come from Anna Clark."

You could say we're literally in the dark, but hopefully listening to the voice of reason. We're back in the dimly lit, roped-off booth at Captain Elmo's Saloon listening to the captain himself.

"People die down here. Some days, we get several deaths from diving accidents, fishermen who go overboard with the nets, and tourists who drop dead from too much good life. The tourist industry tries to kick it under the rug. We do a New Orleans-style funeral when one of our Bahamians dies. They do the jazz walk to the cemetery. I had some tourists ask me if we do that every Saturday. It was so much fun.

"You got to remember that Key West is a couple hundred years old, but it's still a frontier town. Half the politicians down here had trouble graduating from high school. Would a medical examiner's report on a stiff be different from the lead detective's report? Hey, this is the town where the assistant chief of police and some of his trusted boys in blue went to federal prison on drug smuggling charges."

Thanks to Captain Elmo's assistant Lucy, we're eating large slices of key lime pie and drinking café con leche from the Cuban restaurant down the street.

"Great stuff," Jimmy says.

"I do this a lot," Elmo says. "If I drank booze the way people say I do, I would have been dead a week after I opened. Remember. There's the image, and then there's the truth."

We nod. Elmo continues.

"Back in the day, a guy ran a weekly paper. A crusader against corruption. He had politicians scared they'd get caught with their pants down or their hand in the till. It worked fine for a while. Then they found out the hotshot editor was a child molester. Some crusader."

"Jesus," Jimmy says.

"It goes on. Another guy owned a radio station. Very popular. The local powers-that-be found his name on the voter rolls and figured he'd be great to have on the board of one of their pet projects. He'd be one of the people who'd decide who'd develop the project. That lasted until they found that he was registered to vote in Florida and two other states where he owned stations. He was on county boards in those places, too."

I get my iPhone out and show the photo of Bonnie, Sherry, and Ronnie to Captain Elmo.

"I've seen them before. They've been in here. The red wig with the boob job shows up when there's out-of-town money around: powerboat races, Fantasy Fest. If there's a crowd with money, she works it. Usually targets older guys. Never saw her with the gigolo in the picture. I've seen him in here with different women, mainly older."

"What about the one with the red leather shoulder bag?" I ask.

"Once, she was in with the guy in the photo. It wasn't a romantic date. Whatever it was, it was serious business. They argued, and it got loud. I had to tell them that people come to my place to have a good time. There would be trouble if their idea of a good time was to make other people leave my bar. I told them I didn't want to call the cops."

"Did they leave?" Jimmy asks.

"Eventually. First, I get some serious sass back, but then gigolo man cuts her off and says something like, we got too much riding on this, Bunny or Bonnie. I couldn't catch which name. When he finally got her out the door, I got a standing ovation from the crowd."

"You were lucky," Jimmy says.

Captain Elmo listens as Jimmy talks about our trio. When he finishes, there's silence.

"She had a .38 in that red leather bag?" Elmo finally says. "She shot her husband and the rest of those people? The red wig boob job ratted her out. And the gigolo? Clark says the guy was sliced up and fed to a shark, but the M.E. says he took one to the head and one to the chest?"

"Interesting puzzle," I say.

"Hey, maybe Clark and the M.E. are both lying," Elmo says. "That Ronnie could walk in here any minute and order a beer."

We nod.

"You should talk with Valerie Masters. Maybe she'll tell you what really happened with this Ronnie guy. She was there."

"Don't know if she'll cooperate," Jimmy says. "We hear she's easy to resort to violence."

"You hear that from people who hate her," Elmo says. "She may be different."

Chapter 36

Captain Elmo is right. Valerie Masters is different.

It's mid-afternoon when the freckle-faced blonde with deep blue eyes comes to the wrought iron gate to let us into her yard. She walks us through a garden full of flowers and tropical plants. Bananas and papayas are ripening next to bougainvillea shrubs.

"This is my humble attempt at paradise," she says as we move toward the front door of what looks to be a 12-room house. "We can sit in the backyard pool area and talk. I hope you like mangos and iced coffee."

"Great," Jimmy says. "We weren't expecting the red-carpet treatment."

"Is that your polite way of saying you were expecting an out-of-control sex monster rather than a short sunflower gal from Kansas?"

Her description isn't far from the mark. She's slim, tan, and a bit over five feet tall. Her blue button-down shirt with epaulets, white shorts, and leather boat shoes would work at a millionaire's yacht club or a chamber of commerce picnic.

"We're used to a lot of surprises," Jimmy says. "Our type of business runs on them."

"Mine, too. Shall we sit?"

The pool area is another paradise garden. One pool is for swimming. Pool number two has a bubbling fountain in the middle. It's for floating plants and small birds to enjoy. We're surrounded by tropical beauty.

A woman named Emma brings the sliced mangos and iced coffee on a tray and sets them on the wrought iron table. Before we can thank her, she disappears.

"I've always gone against the grain," Valerie says. "That's really been the secret to my success."

"I have to confess," Jimmy says. "We weren't aware of your work, your success."

Valerie grins.

"I'm not surprised. Neither one of you is a conservative woman from middle America, secretly fed up playing second fiddle to the boys wearing vests. I've done some digging. I'm really in the same business as you guys. We both get our customers to indulge in fantasy before sending them back to being pillars of the community."

"You know about the Galloping Dominos Casino?" Jimmy laughs. "Then, you know how we try to make our guests feel like George Clooney or Julia Roberts."

"Yes, while taking their money," Valerie says. "No need to deny it. I do the same thing. I tried playing it straight, doing the second fiddle act to the boys. It was a dead end. What do you know? I found that jumping the line was a good way to get ahead and the only way for me to go."

"My wife would agree with you," Jimmy says. "She has no patience for being the little woman."

"I bet we'd get along great," Valerie says. "I grew up in Kansas, did all the good girl stuff: cheerleader, the church choir, married a basketball star I went to school with at the University of Kansas. We were the Jayhawks couple. Then we graduated, and it was all downhill. I was no longer a star. I was the little woman, stuck in a starched blouse by day and trying to be Little Miss Homemaker at night. I had to get out."

"Divorce?" Jimmy asks.

"Not only from my husband but from everything else that was tying me down. There was this way that you were supposed to act. No rocking the boat. If you wanted to go against the grain, you got ostracized. I enjoy Shakespeare and Beat poetry, and I believe in the equality of the races and sexes. I like reggae and free-form jazz. That didn't go over well. No one in Emporia wanted to hear any of that."

She stops and sips her iced coffee. A flock of small birds lands in the bushes next to the pool of floating plants. The flowering trees point to a deep blue afternoon sky filled with white clouds, the kind you can get lost in.

"But that didn't stop you," Jimmy says.

"No, it drove me to New York, London, and San Francisco. I pursued the fine arts in those places. I even became a minor expert making a decent living by writing about them. It was better than Kansas, but I had a long way to go before becoming the lead critic for the New York Times. It was then I had the strangest epiphany."

She stops to sip iced coffee. Her broad smile stops just short of a giggle, and she goes on.

"I was driving through Mill Valley in Marin County. There was an interview show on NPR about success in America. One of the panelists quoted the bandleader Xavier Cugat saying something like, 'My orchestra has highly trained musicians. We could play an excellent Bach or Beethoven symphony, and we'd make a decent living. On the other hand, we can play Chiquita Banana and have large houses with swimming pools.'"

"I've heard versions of that before," Jimmy says. "A lot of truth there."

"Yes," Valerie says. "I had to think about that. Was I like Hemingway's old man Santiago, going after the one big fish but ignoring all the smaller hungry fish waiting for what I had to cast on the waters? I realized that I had an audience waiting. They were hungry. Their oh-so-respectable lives were giving them just enough passable Bach. I could make them dance to my version of Chiquita Banana."

"And boy toys became the answer," Jimmy says.

"Guilty as charged," Valerie says. "Every woman playing second fiddle to some three-piece suit know-it-all jumped to get an inside look at handling a boy toy. My books are bestsellers in all the red states. If I do a book signing in Tulsa or Houston, my writing hand will be sore for the next week. In LA or Boston, I'm just another writer of sexy chick-lit. I'm not the lead critic for the New York Times. Instead, I'm on their bestseller list."

Jimmy asks about Valerie's publishing house.

I sit, half-listening, and try to balance Valerie with the woman who teaches her houseboy to hack up Burmese pythons.

Is this the woman who shacked up with Ronnie Nolan at the Sea Change and maybe took a blade to him somewhere near Content Key? Did this woman throw an electric fan at her toy boy and whip him with the cord?

What about Norbert Kent, the tough-guy actor, I wonder? Didn't the Key West cops have to come over four times a night because the sex got so heavy with Valerie that they thought someone was getting killed? Didn't Anna Clark say that Valerie referred to him as a loser at lovemaking after Norbert left town?

Anna Clark? How much of her can anyone believe? I wonder.

I tune back into what Jimmy is saying.

"Your editor is helping with the book Norbert Kent wants to do?"

"Yeah, Norbert and Amanda Stark, his love mate, were down here for a week to meet with my editor, crusty old Mort Sweeney. They were heading to London for the filming of that Bond movie. We had quite a time. Everyone loves Norbert's work. Amanda's now the hot actress since she did that murder on the Riviera movie. I pretty much opened the house to Key West people. Folks were stopping by at all hours, having refreshments, and seeking autographs. Even some local cops came by for selfies with their favorite stars."

"Detective Anna Clark mentioned it got busy here," Jimmy says.

Valerie smiles.

"I'm sure dear old Anna Banana put the most negative spin on it for you guys."

We nod.

"Anna has her own agenda," Valerie says. "I think she does a little too much coke. I don't know what her goal is; I know that successful women are a big threat to her."

"We know the type," Jimmy says.

"But you guys didn't come over to hear me talk about Anna Clark," Valerie says. "You want to hear about what happened with Ronnie Nolan and me."

Chapter 37

"I should start by telling you about boy toy versus gigolo," Valerie says. "I wouldn't want you getting confused. My many loyal readers know that a boy toy is for the short term. A boy toy could be the college kid who works at the country club during the summer. They're prone to sex, love expensive gifts, and figure that making love to an older rich woman is a much better gig than trying to deflower virgins."

We laugh and sip iced coffee.

"My first book was about boy toy experiences I had," Valerie says. "I was fixed enough from the divorce settlement to spend some crazy money. I found five boy toys: a surfing instructor, a day camp counselor, a veterinarian assistant, a barista, and a yoga instructor. Those five were the book. How we seduced each other during summer break from college. Theirs, not mine. I was already in my early thirties, an older woman to my five toys."

"Was that a problem for any of them?" Jimmy says.

"No, I had what they couldn't get from women their own age, experience, and money."

"How much money?" Jimmy says. "Did you drop a bundle on the sex maniacs?"

"No, that surprised me. We went to nicer restaurants, danced in great clubs, and got prime concert tickets. I bought them a few mid-range watches, a couple surfboards, and five tennis rackets from the same shop. The pro who ran the business said I was his best salesperson. Anyway, by the end of the summer, I had the makings of my first book, *Care and Feeding of Your Boy Toy.* It practically wrote itself. I shopped it to a few agents at book conferences, which was all it took. The publisher got me on some women's shows, and the book took off. It even started a minor culture war when one of those Jerry Falwell types condemned me from the pulpit, saying it wasn't the sort of thing a woman should be doing."

"Yeah, like it would be okay for a guy to do it with young women," Jimmy says.

"Isn't it?" Valerie smiles. "It's been the accepted way for centuries."

We laugh.

"I began to worry," Valerie says. "*Would Care and Feeding* be a one-shot success, and I'd have to find something else to write about? But then I started hearing from women who had boy toy stories of their own. 'Put this in your next book,' they'd say. So, I did. Every time I publish, I get more stories. There's even a movie in the works. It's been great. I have the house in Coral Gables, the home here, and my apartment in Manhattan. That's Manhattan, New York City, definitely not Manhattan, Kansas."

"But gigolos are a different breed from boy toys?" Jimmy says.

"One of my readers cornered me with that," Valerie says. "I was at a book signing in Houston. She came up to me and told her story. Her wealth was from old oil and plenty of it. 'Valerie, honey,' she said. 'You wouldn't believe the gigolos. They're the ones who play for high stakes. We ain't talking surfboards and tennis rackets. These boys are Cartier all the way. You need to do a book on them.'"

"So, that eventually led you to Ronnie Nolan," Jimmy says.

"Yeah, to start with, I got some first-hand stories from my readers, women who had been involved with gigolos. It got so I could tell a gigolo just by a certain pattern of behavior."

"You got to tell us," Jimmy says. "I'll take one guess. They dress too well."

"You get one point," Valerie says. "They also have a fascinating project going that has a lot of promise but needs funding. In Ronnie's case, it was going after the lost treasure, the Atocha's remains, and other shipwrecks that came apart off South Florida. He had a lot of props for that, nautical charts, binoculars, depth sounder printouts. A lot of scientific mumbo jumbo. I couldn't tell how much of what he said was real or how much of it he was making up as he went along."

"It sounds like he put on a good show for you," Jimmy says.

"Yes, for a time, I thought I had found the perfect gigolo. He had no idea who I really was. To him, I was the heiress to a large meatpacker in Kansas in search of adventure in the tropics. It was fun with both of us playing out our invented characters. I picked him up at the Scarlet Tide. One of my readers said she had successfully found a gigolo at the Tide. Hers was a guy who had a growing wholesale jewelry business, or so he claimed. The only jewelry involved in that relationship was a missing diamond bracelet her jeweler gigolo took with him when he disappeared."

"Wonder what that cost her?" I say.

"Probably twenty thousand," Valerie says. "To my friend, it was a drop in the bucket. She loved the adventure and the sex."

"Was that true of Ronnie, too?" I say.

"For a while. He was charming, sexy, and phony as a three-dollar bill. We ended up at the Sea Change because I told him I wanted a quaint place for our affair to begin."

"Did you freak out when you saw what a dump it was?" Jimmy says.

"No, he told me it was a bit rundown, but the people who owned the place were part of his treasure-hunting crew. Later in the week, we'd go out on one of their vessels to survey the Lower Keys."

"Was your bullshit detector going wild?" Jimmy says.

"Of course. I was prepared, though. Part of my leaving Kansas diaspora included self-defense classes with the best. You probably heard how I've had a few run-ins with boy toys who wanted to get rough with me. I've had to pay settlements for dental implants and scar removals. I already had figured out how I'd take Ronnie apart if he got too vigorous during our stay together. I'm pretty tough when it needs to happen."

"Hey, we come in peace," Jimmy says.

We laugh.

"We hung around the Sea Change for a few days," Valerie says. "I'd spend some money taking Ronnie shopping for that perfect silk shirt or watch he said he didn't want but took anyway. We hit the expensive cafes, and soon it was time for Maroon Key Marina. We took out one of the boats with the Zodiac attached and got ourselves sunburned all over during the day and absolutely stunned by the stars out there at night. For several days a school of bottlenose porpoises followed us."

"It sounds wonderful," Jimmy says.

Valerie sips some iced coffee and continues.

"It was, but things went off the track the third night out. We were near Content Key. Ronnie said he saw something in the water with a green glow. I figured it was marine life. No, he insisted. It could be lost treasure. I tried to look at it. All I could see was marine life shining blues and greens. Beautiful. 'Don't you see the skull? Don't you see the skull with emeralds?'

he said. I shook my head. He was tripping on acid. He'd offered me LSD several times."

"So, what happened then?" Jimmy asks.

"He grabbed my head like I was a bad dog and tried to turn it to where he wanted me to look. I walloped him. I think I broke his nose. He shoved me, and I hit the railing. I jumped up and kicked him in the groin. He went down hard. That was enough. I got my things into the Zodiac and took off toward Marathon. I'd had enough. I was bruised, insect-bitten, and sunburned."

She stops to sip some iced coffee, smiles, and continues.

"Like the true genius that I must confess to being, I ran out of gas about six miles out of Marathon and had to paddle my way in through the hot morning sun. That ended my one and hopefully my only hands-on experience with a gigolo."

"What did you do when you finally made it to Marathon?" I ask.

"That guy that handles your boats at Maroon Key, Zimmer, is it? He took one look at me and ran me to the hospital. I looked like a walking wreck. I was suffering from dehydration, exposure, bruising, you name it. I got the overnight stay treatment and felt better the next day. I looked into the mirror at what a mess I was. 'Val,' I said to myself, 'Don't say you've got nothing to write about now.'"

"So, the emeralds and the skull?" Jimmy asks.

"Never saw any of it. I heard rumors around Key West that someone had found emeralds. Was it Ronnie? Couldn't say. He might have said he did to lure some sucker into investing in his scheme. Thinking back, I wonder if those people that you had running the Sea Change were involved in Ronnie's scams. They left a lot to be desired if you don't mind me saying."

"Not at all," I say. "All that was before we came down to straighten out the mess."

"You had a first-class bimbo running the office. She and her boob job friend had a revolving door turning tricks. A lot of men. You could hear them moaning, 'Oh, oh.' It got so I couldn't sleep."

"What about the manager, Billy?" Jimmy asks.

"The old guy with the tattoos? Didn't see much of him. He and the Haitian guy they had working there were out at sea most of the time."

"And Ronnie Nolan?" Jimmy asks. "Some think that he never made it back to Key West from where you left him."

"Yeah, I heard that going around when I came here to recuperate. Some said the sharks got him, or maybe his so-called friends cut him up. I don't think so."

"How's that?" Jimmy asks.

"I'm sure I've seen him driving down Duval Street. He's got a red VW bus."

Chapter 38

Once again, the more we find answers, the more we find more questions to be answered.

We're sitting in our apartment at the Hurricane Oceanfront Suites, where we're staying on the Johnny Sorrento plan.

"Now we know that Ronnie Nolan was sliced and fed to a shark, according to Detective Anna Clark. Or he took one to the head and one to the gut, according to the Monroe County Medical Examiner. Or he's hustling dope out of his red VW camper," Jimmy says.

I toss my hands in the air in frustration.

"Valerie Masters says Ronnie was tripping on acid when he said he saw the emerald-covered skull in the water. Maybe no one found any emeralds on their voyage."

Jimmy pops the tops off a couple Beck's and hands one to me.

"We heard a similar story about the skull from that guy Earl at Brewster's. It might be one of those urban legend stories that everyone down here has heard about. I'll bet Valerie Masters told Uncle Billy about Ronnie tripping on acid and seeing emeralds in the water."

"So, can we be sure that anyone found emeralds?"

"We saw what Chuck and Buddy showed us at the Fontainebleau," Jimmy says.

"Yeah. We heard what they said. We saw what they showed us, but were the emeralds real?"

"They could have been. Bonnie tried to grab them all for herself. Hell, she took Billy's share and Mandingo's too. She said she was going to have them appraised. They're probably in her safe deposit box somewhere. Don't forget, someone dropped one on the floor at the Sea Change office. Harry took it to that retired jeweler friend of his. He said it was worth fifteen hundred bucks."

I nod.

"Yeah, Colette found it on the floor. I don't know about you, but if I'm taking the loot, I'm going to count and make sure I've got it all, not leave one on the floor."

"But if I'm running a scam," Jimmy says, "I've got to have one genuine article. I'd have an appraisal slip on it to show people. I'd buy an emerald from a reputable jeweler the same size and shape as the phonies. I'd keep it separate from the others and just produce it when I needed to impress one of my marks."

I nod.

"Try this on for size," Jimmy says. "Billy took the guys down to Marathon to straighten out the mess with Valerie and the missing boat. They also spent time searching for the missing Ronnie. Billy hears the emerald skull story and thinks, why not make up a found treasure story?"

"Maybe. It could be a way out of the Sea Change with big bucks attached. He lets the word out to Malone, Fuentes, and Boyer that he's got a lead on where some old treasure's hiding. He tells them there are millions worth of emeralds and other precious stones. But he needs sophisticated equipment to dig it out. He tells them he needs to sell the Sea Change to fund the treasure hunt."

"I like it," Jimmy says. "He puts the Sea Change up for sale for way more than it's worth. Whoever buys it, he says, could get a healthy share of the treasure. He figures he'll take his piece from the sale of the Sea Change and split with Mandingo and the Townsends. Even Ronnie Nolan gets wind of Billy's treasure finds. All the Townsends and Mandingo have to do is show off some fake jewels and talk up the hunt."

I nod.

"Only something goes wrong," Jimmy says. "Bonnie believes Billy so much she's willing to kill him for the treasure. Maybe he gets drunk one night. He tells her that the GPS coordinates for where the treasure might be found are tucked away in the cash register. She half listens, and later after she splits, she remembers and has to return to retrieve the information. She can't get it, so Malone sends your buddy Slime Ball."

"That would explain why no one went back to the Keys to do a treasure hunt," I say. "Billy and the boys knew it was a scam. There was nothing there."

"Yeah, but here's the strange part," Jimmy says. "Ronnie's the one who set it all in motion by taking Valerie to the Sea Change. He knows the place is a dump, but he's on safe turf. Two of his hooker girlfriends work there. Sea Change even has boats in the Keys where he can play treasure hunter for Valerie and maybe get her to invest in his own treasure hunt scam."

"So, if Ronnie doesn't take Valerie to the Sea Change, none of this ever goes down," I say. "Jacky sells the Sea Change, Billy moves on, and none of our newfound friends are in jail or dead. We should check to see how much of this holds water."

It doesn't take long to make a few calls to cops that we know.

"It's the damnedest thing," Detective Cohen says. "You called it to a tee. Yesterday, we executed a search warrant on Bonnie's safe deposit box. She had some cash tucked away and a bunch of emeralds that turned out to be phonies. Olivine. It's costume jewelry. There were other jewelry pieces, costume jewelry. There was an appraisal slip for one stone valued at twelve to fifteen hundred, but the stone wasn't there. Maybe she pawned it to buy condoms and bullets."

We thank Cohen and ring off.

"Christ's sake, don't you read what I send you guys," Detective Jake Glover says. "I told you this Ronnie had warrants out on him for grand theft, burglary, false imprisonment, and drug smuggling. There was even an accessory to commit murder warrant he was named in. When I told you that the M.E. in Monroe County said he took one to the head and one to the chest, you heard that. Then I said that his getting killed was probably a favor to him, considering he would have probably gone away for twenty, plus."

"So, of course, everybody has quit looking for him," Jimmy says.

"Yep. It's hard enough chasing the live ones. No one wants to chase a stiff."

"So, someone could have done Ronnie Nolan a huge favor by listing him as dead and sending it out to whoever's looking for him."

"Yeah," Glover says. "From what I know about Ronnie, he ain't worried about filing taxes and collecting a pension. For him, walking around dead is better than being listed as alive and looking over your shoulder."

We tell Glover that we've met Captain Elmo.

"He can help you," Glover says. "Talk to him some more. Give him my best."

We ring off.

I look at Jimmy. He's doing the slow head shake with a "woe is me" look.

"We got some shit," he says. "Think of it this way. Before we got here from Vegas, no one was down here looking for that treasure. Why? Because everyone involved in the scam knew that it didn't exist. The others were waiting for someone who knew where it was to lead them to it. You know that saying about getting invited to the poker game and wondering who the patsy is?"

"Yeah, if you don't know, you're the patsy."

"I'm thinking about all the players in the hunt," Jimmy says. "We've made ourselves visible to a bunch of them. If Anna Clark is protecting Ronnie, she's got a stake in finding the treasure. She's probably got a tail on us. We know that Boyer and Father Jacques are down here looking. Ronnie's connected to the Everett brothers and that Buckshot guy, the freelance druggist."

"So, what we're telling people by the fact of us being down here is that we know where the treasure is?" I ask. "They follow us, and they'll get it?"

"Follow us?" Jimmy says. "How about putting the muscle on us, threatening to shoot us? Remember the wisdom of Al Capone: 'A smile and a gun gets you further than just a smile.'"

"So, what choices do we have? We could just leave. How far could they follow us?"

"How far would they go for five million bucks?" Jimmy asks. "That's what Boyer and Father Jacques are offering for the Columbus skull. You don't think that we're the only ones who have heard that offer, do you?"

"The Atocha treasure they found down here in the eighties came to about 400 million dollars. If they think another piece of it could be where the emeralds were allegedly found, that raises the interest."

"Yeah," Jimmy says. "I don't think this is one of those 'let's walk away Jose' situations."

"So, the GPS coordinates," I say. "What do you think...?"

"What do I think they signify? It's probably where they recovered the boat that Ronnie and Valerie took out. According to Buddy and Chuck, it was getting dark as they got the boat free from the mangrove. They still had no idea about what happened to Ronnie. And they didn't know what kind of a fuss Valerie would kick up over her lost lover. Maybe it was just a way of keeping track of where they were. They could use the GPS coordinates with the Coast Guard or the Marine Patrol if anyone wanted to do a proper search for Ronnie."

"Yeah, and as it turned out," I say, "No one cared about whether he made it to Key West or became dinner for the sharks."

"But someone cared enough," Jimmy says, "They cared enough to file a police report on Ronnie's corpse being found sliced and diced and snacked on by a shark. For whatever reason, someone else filed a Monroe County Medical Examiner's Report stating that dear old Ronnie took one to the head and one to the gut."

"Yeah, that's all true, so where does it lead?"

Chapter 39

Detective Jake Glover is right. Captain Elmo can help.

"My daughter Inez works for Monroe County," he says. "She can get the medical examiner's report on Ronnie Nolan's shooting. She can email that and the one from Detective Anna Clark about how poor Ronnie got sliced and fed to a shark."

"Remarkably, Ronnie still managed to hop into a conveniently placed rowboat," Jimmy says. "The report on his making it through all of that and going into dope sales on Stock Island probably isn't ready yet."

We're back in the roped-off booth at the back of Captain Elmo's Saloon. We keep one eye on the front door to see if anyone threatening is entering. The problem with that is we're sitting with Captain Elmo. Everyone who comes through the front door scans the place to see if he's here. Half the saloon crowd is staring at us, waiting for a wave and a "How ya doin'?" from the captain. Two bartenders are busy keeping up with the thirsty crowd.

The jukebox plays the Creedence Clearwater song about a bad moon on the rise. Is it an omen? Am I jumpy? Short answers: maybe, and yes.

We've become the lead dogs on the road to riches to people hunting for an alleged treasure. I still have flashbacks from my deadly encounter with Myron Moran, aka Slime Ball. I catch myself pulling on my shirt, checking to see if my Glock is still in my waistband.

Captain Elmo's faithful waitress/assistant manager Lucy has just left the booth with an order we've given her. We're sending a thousand bucks worth of Captain Elmo t-shirts to people in Vegas. She's putting the bill on our company credit card and sending the shirts out via next-day delivery. We've had fun guessing sizes and colors for people like Jake Glover and our players on the Vegas Dykes-- our casino-sponsored LGBT softball team. Even Zorro, Jimmy's Labradoodle, is getting a Captain Elmo shirt.

"You didn't have to do that," Captain Elmo says. "I'm guessing it's your way of saying there's no treasure. The shirt order is my taste."

"We would have bought some shirts anyway," Jimmy says. "We're pretty sure that this treasure is all a scam worked by Billy Teller. A scam that backfired on him, getting him killed by his wife. Now he's put us in the crosshairs. We don't like that. But, hey, if we strike it rich, you're definitely in for a large slice."

"I'm still with you guys, shirts or no shirts, treasure, or no treasure. From what I gather, we're dealing with a bunch of backstabbers," Captain Elmo says. "We got a crooked cop in Detective Anna Clark. This crazy Ronnie has a bunch of warrants out on him. He's got those bums from the Spider Dog Tap ready to do his bidding. Probably worse than those characters, we've got the Haitian, Henri Boyer, of Tonton Macoute fame. What kind of scum is he bringing to the party? Those bastards love to torture people, even after you've given them what they want."

"You left out Father Jacques Dupres," Jimmy says. "He claims he's doing this for the good of his people."

"Yeah, don't they all?" Captain Elmo says. "Did he promise to make the trains run on time, too? If he's such a great guy, what's he doing with a piece of shit like Boyer?"

I'm about to answer him when my iPhone buzzes. The display says, "Boyer."

"It's our favorite Haitian," I say.

I hit the speaker button and push the phone toward the center of the table.

"Nick here. What can I do for you?"

"Maybe, it's what I can do for you," Boyer says. "I've seen you and your associate running loose in Key West. I think you've come down to find the Columbus skull, yes?"

Jimmy and Captain Elmo roll their eyes. Boyer has been drinking.

"What do you think?" I say. "You think it might be down here somewhere?"

"Of course. I'm no fool. I think Billy Teller maybe left you some good clues. I'm going to help you retrieve it. I have four former associates from Port-au-Prince ready to recapture the skull. They're tough guys who aren't afraid of sharks in the water. They see a shark, and they piss on it and then blow it apart with an M-16."

"What about Father Dupres? Is he down here with an M-16 to help recapture the skull?"

"He'll give his blessing, certainly. I don't think he's going to piss on the shark. He's better at pissing in his pants. Ha. Ha. When are you going to go out? I want to be informed."

"Not for a day or two. We're waiting for some special equipment."

"Of course. Someday after we find the skull, I will visit you in Las Vegas. It will be nice to meet your family and the family of your associate, Jimmy. Keep in touch with me. I'm here to recapture the skull."

A sudden click. The call ends.

"Stay cool," Jimmy says. "I know it's a threat. Stay cool."

"Goddamn right, it's a threat," Captain Elmo says. "Did you think this was paddy cakes? This guy has got to go."

I take a swig from my beer.

"Goddamn right, he's got to go," I say.

"Lucy," Captain Elmo says. "Bring another round for my partners in crime. We've got some planning to do."

It's past closing time.

The streets are wet, dark, and quiet when we leave Captain Elmo's Saloon.

We've hashed out the details of our plan. It's a matter of putting all the pieces in place. We feel confident. But then, a part of me sees the negatives. Can it come together before we get killed?

I look into the shadows as we walk down lower Duval Street toward our hotel.

A sharp rattling sound comes from my left.

I've got my hand on the Glock, ready to pull it and point, when an old man steps out of the shadows. He's pushing a rusty cart carrying fishing poles and bait buckets. He tips his greasy cap and says, *"Bueno."* In seconds he's across Duval Street and disappears into the shadows.

"Jesus, he had me reaching there for a minute."

"Me too," Jimmy says. "Stay cool. He's just some old fart."

We walk on, our steps echoing off the closed storefronts.

Or are they steps of someone else? Someone behind us?

We stop and turn.

No one.

But there's a sound from a doorway, a half-block behind us.

We listen.

Silence.

Someone's tracking us.

I can feel it.

It's almost something I can taste.

I feel the back of my shirt. I've been sweating.

The Glock is there at the ready.

There's no fumbling with a safety on a Glock. The trigger is the safety. A slight pull releases the safety. A harder pull and you're pushing lead.

We turn again to look behind us.

Nothing.

The only sound is the ocean crashing against a nearby seawall.

We finally get to the hotel grounds and head toward our suite. I'm reaching into my pants pocket to check for my extra magazine for the Glock when someone runs behind us down the darkened hall. I turn, ready to grab and fire.

Then I stop.

It's Marvin, the coordinator for the Johnny Sorrento discount plan.

"Is everything to your liking with your accommodations?" he asks.

I stare at him in silence, wondering how close I came to killing him.

"Yeah. It couldn't be better," Jimmy says. "The room is nice. The food is damn good, too."

"Some friends of yours stopped by earlier. They wanted to know if you were staying here at the Suites. They asked if you were enjoying yourselves here."

"Friends?" Jimmy says. "They leave their name, a message?"

"Didn't have to," Marvin says. "It was Detective Anna Clark from the county sheriff's office. She said she'd catch up to you. She had a guy with her who waited in the squad car."

"Another cop?" Jimmy asks.

"Couldn't say for sure. He might be undercover DEA or ATF. I've seen him hanging around places like Hooky John's and the Spider Dog. He's got a red VW bus with a surfboard rack."

Chapter 40

Tired of looking behind us to see who's closing in, we've decided it's time to act. Our morning starts with a drive to see a local official, Charles Taylor, the county medical examiner.

"It's nothing to sweat," he says. "I was visiting relatives in Tampa when that guy got killed over some drug deal. One to the head and one to the chest. Deader than a frickin' doornail. Ronnie. That was his name. Ronnie Nolan. They said he was dead a couple days in a leaky rowboat. He was covered with flies and stinking bad. I made a few notes and told them what to do to fill it out. I'd take care of it when I got back. We were on our way to Disney with the grandkids. I wasn't going to blow my vacation over some dirtbag."

It's after nine in the morning. We're sitting in Charles Taylor's Grassy Key office. My guess is that Charles has had three or four shots of bourbon to start his day. Jimmy tells him we're tracing Ronnie over a bad debt from the Galloping Dominos Casino in Vegas.

Taylor glances around his office, checking to see who's listening to our conversation. It's a familiar Chicago move, done immediately before suggesting that money in an envelope will go a long way toward solving a problem. The trouble with Taylor's overture is we're not interested in bribing him. What can he possibly do for us? Send a report saying Ronnie Nolan is alive?

"Wish I could help you, but dead is dead," Taylor says. "You can't collect from a corpse."

"True," I say, thinking you can't collect from us either.

"Couldn't even tell you if he had gold fillings," Taylor says. "They could've been worth a few shekels. They cremated him before I got back from

Mickey Mouse Town. We get a lot of drug deals gone bad down here. A lot of dirtbags, too. There's no respect for the law anymore."

"We thought we'd get your statement to make sure," Jimmy says.

"Sure," Taylor says. "Doris, down the hall, will give you a copy of my report so you can tell your boss that Ronnie ain't around no more to collect from."

We thank Taylor and head to where Doris, down the hall, has her office.

Thanks to Captain Elmo's daughter Inez, we already have an emailed copy of Taylor's report. We're happy to get another from Doris, who, on the fifth try, manages to get it into an official envelope with the Monroe County logo on it.

"I remember this one, man," Doris says. "Like Chuck was visiting his grandkids up north. There was some confusion about how this Ronnie dude boogied. One of the detectives said he had his good time ruined by a shark. Chuck dictated his report from Tampa to Amanda, a work-release sister doing community service on the weekend. Pretty far out. The shark turns into a gun. Two pops. One to the head, one to the heart. Guess it don't make much difference, does it? Dead is dead, ain't it?"

We both agree on the concept that dead is dead and thank Doris, down the hall, for helping us.

"Remind me never to have brain surgery in this town," Jimmy says as we get back into our Jeep.

I put a copy of the report from Detective Anna Clark into the envelope with Charles Taylor's statement. The two can argue it out. Shark attack. Gunshots. Shark attack. Gunshots. There's nothing like overkill when you're trying to tell the world that the guy running around hustling women and dope on Stock Island has been documented DOA twice over.

Jimmy says we're putting together a court case that we won't have to take to court.

"We're setting it up," he says. "Just like we did in Miami. We need to present our case to someone who can carry the ball."

"Didn't we recently meet someone who carried the ball for South Miami High?" I ask.

"The Cobras," Jimmy says. "He said he was a running back, all-conference team. You don't suppose that was the beer talking, do you?"

"Maybe the pizza. We should at least talk to him."

Cortez answers on the first ring.

"It's Nick and Jimmy," we shout.

"Yeah. Hey, what's on your mind? You guys in Marathon?"

"Near there, we're driving toward Key West," Jimmy says. "We got something we wanted to run past you to see if you're interested. It connects with some of the people involved in the South Beach investigation you guys are working on."

"Yeah? How so?"

"We emailed you a couple documents from Monroe County. Take a look."

"Okay, give me a minute."

Jimmy and I look at each other and shrug the "what the hell, we tried" shrug.

"Those people down there are all on dope," Cortez says, returning to the phone. "They can't tell the difference between a gunshot and a shark attack? Who in the hell is this guy? How'd you get a hold of this?"

"It fell into our hands," I say. "Funny thing is this guy who's officially dead twice is still walking around live. He's selling dope out of a place called the Spider Dog Tap."

"I know it," Cortez says. "It's a loser joint out on Stock Island. Cohen and I were down there last summer as part of the drug task force. I think we got a few of their customers on possession of small amounts of cocaine."

"You should run Ronnie Nolan through the system," Jimmy says. "He's got priors, but there are also warrants for heavy raps. He fits into what you're working on. He has connections to Bonnie Teller, Sherry the hooker, Malone, and the Scarlet Tide."

"This Ronnie guy was maybe getting his dope from Malone or Fuentes and running it down to sell in Key West?" Cortez asks. "That seems logical, no?"

"We know he hung out at the Scarlet Tide, hustling dope and trying to play the gigolo to women with money," Jimmy says.

"This Detective Anna Clark? Maybe he's hustling her, too," Cortez says. "Maybe she's part of the drug sales. It looks like she's tried to help him out of his fugitive-on-the-run problem. We had doubts about her last summer. If she knew about a planned bust at a place, we'd get almost nothing when we showed up. We'd get a couple of losers holding a nickel bag or a small bit of oxy. Anyone doing serious pushing would be far from the scene. Someone was tipping them off. The search warrants produced nothing."

"You could check out the M.E., Charles Taylor," Jimmy says. "I don't think you'll get much there beyond incompetence. He's the four-drinks-before-breakfast type."

"It all sounds charming," Cortez says. "What else you got?"

We tell him about Buckshot, the Everett brothers, and the photos of Ronnie Nolan with Bonnie Teller and Sherry the hooker.

"How cozy," Cortez says. "I've got Nolan's file up on my screen. He looks like he could be good for helping Bonnie get rid of her husband and the Haitian. I think the drag queen and the junky were there to take the fall. Maybe Nolan helped her. We don't think the junky and the queen were capable of heavy lifting to pull off the Billy and Mandingo disposals."

"Ronnie Nolan's a man of multiple talents," Jimmy says.

"Yeah, none of them legal," Cortez says. "If he was hanging around the Tide when Scarlet got attacked, we'll look at him. He could have helped Fuentes get a five-million-dollar payday from the insurance company. Fuentes' assistant, Stormin' Norman, is cooperating. He claims he was nowhere near Key Largo when Scarlet got killed by the shark. He says some other guy was down there. This Ronnie fits the description. Norman says Fuentes pressed him to make a false statement on the insurance claim. He promised Norman a bundle of cash. The bundle turned out to be five hundred bucks. Talk about cheap. It makes sense. Ronnie Nolan couldn't make an official statement on a large payout like that. One check on him, and cops all over Florida would be on his tail."

"This guy Ronnie works out of a red VW bus set up with a surfer rack on top," Jimmy says.

"That could help us," Cortez says. "This guy looks like he's dangerous. He needs to be off the street ASAP. One question: why are you turning him in? He do something to piss you off?"

"A few weeks back, he rented a boat from our marina in Marathon and ran it up into some mangrove," Jimmy says. "Our people had to go down there to find it and haul it back to the dock."

"What, he left it and swam away?"

"Don't know how he got away," Jimmy says. "Maybe his buddies, the Everett brothers, hauled him back. Maybe they were going to haul the boat back to Key West and sell it with phony papers. Our people got to it first."

"Tell you what," Cortez says. "I'm going to make a few calls and see how soon we can get it all together. If I have questions, I'll phone you back."

"Good," Jimmy says. "How soon do you think...?"

"I'll call you back? Or how soon will we get Nolan off the street and into a cage?"

"Into a cage," Jimmy says.

"I'll keep you posted. Jerry Cohen and I might be having a late dinner tonight with you in Key West."

"Bring your appetites," Jimmy says. "Nick's picking up the tab."

Chapter 41

They say the sunsets in Key West are unforgettable. The one on Stock Island comes with sirens and flashing blue lights. Happy hour at the Spider Dog Tap comes to a sudden end when agents from the DEA, ATF, and the South Florida Interagency Task Force arrive en masse.

Ronnie Nolan's attempt to roll away from the festivities is stymied by two squad cars that block his tricked-out red surfer VW bus. The Everett brothers, Buckshot, and the recently back-from-the-dead Ronnie are perp-walked away in handcuffs in front of TV cameras.

Ronnie's exit line draws laughs from the assembled group of drunks, dopers, and law enforcement personnel:

"I'm being set up by the cops. I'm a political prisoner. They planted dope to shut me up."

In Key West, the action is a bit subdued one island over. On Whitehead Street, six DEA agents take custody of a snarling Detective Anna Clark, and search her house for evidence. A similar scene happens at the Flagler Street home of Medical Examiner Charles Taylor.

"It went well," Detective Alberto Cortez says as he finishes his shrimp scampi. "I especially enjoyed Ronnie Nolan's claims of innocence after we found a half kilo of blow in his bus."

We're sitting on the veranda at the Hurricane Oceanfront Suites restaurant, looking at moonlit sailboats in Key West Bight. Detective Jerry Cohen is finishing a 24-ounce steak.

"I haven't eaten all day. Your phone call got us moving fast. Jesus, what a fucking haul."

Cortez laughs and nods as our faithful waitress Corinne hands him the dessert menu.

"Jerry's right," Cortez says. "They found a kilo of coke at Anna Clark's home. There were a dozen vials of oxy and enough weed to bring back the Grateful Dead for a week. She was the warehouse for the Spider Dog Tap. Ronnie Nolan was living at her place. His clothes were in her closet. There were pictures of the two of them next to the red VW bus."

"So, is Ronnie going away for the long term?" Jimmy asks.

"Grand larceny in Orlando, burglary in Palm Beach, attempted murder in St. Pete, all look like slam dunks," Cohen says. "The drug charges on Ronnie will be complex. It's an organized crime thing with Clark, the Everetts, that guy Buckshot whose name, believe it or not, turns out to be Clarence Thomas. It's your standard crew of parole violators, petty thieves, muggers, and dirtbags. They're all going to go away for some time."

"We'll get some of the mopes to start ratting on the others," Cortez says. "I figure Ronnie will try to cut a deal to help send Fuentes and Malone to prison. On the other hand, maybe they'll have some interesting things to tell us about Ronnie."

"What about the M.E., Charles Taylor?" I ask.

"He'll suffer the embarrassment of being the stupid guy in the news," Cohen says. "We'll squeeze him for info about Clark and the others. I don't think he'll be back refereeing football at Key West High, but then again, knowing Key West, maybe he'll run for mayor."

"So, tell us how you guys found out about all this," Cortez says. "You must know someone who can access the database."

"We have friends on the South Vegas PD," Jimmy says. "We wanted to follow up on Ronnie. We ran him with a few other names from South Florida. We didn't know what happened to him after he ran our boat into the mangrove. For all we knew, he was dead. Detective Clark said he was attacked by a shark. The ME had a different story. We heard through the coconut wireless that Ronnie had friends at the Spider Dog. That's where we found the photo of him with Bonnie Teller and Sherry the hooker."

"Excellent work," Cohen says. "Jesus, we could use a few guys like you on our squad."

"Don't tempt me," Jimmy says. "My wife would kill me if I did. We're supposed to be helping to run a casino, not playing detective."

"So, what's next?" Cortez says. "You guys going back to Vegas?"

"We got a few loose ends," I say. "The Maroon Key Marina is a fancy name for two piers and a couple cabin cruisers with Zodiacs. Our boss will decide. It could be a sale. Maybe he'll hang onto it. We need check where

Ronnie ran our boat aground. We're short an anchor, a large cooler, and a ten-horse motor that was stored on the boat. Did dear old Ronnie swipe them? Who knows what happened out there? The four guys who went to get the boat are all dead. The Townsend boys said it was a mess to get it loose from the mangroves."

"Some of our people are in Marathon evaluating what the property might be worth," Jimmy says. "Harry Feldstein is there. He follows real estate pretty close. He and his wife, Colette, live at that tennis condo on Miami Beach. Bruno and Angie are there. They know about sports fishing. They compete in Catalina Billfish Tourneys. We're trying to figure how much life the property has in it."

"You didn't give Bruno any linseed oil, did you?" Cortez says.

We all laugh.

"No," Jimmy says. "It would be pretty hard for him to burn it down. It's a few steel piers on concrete pilings hooked to the gravel parking lot. There's an ice-maker and a coke machine under a small plywood roof, but that's about it."

The conversation leads to what it's like to live in Vegas. Jimmy describes the Galloping Dominos Casino. He starts telling stories about the characters-doing their version of "what you do in Vegas stays in Vegas."

I supply the smile and the laughs.

Cohen and Cortez remind me of South Vegas Detective Jake Glover. It feels good sitting with these guys. Are they friends? Friends in the making? Maybe I'm just relieved that some of the dangerous people after us are in custody.

"Justice isn't perfect," Glover is fond of saying. "But we do our damnedest to balance the books."

I think about balancing the books. We've done that, getting rid of problems with the Sea Change and getting felons into the slammer. Somehow, we'll clear it all up and head back to Vegas. There's just this other thing that we need to do.

Jerry Cohen notices.

"Nick, you look like you're in deep thought," he says. "Let us in on what you're thinking."

"Just how nice it is to sit here having good food and conversation," I say. "You guys are okay."

"Hey, same here," everyone echoes, raising their glasses.

I raise my glass and smile.

I'm thinking about the drunken threats to our families from Henri Boyer.

I'm thinking about his quartet of M-16 toting thugs from the Tonton Macoute.

I'm going to stop them all before they take one step toward my family.

Jerry Cohen tells a story about catching a couple riding down Collins Avenue on a Harley.

"I pull them over, and the guy asks me if they were going too fast. I said that maybe they left home too fast, considering that neither of the two had any clothes on."

Everyone laughs.

"We had one similar at Galloping Dominos," Jimmy says. "A naked drunk rides an expensive racing bike off the low dive. Then he complains that we took too long to retrieve his ride out of our pool, and now it's water-damaged."

After a few more stories, we say goodbye to Cortez and Cohen. They're supposed to catch a late-night flight that will get them back to Miami after midnight. They'll start to sort out the charges on Ronnie and his crew and connect them with the Scarlet Tide group.

One last thing: we check in with Captain Elmo.

"It worked fine," Captain Elmo says. "Lucy tracked Boyer and his crew. They were staying at a hotel down the street. She told them I had news about the treasure they were hunting."

"And they took the bait?" Jimmy asks. "They come over to the saloon?"

"Yeah, I played the part of a greedy drunk who wanted money for the tip I gave them. I said you guys got drunk and spilled your guts about the treasure. If they wanted the info, it was worth a grand. That asshole Boyer tried to weasel me down to six hundred. I told him I'd sell the info to some Cubans. I'd get twelve hundred from them. That's when he forked over."

"So, you hit him up for a grand?"

"Twelve hundred. Then I got Boyer all defensive about his manhood. I told him that I'd rent him mine if he didn't have a decent boat. If he didn't know how to handle it, I could skipper it for a price. Hey, I told him, it even has big life preservers to wear if you're scared of the water or your guys can't swim."

"What happened then?" I ask.

"He had to lecture me about what a great boat he had. It's called "Jesus M'aime Enormément." It means something like Jesus loves me very much. I had to listen to how he got a captain's license and how his men were tough guys who piss on the shark before shooting it. If I didn't believe it, he'd show me the boat. It was docked nearby and ready for anything."

"Did he leave after that?" Jimmy asks.

"I had to buy them all a drink, tell them some shit about how Hemingway fell asleep under the table back in the thirties when Charlie Lancaster owned the joint. After a little more back and forth, they went away."

"He had the Tonton Macoute quartet with him?" I ask.

"Yeah, humorless fucks. I thought they'd start biting people. Anyway, they left after that. That's when I did like we talked about, and as far as I can tell, everything's fine."

"It's going to plan," I say.

"Yeah, if it doesn't work, they'll kill us. Get some sleep. Tomorrow's quite a day."

Sleep comes easy at first. We've moved from the Hurricane Oceanside Suites to a cookie-cutter motel on the other side of town. If Boyer and his Tonton Macoute thugs want to play the midnight visit game, they can bust into an empty suite. We're both worn out from their crap.

Boyer and his four M-16 toting thugs are at our pool in Vegas in my nightmare. They point M-16s at my daughter Molly and my wife, Dawn. Somehow, I'm underwater and, despite my struggle, can't surface to help out. Screams from Molly and Dawn bring me awake.

It's four am.

I'm sweating and shaking.

It's quiet in the motel. The sound of an idling car in the parking lot is all I hear. I get up and peek out between the curtains. Someone is walking in the dark past the pool. It's a guy carrying something heading toward our door.

I grab the Glock, slip on my pants, and stand to the side of the door.

He's just outside our room.

I ease the door handle to "unlock." I'm ready to fling the door open and take out Boyer's goon.

A woman's voice outside the door stops me.

"Glad you got here," she says to the guy outside my door. "I just made my first cup of java. Here's a couple bucks. Gimme a Herald before you put them in the machine. I want to read about my Dolphins. They're playing like a high school team. They need a new coach."

"Story inside says they're thinking of changing quarterbacks," the guy says.

"They gonna bring back Dan Marino?" she asks.

"Yeah, probably Bob Griese," the man says.

They laugh.

"Ain't they the shit?" she says.

I slip the Glock into the back of my waistband, reach for some money, and open the door.

"I'll take one of those Heralds. Here's a fin. Keep the change."

I make myself one of those coffees that come in a small plastic cup that is shoved through a machine next to the sink. Somehow it comes out decent enough. I slip into my bed with the Herald and turn on the small light next to my bed.

"Monroe County Detective, Medical Examiner Arrested in Drug Raid," the headline reads. Below are photos of Anna Clark and Charles Taylor. The subhead reads, "Police Say Drug Ring Has Connections to South Beach Dope and Murder Scandal." Beneath that are mugshots of Ronnie Nolan, Clarence "Buckshot" Thomas, and the Everett brothers.

"You up already?" Jimmy asks from his bed. He's half-asleep.

"It's all a dream," I say. "Go back to sleep. We got a big day ahead of ourselves."

"Good. Wake me when it's over."

I fall asleep somewhere between the front page drug bust story and the Dolphins' debacle.

"Hey Sunshine, get your ass moving," Jimmy says, kicking the foot of my bed.

It's seven am. He's up and ready to go.

I head for the shower. It's an important day.

Chapter 42

When valuable things stumble into your life, you need to honor them and realize that friendly spirits might be helping to balance the books.

"All the lost treasure talk got me thinking the outside of the box, no?" Colette said when she heard about the emeralds and some other lost treasure waiting to be found. "Maybe no *emeraude* or the gold of the bars, but I like to have a treasure chest, maybe at the foot of our bed. Harry liked the idea. Angie wanted one, too. So, we girls went shopping."

"We tried the antique dealers," Angie said. "Prices too high. Plus, they wanted you to kiss their ass over some relic that Louie the umpteenth spit on. I asked one of the guys that waited on us if he could do better off the books. Turns out he's got a buddy that makes fake antique strongboxes. Metal strapping, rusted, and they even have an old-fashioned lock with a big key. Then he asks if we want French style, Italian style, or German. Which century?"

"We should ship one each for our wives and one for Molly," Jimmy said. "The girls will love them."

I think about that as we approach our day with Henri Boyer and the four horsemen of the *Tonton Macoute.*

"It's a good thing, the strongboxes," Jimmy says. "Having that guy engrave some with *'Propriété de Maurice Levant'* costs a few bucks, but what the hell. Jacky's got millions. Besides, we sent one to his loving wife Muriel, no extra charge."

We're on the veranda at the Hurricane Ocean Suites having brunch on the Johnny Sorento Plan.

In the distance, we can see the Maroon Key anchored a mile to the southwest. Small wafts of smoke drift from beneath her motor mounts, courtesy of slow-burning smudge pots supplied by Bruno.

"They'll burn forever," he says. "All they do is smoke the place up."

We have binoculars focused on the scene. A large sportfishing boat approaches and circles the Maroon Key.

"It's our friends aboard the French version of 'Jesus is Nuts About Me,'" Jimmy says. "Odd way for missionaries to act, pointing M-16s at a disabled vessel."

"It's religious conversion at gunpoint. There's a lot of that going around. The weaker the god, the more violent the fanatic," Bruno says, getting up from the table.

I'm about to bite into some smoked octopus when my phone buzzes. It's Boyer.

"Hey, Nick, my friend. It looks like you have had a bad boating experience. What happened with the Maroon Key? Did you forget to put oil in the engine?"

"We were about to call you, Henri. Can you give us a lift out to where we think the treasure is? We could find it together, just like we've been planning."

I look at Jimmy. He's got an ear-to-ear grin.

"Oh, Nick, you and your Jimmy are amateurs," Boyer says. "We don't need you, except to tell you goodbye. The Captain Elmo drunk, your confidant, has sold you out for a hundred dollars. We know where the treasure is, and we'll collect it. I can't believe your stupidity. You find the chests, but then you haven't the tools to dig them out or unlock them."

"You can't do this," I say. "We'll take you to court. We'll tell our story to the Miami Herald. They know what a crook you are."

"Hah. One step in that direction, and you and Jimmy will need funeral arrangements for your families."

A click ends the conversation.

"Gee, what a swell guy," Jimmy says. "To think about how we used to make fun of him. He deserves everything that he's got coming."

Bruno comes back to the table and sits.

"Elmo and Harry are at the docks. They just called. Everything's ready to go. They want us to bring back some more onion rolls."

Our faithful waitress Corinne tops off our coffee.

"I'll get you a sack of onion rolls with extra butter packs," she says. "Mango jelly, too."

"I'll settle the bill for the whole gang," Jimmy says.

"Two hundred, if you think that's fair."

"Hey, it's been great." Jimmy hands her three C-notes.

We board Captain Elmo's boat at the marina. Lady Day is a 25-foot Boston Whaler with a Bimini top. She's ideal for where we're going. She draws just over a foot of water, and she'll have no trouble towing our two shallow draft Zodiacs.

If you look at where we're going on Google Maps, you'll see satellite views of the low-lying islands on coral flats— Big Mullet Key, Little Mullet Key, Barracouta Keys, Man Key, Woman Key. Low tide gives maybe a foot of water in places. We shouldn't have much trouble getting into where we want to go.

Henri Boyer and his crew of fascist maniacs may have a problem. Their craft, *Jesus M'aime Enormément*, Jesus Loves Me Very Much, to those who can't *parlez Francais*, suffers from its owner's outsized ego. Dear old Henri wanted a boat that would impress people in Miami. The Hatteras 36 Convertible has plenty of room to store treasure and luxurious accommodations for honored *Tonton Macoute* and other lowlifes. It also draws four-and-a-half feet of water.

Captain Elmo squints through his sunglasses and steers us out of Key West boat traffic.

"That small fiberglass dinghy Boyer's got lashed to his foredeck isn't going to hold him and his crew," Captain Elmo says. "Maybe he's got a small inflatable below deck, but they may have to paddle it some distance to get to shore."

We head northwest out of Key West. Our plan is to come from the north side to our targeted key. Boyer and his crew are heading Southwest out of Key West. The draft is deep on that route until they swing to the north to approach the target. That's where the depth sounder will go from two fathoms to half a fathom in seconds.

"If they don't pay attention to the depth sounder, something else will alert them," Captain Elmo says. "They'll hear a crunch as they run into coral. If they're going fast, they'll get tossed on their fannies."

We move under clear blue skies. Our radio tuned to the marine weather channel tells the story: "Variable winds five to ten knots, mainly from the east. Temperatures in the low eighties...."

"You don't need a weatherman," Jimmy says. "It's a gorgeous day. Look. Manta ray."

A ray passes within yards of our port railing. Off starboard, a turtle surfaces and then dives.

"Ten knots," Captain Elmo says. "It's a good speed for seeing the turtles and rays."

We splash along. Our Zodiacs bump and rub on each side of *Lady Day*. It's a perfect morning, the kind you want to share with people you love.

Except, of course, the day isn't perfect. We're dealing with cutthroats. This is no place for loved ones. It takes all the charm out of the old pirate stories when you realize Boyer and his choir boys are here to steal treasure from us –the treasure that we don't have. If they fail to find treasure, they'll come after us and kill us.

Behind us, Key West disappears beneath the horizon. Only the taller buildings are visible. A small Coast Guard vessel passes us, heading east toward the Lower Keys, but then it turns north toward Marco Island on Florida's west coast. In a minute, it disappears.

A cormorant on a rusty buoy spreads its wings to dry them. It looks at us as we pass by. We're brief intruders to its part of the ocean.

The *Lady Day* hums on through the damp, salty air.

We scan the horizon for several minutes. No vessels are in sight, and Key West is gone. Soon, we're alone, moving through a light chop.

The Lady Day makes a broad swing to port.

"We'll ease our way into the short beach," Captain Elmo says. "Time to get it all together."

I look at our crew. We're ready

The Lady Day idles down. The engine stops. We drift toward the mangrove covering the shallow beach. We're a hundred yards from shore. We ease the anchor into the sandy bottom and get into the Zodiacs.

We paddle toward shore, listening for sounds from Boyer and his crew. They'll come ashore where Captain Elmo told them to on the south end of the key, close to the half-buried strongboxes, several hundred yards from where we land.

Small fish swim in the shade beneath the Zodiacs, darting in and out between sponges. The only sound comes from our paddles and the small waves breaking on the shallow beach.

It’s a beautiful place to avoid dying.

Chapter 43

The Zodiacs float us onto the beach, scattering hundreds of black crabs. The crabs seem offended. We've crashed their party.

We pull the Zodiacs under mangroves and tie their painters to thick branches. A few yards from the trees, nature has sculpted a cluster of small sand dunes, each about four feet high. Captain Elmo says the dunes are probably from the king tides pushing things around. Each dune has bleached-out coconuts and palm fronds topping it. Bleached-out beer cans and plastic six-pack holders serve as reminders that nature has a big fight on her hands with you know who.

A quick look over the top of a dune reveals more thickly grouped mangroves yards away. Beyond is a small clearing just off the small beach on the key's south end. The fake strongboxes are there. They poke their heads out of the sand, waiting for Henri Boyer and his *Tonton Macoute* quartet.

"They're not ashore yet," Jimmy says. "I can see their boat through the binocs. Looks like they're maybe two hundred yards offshore."

"Yeah, like I figured," Captain Elmo says. "They're untying the small dinghy from the bow."

"Looks like they've got a small outboard to put on it," Jimmy says. "Maybe a two-horse."

Jimmy hands me the binoculars.

"They've got a small inflatable. Wait. This doesn't look like any Zodiac. Jesus, it looks like some kind of a large pool toy."

"I've seen them," Captain Elmo says. "They rent them to tourists in Key West down at the beach off Roosevelt Road. Comes with two paddles. Most people give up after paddling a few strokes. They don't move like Zodiacs."

The activity aboard the French version of "Jesus is Nuts About Me" continues. Getting a fiberglass dinghy with small outboard ready for the trip to the beach has become a significant undertaking. The honcho-in-charge, Henri Boyer, barks the names Marcel, Armond, Leroi, and Pascal in staccato sentences.

"If I didn't know better, I'd think I was listening to a Montreal hockey game," Jimmy says.

"Typical tin horn." Captain Elmo hands his binoculars to Harry. "Take a look. These are the clowns coming for the treasure."

"Somehow, they're all getting into the dinghy or the fancy pool float and coming here to haul off heavy strongboxes. Is that the plan?" Harry asks.

"You left out their M-16s," Captain Elmo says. "They may have to shoot the treasure."

Shooting the treasure could bring about an explosive result. All three strongboxes are rigged with a simple detonator attached to several sticks of dynamite. Lift the lid at your peril. Bruno says the safe way to get into the strong boxes is to soak them in water or tear off their bottoms.

It takes time to get Boyer's armada together, but he finally gets it to his liking. His Jesus boat is in a naturally deep channel next to shallow coral, where the water is about three feet deep. Two *Tonton Macoute* quartet members will tow the dinghy, while the remaining two will tow the pool toy. Multiple attempts to start the small outboard motor result in Boyer ripping it off the dinghy transom and tossing it into the water.

The payload aboard the two vessels consists of tools and M-16s. The only difference we can see from our hiding place is that vessel number one, the dinghy, has the honor of hauling Henri Boyer and the heavy metal. Vessel number two, the pool party float, has another unforgettable onboard, Father Jacques Dupres. The good padre and two Tonton Macoute warriors have opted to wear loosely fitting pink ski belts that look like they were bought at a garage sale.

"It's nice to see the religious community getting involved," Jimmy says. "I wonder if he's aware that he's in the company of sharks?"

The two vessels move toward shore with the aid of *Tonton Macoute* - propulsion. About fifty yards from the beach, they stop.

"*Requin des sables*," one of the dinghy pullers yells. He grabs an M-16 from the dinghy where Boyer sits. Boyer holds one, too.

"Sand shark," Harry says, translating for us. "They're worried about sand sharks."

"Yeah, probably Blacknose or Sharpnose sharks," Captain Elmo says. "They're no big threat to anyone."

The *Tonton Macoute* brigade disagrees. Dinghy puller number one empties a magazine into the water, trying to eradicate the threat. Boyer, not to be outdone by a person of lower rank, also fires a full magazine into the water. The sound of bullets slamming into peaceful waters and schools of fish alerts a thousand birds sitting in the mangroves. They take off screeching. A third member of the *Tonton Macoute* expedition grabs an M-16 from the pool toy float and fires it above the mangroves where the birds were a second earlier.

"Are these guys spooked or what?" Bruno asks.

"Must be," Jimmy says. "I thought they were supposed to piss on the shark before they shot it."

The birds come to rest again on the mangrove.

Boyer yells something at his crew and turns back toward the beach. For a second, I think he's spotted us hiding behind the dunes and the scruffy mangrove. But no.

He's spotted the tops of the strongboxes sticking out of the sand. His treasure is waiting, but he's not about to wait. He's out of the dinghy and sloshing his way toward shore.

The rest of his crew sees the strongboxes, too. They also slosh.

This amphibious landing on our small Key isn't a replay of the Marines storming Iwo Jima or MacArthur returning to Manila.

Drunks stumbling over the shaking floor at a funhouse is closer to the truth.

The six stagger onto the beach, dragging the dinghy and the pool float. Boyer runs to the strongboxes and circles them. He stops, faces the ocean, and spots the engraving on the strongbox. Down on his knees, he examines the first treasure chest and reads out loud.

"*Propriété de Maurice Levant.*"

Father Jacques drops to his knees next to Boyer and crosses himself.

"*Le Corps et le Sang de Jésus.*"

"The body and blood of Jesus." Harry translates.

Boyer runs his finger along the minor groove that separates the locked strongbox from its lid. He turns to face the others. He has something in the palm of his hand.

"Emaraude. Emaraude. Emaraude," Boyer says.

"If all this French keeps up, we'll have to install subtitles," Harry says.

Boyer has a plan to prevent that. He stands and looks at the four horsemen of the *Tonton Macoute.*

"Marcel," Boyer says in his best Miami-let's-cut-the-bullshit English. "Do your duty."

"About fuckin' time," Marcel says, emptying an M-16 magazine into Father Jacques and the strongbox in front of him.

Again, a large flock of birds squawk their way out of the mangrove and take flight.

We hold our breaths, waiting for dynamite to explode from a direct hit.

Nothing happens.

Then, to add insult to fatal injury, Marcel kicks what's left of Father Jacques in the head.

He adds a eulogy for the fallen priest, "Everyone's had enough of your holy roller shit."

Green jewels fall through the bullet holes to mix with the blood of Father Jacques on the sand. The birds come to rest again on the mangrove.

Boyer turns to the two crew members holding the dinghy and the pool toy lines.

"Pascal, Leroi, get rid of this asshole. He's bleeding all over the emeralds."

The two drop the lines and grab the departed priest by his life-saving ski belt. Boyer watches with his hands on his hips as the two drag what's left of Father Jacques to the water and shove him in.

"Big fucking mistake," Captain Elmo says.

"Blood in the water," Harry says.

"We've found it," Boyer says. "Look at these emeralds. We've got all three cases that Maurice Levant shipped over two hundred years ago."

Marcel stoops to grab a handful of the olivine costume jewels.

He slaps another magazine into his M-16.

"We must be rich, boss," Pascal says, standing at the water's edge. "This must be a five-way split now, no?"

"No, Pascal. Only three-way." Boyer nods toward Marcel, who stands and unloads another magazine into Pascal and Leroi. They fall into the water next to Father Jacques and the pool toy. The pool toy quickly loses air from one of Marcel's fired bullets.

"Let's get to work," Boyer says. "Get the chests into the dinghy. We'll open them after we get them on board the boat. Let's not hang around with these three stiffs."

The strongboxes come out of their nesting in the sand with ease.

"Fucking weaklings," Boyer says. "Nick and his asshole partner Jimmy didn't have the strength to carry off three strongboxes. Lazy bastards."

Soon, the beach is clear of strongboxes and fake emeralds. The treasures are aboard the dinghy, along with the five M-16s and their extra magazines.

The bodies of Father Jacques, Pascal, and Leroi, kept afloat by their ski belts, move slowly into deeper water.

Armond and Marcel wade toward the 36-foot-long *"Jesus M'aime Enormément*," pulling the dinghy. Boyer sits with the three strongboxes. He pushes the three dead men out of the way with the butt of his M-16 as they float past.

Halfway to their anchored Hatteras, Armond yells.

"Something big just bumped me. Did you see it? You got the gun? What was it?"

"Settle down," Boyer says. "You've got the shakes from all that excitement back there. Keep pulling. We're almost there."

The dead body of Father Jacques shakes and suddenly submerges.

"Shark," Armond says. "Shark. Your gun, can you...?"

That's all he can manage before he's pulled under.

Boyer levels his M-16 at the powerful shark that now has Armond above the water, shaking him. Boyer's bullets go through the shark's head and tear through Armond. Now there's more blood in the water.

Boyer turns to look for Marcel. He's not where he should be. Boyer stands and pivots with the M-16 in his hands. He fires again at the shark that has

Armond. It's no use. Something bumps the small dinghy. Boyer turns to fire, but his magazine is empty.

Another bump capsizes the boat.

The strongboxes fall to the bottom.

Boyer tries to stand in four-foot-high water. Then something pulls him down.

The turbulence lasts for several minutes, then all is calm. The pool toy rests on the sand beach. Spots of blood from Pascal and Leroi dot its plastic blue and white skin. Waves that have a red tint break on the beach. Three pink ski belts float from shore. The white dinghy rights itself a hundred yards offshore. It floats off, the lone survivor heading for a beach on another key.

"Someday, someone will find the strongboxes," Captain Elmo says. "They'll be crusted over with marine growth. Maybe they'll find the M-16s, too. They won't be much good. As far as the Boyer bunch goes, there are a lot of bones under the sea. The sea life here has strong appetites. They'll be picked clean."

Cleaning up a messy key takes some time. Our crew picks up the old beer cans, the pool toy, and the leftover mess from Boyer's bunch. Being the good guys can mean hard work.

We bring Lady Day and the Zodiacs next to the Hatteras as the sun sets.

A thorough search of Boyer's boat gives us the personal effects of the Tonton Macoute quartet. Passports, driver's licenses, and keys to cars and houses get tossed into a bag in case we need any of them for follow-ups. We also find the leather-bound valise with the picture of the Columbus skull. A few notes accompany it, some in French, some in English. The valise is labeled in Haitian Creole, "*Zo bwa Tèt esklav Kristòf Kolon*."

"Pretty sure that says, 'the skull of the slave of Christopher Columbus,'" Captain Elmo says. "When you've hung around Key West long enough, you get to know stuff you never thought you'd be learning about."

The rest of the *Jesus M'aime Enormément* cargo is boat junk.

We double-check everything and power her up. She runs rough.

We manage to work the Hatteras out of the tight channel and make our way south in the dark. Ten miles south of the Keys, Bruno places a small charge with a timer on the anchored *Jesus M'aime Enormément*. He hops aboard one of the Zodiacs, and Harry motors him over to the *Lady Day*. We watch in a light shower from several hundred yards away. The explosive blows out the transom of Boyer's boat and sends her to the bottom 300 feet below.

It's shortly before midnight when we near Key West. The rain stops, and the stars are out.

"I think we're finally out of this Uncle Billy mess," Jimmy says.

My cell phone gets some bars and tells me I have messages. Dawn has called, and Jacky has, too. He wants to know what we think. He can wait. We will have a few drinks at Captain Elmo's and head for the Oceanfront Suites.

Then I notice another message. It's from Valerie Masters.

"I need to see you and Jimmy. Call me tomorrow. I know more about Ronnie Nolan. There's something important I have to tell you. Something I left out has been troubling me."

Chapter 44

It's never over 'til it's over, according to the Yogi man. Or maybe it's over when the fat lady sings.

"Same difference," Jimmy says. "No matter. For you and me, it's never over. Look at it. We work for a rich egomaniac with a whacked-out sense of the real world. Why are we surprised when a simple real estate deal Jacky sends us to turns into what? Thirteen people dead and another ten in jail?"

"I wasn't keeping a scorecard," I say. "That does sound about right, though."

"It is right, damn it. I kept the count on my iPhone. We arrive for a fishing trip, and we end up at a shark attack."

"Maybe it was something that one of us said."

"Like, 'okay, we'll go down there and take a look at it?' We need to quit saying yes to Jacky."

It's later in the day, and the fat lady hasn't sung. In fact, she isn't fat. She's sitting on her porch swing with her bare feet tucked under her five-foot-two-inch frame. She's the very picture of middle America's wealth and respectability. I wonder what happened to that combination. Where did it go? Did everyone opt out for becoming either a money-grubber or a lackey? I know someone is getting wealthy on Miami Beach, charging tourists high prices to swim in shit.

"I wanted to come clean," says the blond lady with deep blue eyes. "This whole boy toy thing has done a number on me. I'm ready to move on, to do something good for the world. Getting involved with the Ronnie Nolans of the world was not just tacky. It was damn dangerous."

"I wouldn't worry about Ronnie and Anna," Jimmy says. "They'll be in the slammer for a long time."

"They're the ones that got this skull of the slave of Columbus thing started again," Valerie says. "They knew some Haitians that were looking for it. They had a couple old charts where it might be found. One had it buried on a key somewhere west of Key West. The other chart was crudely done, showing the skull was in the lower Keys. Everyone here thought it was bullshit. The Columbus skull story was some kind of a Halloween story. Every kid knew a version of it."

"Yeah, we know," Jimmy says. "Urban legend. As far as the Haitians, you can rest easy. They're not in the picture anymore."

"That's about all Captain Elmo would say about Boyer and his crowd, too. I talked with him earlier. I bet you boys had a big part in that. Anything you can elaborate on?"

"We can guarantee that Captain Elmo is one hundred percent right," Jimmy says. "Rest easy. Things should quiet down. Maybe this Christopher Columbus skull story will slowly disappear."

"Not if I have anything to do with it." Valerie smiles and winks.

Valerie's housekeeper Emma places a tray of coffees and toasted Cuban bread on the wicker table. She pours ice water into our glasses and disappears.

"Did I hear you, right?" Jimmy says. "You want this story about the Columbus skull sitting out there on some outer Key to continue? Isn't that the kind of story that gets people ready to kill each other over something that, as far as we know for sure, doesn't exist?"

Valerie smiles and spoons some sugar into her small black coffee cup.

"I love you guys. You're like the brothers I always wish I had. Streetwise, always sensing an angle somewhere. I'll bet your street smarts have gotten you out of tight spaces. When you tell me that Boyer and his bums will never bother anyone or that Ronnie and his ilk are going away for a long stretch, I believe you. But as you know, the world keeps turning out Boyers and Ronnie Nolans. If there were no stories about Columbus skulls or strongboxes full of emeralds, the sharpies would make up others."

"Good point," I say. "We know what treasure fever can do to people. We try to prevent people from going bust at the Galloping Dominos. Some of our pit bosses can tell when someone's gone to their limit. We want happy customers to come back. You'd be surprised how many free tickets to top shows we give to people just so we can get Daddy away from the craps table and maybe preserve his marriage."

"Yeah," Jimmy says. "If the guy wants to go bust after that, he can do it at another casino. Don't get me wrong. We're happy to take down high-rollers who think they own the world. Fact is, though, there aren't enough of those around anymore."

"I know," Valerie says. "We're all in the fantasy business. That's how Captain Elmo puts it. People think that it's one glamorous night after another at his place. He jokes about how people expect Humphrey Bogart to walk through the door and order whiskey. Do you know what Captain Elmo really likes to do? The crossword puzzle in the Sunday New York Times."

A breeze dances through the bamboo wind chimes hanging from the corner of the porch. The melody sings "relax." We raise our cups and smile at each other.

"This whole thing has changed me," Valerie says. "That's part of what I want to say. I left you that message last night. I realize now how dangerous the people I got involved with were."

"We figure a bunch dead and ten in jail," Jimmy says. "You're not going to add any more to the list, are you?"

"No, but this Columbus skull thing got me thinking. He was a sex slaver, you know. I have to confess. The boy toy thing was a form of that. It wasn't an honest attempt at love. I was like some guy trying to put notches on his headboard. I was super cool Valerie, the tough gal from Kansas who knew how to hustle up some fine piece of ass. Isn't that how the cool boys put it?"

"Hey, you didn't carve your signature into anyone's skull," Jimmy says. "You let everyone involved have their fantasy. The young guys you got involved with, your readers."

"Maybe, but I'm not sure that no one got hurt. What kind of message was I sending? Telling women that they should go out and buy a boy toy? Or go long and invest in a gigolo? No, I've got to confess. The fact that this prick who carved his name into his sex slaves' skulls can go down as some kind of hero just bugs the crap out of me."

"I hear you," Jimmy says. "It's part of the irony of history. It says something about how people heal by trying to put the best face on something awful that's happened. Think about it. How many movie makers and writers of thrillers and history books owe their careers to a jerk like Hitler? I hate to say it, but World War II is an industry that keeps on giving. Those writers and filmmakers would all be writing about what with no Adolf? The boredom of middle-of-the-road Germany in the thirties?"

Valerie leans back and drains the last of her coffee. A thin coffee mustache appears above her lip. She smiles.

"Well, I'm not going to sit idle. I've got something to say about this monster who got countries and cities named after him. Remember the brainwashing? 'In fourteen hundred and ninety-two, Columbus sailed the ocean blue'? We got all that hero crap poured into our heads as kids. It reminds me of these people who want to hang a kid for joining the Taliban, but they'll go out of their way to honor their Confederate heritage. Is there a disconnect somewhere? When do slavery and treason become honorable?"

"Valerie," Jimmy says. "We know it's unfair. Maybe the system has been designed that way. But we're still in the game, fighting it. How can we help you?"

She licks the thin coffee mustache from her upper lip, wipes her mouth with a linen napkin, and smiles.

"I have something of yours that I want to return to you."

"What?" Jimmy asks.

"A large ice chest came off your boat that Ronnie Nolan and I were on."

I look at Jimmy. He shrugs.

"Yeah, a few things were missing," I say. "No big deal. We're glad you're safe. Where is it?"

"It's still where I left it on one of the outer Keys, buried under a heavy tangle of mangrove roots and branches. I want you to help me go get it."

"Hey," Jimmy says. "If it's what? An eighty-buck piece of plastic...."

"It's what's inside of it," Valerie says. "I have the skull."

Chapter 45

"I want you to understand how it was for me," Valerie says. "I had a look at some of the friends that Ronnie hung out with when we stayed at the Sea Change. They were hard cases. That Sherry, the red wig with the boob job, was disgusting. She came to our door and offered to do a three-way with us for two hundred dollars. I slammed the door in her face. Bonnie was a cheap whore, too, but she had something else about her that gave me the creeps. You could tell there was a violent streak in her just below the surface, ready to burst out."

"You were right about that," Jimmy says. "She had no qualms about pumping .38 slugs into people who got in the way."

"So, I was happy to get away from Miami Beach and head for the Keys. I figured that Ronnie and I would have our love cruise in paradise with all the erotic trimmings. I could write about it later. I'd bow out of the relationship when we got back to Marathon, going our separate ways. He'd leave with some expensive gifts and some of my money. Knowing he was a gigolo, I figured he'd just move on to the next rich woman."

"That was his pattern, according to people we know," I say. "He'd hustle women, peddle dope, and do some strongarm stuff on the side. There's some stuff you didn't know. He's named in an attempted murder warrant upstate. There's also a strong suspicion that he was in on the murder of Scarlet Fuentes, the fashion designer."

Valerie takes a deep breath and lets it out.

"Oh, Jesus. That bad?"

"Yeah, that bad," Jimmy says. "A cold-blooded son of a bitch."

There's silence for a minute except for the small birds chirping around the banana plants in Valerie's yard. A tear makes its way down her right cheek. She wipes it away with her linen napkin.

"Call me stupid," she says. "Damn lucky, too. I got away before he could kill me."

"You went out on the Maroon Key II with Ronnie. When did the skull show up?" Jimmy says.

Valerie takes a deep breath and continues.

"Ronnie was tripping on acid. He tried to get me to take some, but I told him I'd stay with our champagne. There was no moon. We turned off most of the lights on the boat to see the bright stars. The boat was drifting with the tidal current. It was like a magic carpet ride. We looked at marine life in the water. The phosphorus glowing sea life in green and blue was fascinating. He started to talk about the Columbus skull and how it was lost somewhere in the vicinity some two hundred years back. I had heard versions of the story before. I figured he was retelling an old legend and left it at that."

"What happened then?"

"He started to talk about how some marine life resembled the skull. I figured it was fantasy fun, like when you see bears and lazy dragons in puffy white clouds. Then he got fixated on the skull idea. Everything was a skull. He was sure we had drifted past it in shallow water. Couldn't I see it? I finally had enough. I told him to leave me alone."

"I'm betting he didn't listen," Jimmy says.

"No. He grabbed me with both hands on my head and tried to turn me to where he saw a skull. I went after him. He was stoned, and I was ready to take him down. I struck him in the face a couple times, and he lost his balance. He grabbed the gaff hook as he fell and cut his hand on it. He got up and was about to take a swing at me with it when I kicked him hard in the balls. He was hurting bad. It was my chance to leave."

"You took the Zodiac," Jimmy says.

"Yeah. The cruiser had a lot of room on it, but it couldn't get into the shallows as the Zodiac could. I had been using it during the days to explore the smaller Keys. I loved buzzing around in it. My swim mask and flippers were already on board. My stuff was already in a duffle bag. I tossed it into the Zodiac next to the ice chest. I grabbed a gaff hook and a flashlight from the captain's station and took off into the night."

"What was Ronnie's response?" Jimmy says. "Did he try to stop you?"

"He was incoherent, lying on the deck trying to catch his breath. I turned the flashlight at him. He had blood all over his face. Was it because I hit him in the nose, or was it from him putting his bleeding hand to his face? That was enough Ronnie for me. I boogied."

Valerie untucks her feet from beneath her and leans forward. She grabs the large French press and pours coffee into our cups. For a brief second, there's a look on her face of someone who has lost her place. Maybe in her story? Maybe in her life?

"How did I know where to head?" She says. "It was dark."

"Good question," Jimmy says. "You made one good decision. You headed clear of Ronnie."

"It was strange, but some of what Ronnie had said earlier stuck in my head. He said the tidal flow was taking us southwest toward Key West. That meant Marathon was somewhere to the northeast. There was a small compass aboard the Zodiac. I headed in that general direction, turned off the flashlight, and slowed the motor down to a hum. The Maroon Key II seemed to be going the other way from me. I was putting some good distance between us. I again saw the glowing sea life beneath the Zodiac."

"Maybe you were back where Ronnie started talking about skulls in the water," Jimmy says.

"Maybe. I'll never know for sure. What I do know is that the Zodiac ran into something. I figured it was a mangrove root or maybe a part of a rotting channel marker. I put the engine into neutral and grabbed the gaff hook to push away from whatever it was. Damn. The gaff hook got stuck on something. I tried to twist it. Finally, I could pull it free, but something came up with it."

"The skull?" Jimmy says.

"It was dark. I didn't know what it was at first. It was a small iron bar cage with an old padlock on it. Maybe I had someone's crab trap. I set it in the Zodiac stern while pushing away from what I had run into. I wanted to be free of Ronnie. I got back into deeper water and went to the stern to put the engine in gear."

"Is that when you saw it?"

"If Valerie the Adventuress was telling the story on the History Channel, that would be the storyline. But it was Valerie the Klutz on that Zodiac. Valerie had to have a diet soda out of the ice chest to soothe her fucked up head over what had happened with psycho Ronnie."

Jimmy nods.

Another tear rolls down Valerie's right cheek.

"I sat on the lid of that ice chest, looking back at the disappearing Maroon Key II. It was just a speck. I could make out the small light that held the ensign on the stern, and then I aimed my small flashlight down at the small iron bar cage. I stared at her for a good while. The emerald coqui frog on her head was framed with emeralds. Her lower jaw was missing."

"What did you do then?" Jimmy says.

"I kept saying, 'Omigod, omigod, omigod."

"So, you decided to put the skull into the ice chest for safekeeping," I say.

"Yeah, I thought she should at least have a name. I thought Esmeralda was fitting. It means emerald in Spanish. I wanted to keep her safe. There was nowhere else to hide her. Then I got into this paranoid thought pattern. What if Ronnie caught up with me before I got to Marathon? Maybe he'd grab me in Marathon. Maybe that guy Zimmer who worked at the marina, was in with Ronnie? I couldn't just show up and walk off with the ice chest that said 'Maroon Key II.' I had to think fast.

"I couldn't take her to Marathon, and I sure as hell wasn't taking Esmeralda back to Ronnie. She had to be hidden somewhere in between. Somewhere I could come back to and find her when it was safe. The trouble is it was dark. I pulled the Zodiac into a small cove between two small keys and waited for the sun to come up."

"And that's when you found the hiding place?" Jimmy asks.

"First, there was the long wait, getting attacked by mosquitos and other bugs. About three in the morning, I noticed a bright spotlight beam coming from where the Maroon Key II had been. It flashed out across the water. I thought it might be Ronnie's friends coming to rescue him and maybe do away with me. I didn't know. I pulled in closer to the small key on my left and stayed down in the Zodiac. The beam flashed over me a few times, and then it stopped."

We sip more coffee.

Valerie tucks her feet back under her and continues.

"I fell asleep while hiding in the Zodiac. I awoke to sunshine and birds. There was a small beach before the thick mangroves started. I stumbled through the maze of branches and found a spot that was a struggle to get into. That's where I put the ice chest with her in it. I covered it with more driftwood, and I tied it in with a section of the line from the Zodiac."

"That's when you headed for Marathon?" Jimmy says.

"First, I did my best to mark where I was. I tied a shirt on a tree on the key next to the hidden ice chest. Then I tied a small line on the mangrove branch above her. That done, I cast off and opened the throttle for Marathon. Two minutes later, I ran out of gas."

"Will that be on your History Channel interview?" Jimmy asks.

Everyone laughs.

Valerie's housekeeper, Emma, brings another tray of coffee and Cuban Bread. She pours fresh ice water and hands Valerie a small pack of tissues.

"You gonna be okay, child?"

Valerie nods and smiles.

Emma leaves.

"It was around noon when I finally rowed into Marathon. I was sunburned, bug-bitten, and dehydrated. Zimmer took one look at me and said, 'What happened, little lady? Did that dumb son bitch abandon you?' All I could do was sit there in the Zodiac and cry."

I look at Jimmy. He shakes his head.

"That son of a bitch Ronnie," Jimmy says.

Valerie wipes her face with a tissue and continues.

"Zimmer helped me out of the Zodiac and drove me to the hospital. They took a look at me and said they'd keep me overnight. Dehydration, abrasions, bug bites, severe sunburn. I had it all."

"That goddamn Ronnie," Jimmy says.

"Billy showed up the next day and wanted to know what happened between Ronnie and me. I told him Ronnie got high and talked about buried treasure in the Keys. Then when I didn't want to dive to look for some of it in shark-infested waters, he beat me up."

"What was Billy's response to that?" I ask.

"He kept saying, 'That goddamn Bonnie, and her worthless friends.' He wanted to pay for my hospital stay. I told him my insurance could take the hit. I just wanted to go on with my life."

"What did you do then?" Jimmy says.

"I got a rental car, turned the AC on full blast, and drove away so I could think. I had no idea who I could trust regarding the skull. I knew Ronnie had people who would kill for a treasure like that. For all I knew, they'd kill me for beating up Ronnie. No, I needed to wait for the right help to come along. In the meantime, I had to protect myself."

"Did you head for your house in Coral Gables?" Jimmy says.

"Yeah. I made one stop along the way at Jo-Jo's Gun Shop. I'm now the proud owner of a Glock with two fully loaded magazines. I'm ready to stop creeps in their tracks."

Chapter 46

Lunch at the Oceanfront Suites features outrageous stories told over the best seafood one could want. Captain Elmo talks about locals taking tourists for a ride.

"It's the Hemingway Hustle," he says. "There's always someone buying an old typewriter that Ernest himself used to write *For Whom the Bell Tolls* or *Death in the Afternoon.* I don't know where they find the old typewriters. I also wonder how many bartenders have made an extra C-note or two by selling Ernest's favorite bar stool."

"A while back, there was someone with the idea of putting Ernest's picture on the plastic covering the barstool cushion," Valerie says. "If you were so inclined, you could brag to your friends back home that you had sat on Hemingway's face while you were in Key West."

I think about this desecration of poor Ernest's legend and wonder if a similar fate will happen to Esmeralda. Will there be plastic versions of Columbus's sex slave's skull for sale at the Key West Sunset Celebration?

"Everyone wants to profit from some legend," Captain Elmo says.

"Yeah, in Vegas, places that got built two years ago hang pictures of Sinatra and Bugsy Siegel above the bar," I say. "Ask the bartender, and he'll point out where the two of them sat together drinking Jack Daniels."

Corinne, our faithful waitress, fills our coffee cups and asks if we want anything else.

"No, Hon," Jimmy says. "It's time we got up and did some work. We have a serious boat ride ahead of us."

"Yeah, let's go get it," Captain Elmo says.

We've opted to drive to Marathon. Harry and Bruno have taken the Maroon Key there for service after it played the part of a disabled seacraft. That ploy led the now-departed Boyer and his bunch to think we were out of the hunt for the treasure chests.

We'll pick up the Maroon Key and a Zodiac and head for the area near Content Key. The ice chest with Esmeralda aboard is on one of the nearby keys. We'll retrieve it in the late afternoon and head back to dinner in Marathon with any luck.

"Could be rain moving in," Captain Elmo says as we pull into the lot at Maroon Key Marina. "Those puffy white clouds could turn into a shower before the end of the day."

"If it's only getting wet, I think we can take it," Jimmy says.

We stroll down the dock to where Zimmer is at work on the Maroon Key's engine.

"You'll have to take the Maroon Key II if you're going out," Zimmer says. "We had to take the engine apart on the Maroon Key for an overhaul. Bruno and Harry went to Key Largo to get the parts. They should be back later this afternoon."

"Maroon Key II's the boat Ronnie and I took out on our fateful voyage," Valerie says. "This feels creepy."

"Is that a problem?" Jimmy says. "We could go tomorrow when the engine parts are here."

Valerie looks at the Maroon Key II and sighs.

"We've got to get Esmeralda," she says. "We can't wait any longer. Even though I did a good job hiding her, I'm worried someone could find her. We need to get this done."

I'm about to offer one of my reassuring, tough-guys-in-charge comments when my phone rings. It's Detective Cohen.

I excuse myself and walk up the dock toward the parking lot.

"Jerry, what's up?" I say.

"There's been a few developments that you should know about," Cohen says. "Maybe you guys know something? Maybe you can help us out?"

"Shoot. What's on your mind?"

"Francois Du Pont. You ever hear of him?"

"Can't say he rings a bell. He play for the Dolphins?"

"Only if they move to Port au Prince. He's one of the sleazy characters hanging around with Henri Boyer. Drugs, prostitution, you name it. He runs with the power crowd in Haiti. He often travels into Miami to meet with Boyer. He's not the type you'd go to Disney World with. Anyhow, he came back into town and did something odd. He bailed out the Everett brothers and that flunky they hang out with, Clarence 'Buckshot' Thomas."

"That is odd. How does this guy know the Everetts?"

"Don't know that he does. Maybe he heard about these guys from Boyer. But that's another odd thing. No one's seen or heard from Boyer. A couple of our snitches say that Boyer was headed down to Key West in his Hatteras. He had four thugs with him and that priest he hangs with. We had a GPS tracker on Boyer's boat, but it's no longer working. The last position was several miles south of Key West. Maybe one of his guys found the tracker and destroyed it."

"That is interesting," I say. "Any reason you can think of why this Du Pont guy would want to bail out those bums?"

"He tried to bail out Ronnie Nolan, too. That didn't get very far. Ronnie's not going anywhere. The scuttle from jail is Ronnie keeps talking about lost treasure down in the keys. Probably bullshit. Cortez and I figure this Du Pont guy bought into the lie of Ronnie's and figures he'll have to settle for Ronnie's junior partners."

"He's what?" I ask. "Going treasure hunting with these guys?"

"That's our guess, but here's the kicker. If the Everetts think they're putting one over on the Haitian, they're crazy. Du Pont leaves a lot of dead bodies in his tracks."

Down the dock, Jimmy warms up the Maroon Key II. Captain Elmo and Valerie Masters are aboard, waiting for me.

"I can tell you this," I say to Cohen. "Boyer and that Father Jacques checked in with Detective Anna Clark. They were trying to get a line on Ronnie Nolan. Clark told them Ronnie was dead. Boyer tracked us down a few days later down here. He thought we were looking for some lost treasure. We told him we were just there to see what we could do with the marina in Marathon. He was pretty drunk at the time. I figured it was all bullshit about some lost treasure."

"Are you in Key West?" Cohen asks.

"No, we're in Marathon, about to take a boat ride with Valerie Masters. She might be interested in our holdings down here."

"Good luck with that," Cohen says. "You might want to keep your eyes open for Du Pont and that Spider Dog bunch. Maybe they're thinking about meeting up with Boyer to do some dirty work. You don't suppose there is a treasure, do you?"

"Sure. All you gotta do is pick the right numbers in the Super Lotto."

"Good luck with that one, too. Stay in touch. Gotta run."

Down the dock, Zimmer hands canned drinks and bags of ice from the Maroon Key to the Maroon Key II. Captain Elmo and Valerie stow them away.

Jimmy looks at me and does the let's get going shrug.

I nod and head toward the boat. Halfway there, I notice myself pulling on my shirt, making sure my Glock is tucked where it should be and that the extra magazine is safely in my pocket.

Jimmy notices.

He nods.

He gets it.

There's more to worry about here than getting wet.

Chapter 47

We head northwest past No Name Key and the north end of Big Pine Key. Two people wave as we go past their dock. We enter open water between mangrove-covered keys. We're not alone as we cruise along. We've acquired a school of flying fish that entertains us with daring launches into the open air.

"They can leap fifty yards along the surface," Captain Elmo yells from his position at the forward bow rail.

"Amazing," Valerie says. "We saw them last time I was out here. This place is so alive."

She's moved off the foredeck and has taken a seat in the stern near me.

"Everything okay, Nick?" she says. "I get the feeling you're on edge."

"Yeah, let's get things wrapped up."

She reaches into the ice chest and grabs a beer.

"That phone call, did it have anything to do with what I'm sensing?" she asks.

I glance at Jimmy, following our conversation from the command station. He looks back at me and flips his hand to the side. It's his way of saying, "Go ahead, let it all come out."

I look behind the Maroon Key II. As far as I can see, no one's trailing us.

"There are a few complications, Valerie. Someone else is in the hunt for Esmeralda, and I don't think they run the Smithsonian."

"Oh?"

She lets it hang in the air, waiting for me to fill in the huge blank space. I let it hang, too. I wonder if she's expecting a complete dossier on new characters searching for Columbian atrocities.

"Yeah," I finally say. "There's a new Haitian in the mix. His name is Francois Du Pont. "

Valerie is silent for a moment. She sips from her beer and stares at the wake behind us. It's clear, except for a few brown pelicans flying across our path.

"Is he a friend of Henri Boyer?" She says. "I've heard bad things about that bunch."

"I'm pretty sure there's a connection," I say.

She leans back against the port rail, looks at me, and rubs the soles of her bare feet together. Her toenails are painted bright red—I flashback to Bonnie Teller, putting her feet on the counter at the Sea Change and staring up at her red leather bag with the .38 inside.

I tell myself not to go there. This is different.

Isn't it?

"I thought you said that Boyer and his crew were out of the picture?" Valerie says.

"Boyer's no bother to anyone anymore," I say. "This Du Pont character somehow caught wind of Esmeralda. He and Boyer were involved in running whores and dope. Word is he got some info from your old boyfriend, Ronnie Nolan. He tried to bail Ronnie out of the Dade County slammer, but that didn't work. There's some hesitance on the part of judges in Miami to release the likes of Ronnie. He did manage to bail some of Ronnie's old crew from the Spider Dog Tap. The Everett brothers and some druggy named 'Buckshot' Thomas."

"They're down here?" Valerie asks.

"Don't know," I say. "I know they're headed here. You want to tell us how much we should be worried about Francois and the boys showing up at the spot where you stashed Esmeralda?"

Jimmy throttles down to idle speed. A shower with a waterspout is a half-mile ahead of us.

"Good move," Captain Elmo says. "Let it go past. It won't last long."

We get drizzle and gusts of wind. In minutes the shower is gone, and the late afternoon sun is out.

Jimmy advances the throttle. We're back to throwing a decent-sized wake behind us. As if to celebrate, the flying fish resume their long jumps.

I look at Valerie. I know she's hashing out the next version of what went down between her and Ronnie Nolan the night Esmeralda showed up.

I look at her and think, what's the big deal? You clobbered some thug, found a treasure, and ran off with it. So, what? Why not own up to it?

"It got complicated," she finally says. "It wasn't quite the way I told you."

"I've been getting that vibe," I say. "What happened?"

She smiles and tosses her hands into the air.

"You could say that I stole Esmeralda from a jerk who wanted to take her apart."

"You stole her from Ronnie? How the hell did he get hold of her?"

"Well, we both had her at first. We were diving that afternoon, looking for Florida lobster. It was closed season on them, but Ronnie said we could get away with grabbing a few for our dinner. I was totally corrupted by that time, so, like a total slut, I agreed. We found four lobsters. Locally, they're known as bugs. Like greedy criminals, we went after more. That's when we saw it. There was an iron-strapped trunk encrusted with marine growth. We got a line on one of the handles and went to the surface to haul it up."

"Did you know what you had?" I ask.

"No. We almost gave up on trying to raise it by hand. We tied the line to a cleat and used the boat to pull it up."

"What happened then?"

" We pried open the strongbox. There she was inside, what was left of poor Esmeralda, encrusted with emeralds in a locked iron bar cage."

"I'll bet you both went nuts," I say.

"Yeah, no kidding. I figured it was an archaeological treasure, something for a museum. That wasn't how Ronnie saw it. He wanted to bust open the iron bar cage and chip the emeralds off her skull. 'We can fence this and walk away with a bundle,' he said. I played along. I told him we needed to celebrate our good fortune with lobster, champagne, and sex."

"I guess he went for that," I say.

"Yeah, you could add an acid trip for Ronnie, too. I stayed focused, fed him, and bedded him. When he fell asleep, I went to work. I got the iron bar cage holding Esmeralda out of the strongbox. I grabbed the loose emeralds and gold bars, too. What could I do with all that? The ice chest on the Zodiac had some room. I tucked her in with the other stuff under some ice and soda cans. I could have run with her at that point, but I didn't want anyone chasing me."

"So, how were you going to pull that off?"

"I looked around for something heavy to load the strongbox with. There was an extra anchor with a chain attached. It seemed heavy enough. I wanted it to sink fast and stay down."

"So, you had it ready to give it the deep six," I say. "All you needed was an audience."

"Yeah, I was ready. I found a couple heavy-duty locks to put through the shackles on the chest," Valerie says. "Ronnie woke up, and we had more champagne and dope. We floated along on the tidal current, as I told you before. When I figured it was time, I told him the treasure belonged under the water. There was probably a curse on it. I added I didn't want any part of him. He protested, of course. I called him a few names. He responded likewise, and it escalated enough to where I picked up the strongbox and tossed it overboard."

"I bet he was thrilled."

"Livid. Things got rough as I wanted. I kicked him in the balls. He fell down. I said I couldn't stand to be around a pig like him. I got into the Zodiac and motored away into the night."

"So, if Ronnie could mark the general location of where the strongbox went in...."

"It would be several miles from where Esmeralda is waiting for us."

I think about "several miles." I know you can stand on the shore and see three miles to the horizon on the ocean. Could Ronnie have followed the small light on the Zodiac's outboard motor as Valerie made her getaway and stopped to hide Esmeralda?

I look at Jimmy. He's eased the throttle back again.

We're getting into tight passages between small keys and overgrown mangroves.

Valerie is up next to him, watching the depth sounder. Captain Elmo stands at the bow, trying to find the best route through the natural maze of mangroves and shallows.

The wake behind us has disappeared. Everything aft is clear to the horizon except for an approaching vessel three miles out. I touch my shirt. My Glock is ready.

We turn to port and then back to starboard as we make our way through the obstacle course of trees and shallows. The air is thick, with clouds of insects hovering near the mangroves.

Somewhere ahead is a passage to finding Esmeralda and open seas.

Or a dead end.

Chapter 48

The Maroon Key II crawls through the mangrove maze. The channel is unofficially marked by beer cans on bamboo poles, ropes tied to trees, and sun-bleached wooden arrows on rotting two-by-fours. Other boaters who have found their way through with enough water under their keels have left these markers. Somewhere ahead, we're hoping to find open water that will take us to where Valerie says we'll find Esmeralda.

Right now, we're sweating our way through clouds of mosquitoes and no-see-ums, the local version of flying itching powder. Swarms of bees buzz as they work the white flowers on the red mangroves. A white ibis sits on one of the low-hanging branches ahead. Its orange beak shines in the afternoon sun.

"They're tough birds," Captain Elmo says. "They're the last to leave before a hurricane hits, and they're the first birds back when the storm is over."

The boat we spotted three miles aft when we entered this maze is somewhere behind us. We hear the loud engine as it approaches the mangrove jungle. Then we listen to it get back down to a hum as it enters the winding obstacle course.

We hear their marine radio at first. Whoever it is, they're trying to stay connected to another boat. Now, the sounds are barely audible. They might be having more trouble than we are navigating through the mangroves.

"Any ideas?" Captain Elmo says. "Think it's the Haitian with that Spider Dog crew?"

"That's the hell of it," I say. "Could be anyone back there–an innocent boater or that asshole Du Pont. If it's Du Pont, they're waiting for us to lead them to the treasure, then they'll kill us."

Captain Elmo grabs a beer out of the ice chest.

"Well, we can't shoot first. Can we?"

I nod and look toward the bow. Valerie sits, leaning on the chrome bow rail, dangling her feet over the side of the boat. She gives hand directions to Jimmy, who's still at the wheel. We move along at idle speed, scraping past tangled mangrove branches.

The sun sinks. There might be two hours of light left.

I'm sweating and itching for open seas and the accompanying breeze.

There's a squawk from a marine radio somewhere aft.

"Where you at, Dog? You headed in the right direction?"

Someone mumbles something back, and then there's silence.

"That sounded close," Captain Elmo says. "Dog? Spider Dog?"

"If I had to bet on it," I say. "Yeah. I figure they're five or six minutes behind us. Sounds like there are two boats out here looking around."

"The boat behind us might be seven or eight turns back from where we are," Captain Elmo says. "Could be another boat heading out to where Ronnie saw Valerie deep-six the strongbox."

We pass gaps in the mangroves that look like ways to clear water, but none are marked.

"They're blind alleys," Captain Elmo says. "Navigating this maze is a leap of faith. Just when you're sure that you're lost, another marker shows up to keep you moving forward."

"Like a crooked blackjack dealer tossing aces to keep a rich mark in the game," I say.

"Maybe we could toss a couple aces at our Spider Dog friends," Captain Elmo says. "Lead them down the wrong path?"

Jimmy goes for it right away.

After passing a promising-looking blind alley, we tie a hundred feet of line across the good channel from mangrove to mangrove. The stretched rope is pointing to the proper channel, but it's a dead end. Soon, we're past the line and moving up the actual channel.

We follow our channel to another marker, and we turn to starboard. No one is behind us, we can tell. Has our trick worked?

A few minutes go by as we listen.

We hear shouts.

"Back out. Back out. We're aground."

"Goddamn it."

Loud engine sounds.

"They're trying to reverse out of it," Captain Elmo says. "Might be their only way. Probably no room to turn around in that mess."

We make three more turns in the shallow channel that gets narrower as we go through it. Our turn to port is a squeeze for the Maroon Key II. Mangrove branches scrape the boat's sides as we pass the channel marker, a beer can on an old boat hook pole.

"It's really shallow," Valerie says. "Come on, we've got to make it. We might have to get out and lighten the load to make it over the shallows."

"Let me give her a little more juice," Jimmy says, pushing the throttle forward.

We move forward and run into something that pushes the boat to the side. We hit mangrove branches on our port side and bounce to starboard. Jimmy gives more throttle, and we slide back to port. Only this time, the mangrove branches give way to open water.

We've made it through.

"It's up ahead," Valerie says, pointing at a group of low-lying keys with mangroves on them.

Our goal is about two miles ahead.

We move along at six knots. It's fast enough to blow away the insects that have been biting us, and the cooling breezes are a welcome treat after sweating our way through the maze.

"Going faster out here is a big risk," Captain Elmo says. "Look for sunken hazards. There's stumps, rocks, and wrecked boats waiting just below to tear your bottom."

A look ahead of us shows the sun hovering above the horizon to the west. We're about to get one of those sunsets the Keys are famous for. We'll be grabbing Esmeralda at dusk. The cover of darkness might work for us. Maybe we can slip past all the Spider Dogs and the Du Ponts without incident. We can get what we came for and head for Key West. Dinner at the Oceanfront Suites would suit us all.

"Look to starboard," Captain Elmo says. "That's no sun shower. Maybe we can beat it."

I look to the north. The line of dark clouds covers a quarter of the sky. Lightning zaps from the sea to the sky brings intense thunder. The sky above us is still clear. Can we make it before the storm hits? We move along, getting closer to the mangrove-covered keys and Esmeralda.

Luck might be with us, I think. The flying fish are back jumping beside us.

I'm about to yell how it's a good sign having the jumping fish with us when I look aft. Another vessel has come speeding out of the mangrove maze we left a few minutes back. It only takes a second to register that those aren't flying fish bouncing along the water next to our boat.

Bullets are skipping past.

"Get down," I yell. "Someone's shooting at us."

Jimmy looks behind us and guns the engine. We turn to port and swing back sharply to starboard. Valerie points to the channel where Esmeralda is hiding.

Bullets bang against the side of the boat.

We hit the channel fast and bounce through a small patch of mangroves. The boat spins, chopping its way through sand and small trees. Somehow, we come out upright on the other side.

I look around. We're by ourselves in a small cove surrounded by mangroves. A white ibis points its orange beak at us and takes off, flying south.

Valerie scrambles off the foredeck, trying to stay low. She gets to the transom and ducks. She has her Glock in her hand.

"Where are they?" she asks.

I look over the transom. No one's in view, but I know baddies with guns are out there. Somehow, we've lucked out, bought some time.

I turn to look at Jimmy. He's got his Glock out, too, but he's not looking behind us for the Spider Dog crew.

He's kneeling next to Captain Elmo, lying on the deck, blood coming from his head.

"Jesus," Jimmy says.

There's a loud burst of thunder as lightning hits close by.

A strong gust of wind turns the Maroon Key II and rocks her nearly over. Seawater rushes over the gunwales. We swing back and forth with water pouring in from starboard and then port.

Now the rain is on us in buckets. In seconds it's totally dark, except when lightning strikes. Even then, it's hard to see the boat's bow from the stern.

Jimmy and Valerie drag Captain Elmo under our tattered Bimini top. Valerie yells something at me, but it's impossible to hear her.

The storm has taken charge, howling its commands.

Massive waves push us over the tops of mangroves. The water level is suddenly ten feet higher, and we're bouncing out of control.

I know what I have to do.

I crawl forward on the slippery foredeck, grabbing lifelines and cleats. I get to the anchor and drop it in as a strong wave hits the bow. It nearly knocks me overboard. I manage to tie off the anchor line and crawl back to the stern.

I yell to Jimmy that I've tied off the anchor line, but the howling wind steals my words and sends them flying.

Lightning dances along the lifelines that I grabbed seconds before.

Thunder crashes again and again.

The Maroon Key II turns on its anchor chain. We swing to starboard and then to port. The Zodiac clings to the side of the Maroon Key II like a scared child.

Somehow, we've managed to hook the bottom.

We're riding at anchor in a deadly storm.

Chapter 49

The wind whines and howls as lightning strikes. We rock back and forth and pitch high at anchor on waves, only to be dropped into troughs that plunge our bow underwater as we hold our breaths. We bounce back up, riding the next wave.

I grip the overhead teak handholds in the cabin and hang on tight. The thought crosses my mind –am I holding the boat together, or is it holding me?

The digital anemometer on the bulkhead says, "Wind NW, 67 knots."

The onslaught of rain on the Maroon Key II sounds like a truckload of gravel being poured over the boat. We hear it more than we see it. Our only visuals come when lightning flashes out of the pitch black, giving us a brief still picture of our desperation.

The rear cockpit deck of the Maroon Key II is awash in rain and seawater. The scuppers seem to be handling some of it, sending it out into the sea. Jimmy has managed to get the battery-powered bilge pumps to work, taking some water out of the small cabin.

He and Valerie have dragged Captain Elmo to one of the quarter berths, a foot above the cabin's flooded floor.

Blood covers the right side of his face from his hairline to his chin. Valerie has the first aid kit open and treats his wound. Jimmy kneels beside them in a foot of water, holding them both steady as the boat dives and twists. Empty beer cans and nacho chip bags float past him.

"I slipped and banged my head as I fell, trying to avoid getting shot," Captain Elmo says. Thunder obliterates his words. It takes him three or four attempts to get this message across.

The lightning strikes are close together and right on top of us. Each strike causes a near out-of-body experience. The next strike, I'm sure, will be our last one. We'll either die, or maybe we'll luck out, and the storm will go away.

Wishful thinking?

Scared as hell?

We've lost control.

The thoughts race through my mind.

The most minor pluses seem like significant accomplishments.

We're still afloat.

Captain Elmo has a bandage on his wound.

The pumps are working.

But then there's the deafening roar of thunder, the howling wind that pitches the boat like a cork, and the flash of lightning that makes me think I've just died.

I look at the green glow of the digital clock on the bulkhead. It's after nine pm. We've been under attack by this storm for over two hours.

"Goddamn, that's enough," I yell to the thundering sky. "Go away. We've taken enough shit."

The storm answers with three quick bursts of lightning up close and maybe personal. The thunder is deafening. The screams of the four of us are no match for the storm.

Somehow my ears stop ringing, and my hearing returns to normal. I can hear the wind whistling.

Two quick flashes of lightning are followed by thunder moving off. I hear the waves splashing against the boat.

"You certainly have a way with storms," Valerie says.

I'm surprised that I can hear her.

Something's happened.

We're no longer rocking out of control. The anemometer on the bulkhead says, "Wind NE, 11 knots."

Has the storm quit?

There's a steady rain falling, and the seas are still rocking us with two-foot waves.

It's a definite improvement from what we've been going through.

There's a flash of lightning nearby that lights our boat, but there's no thunder. It flashes again without a sound.

It isn't lightning.

It's a high-powered searchlight from somewhere beyond the mangrove cluster behind us. Maybe a hundred yards from us, there's a boat beyond the trees.

"Everyone quiet," Jimmy says. "If it's the assholes that chased us out of the mangrove maze, they've got a high-powered rifle."

We rock back and forth in the waves. We get a view of the boat with the powerful searchlight through the thick mangroves. It's pointing its bright light at an approaching vessel.

"It's the Spider Dog dive boat," Jimmy says. "It's our old friend, Clarence 'Buckshot' Thomas, and the Everett brothers. That's who was shooting at us."

"Ahoy, Monsieur Du Pont," someone yells from the Spider Dog. "We chased that Maroon Key boat until we hit the storm. I fired off two full magazines at them. No doubt tore the shit out of their boat and probably got a couple of them, too."

"Probably, Clarence? Can you not do better than probably? I'm not paying you for probably."

"I know for sure I gunned down that Captain Elmo. Saw him go down through my scope. We'll get the rest of them. Dead men, you know, don't tell no tales."

"That might be true, Clarence," Du Pont says. "But there's no need to hunt them down. We've retrieved the strongbox from where your friend Ronnie said it was thrown in by some cheap whore. We'll take it to shore and torch open the heavy padlocks."

Du Pont's boat and the Spider Dog boat idle close together, bobbing in the two-foot seas. Coconuts, palm fronds, and branches of mangroves float past in the steady rain.

"We can follow you into Key West," one of the Everett brothers says from under his yellow slicker. "We're heading that way to our dock."

"Certainly," Du Pont says. "That would be nice of you."

"Don't forget about our cut for helping you," Clarence says. "You said we'd get enough to leave the country, where we'd never have to worry about the fuzz."

"Exactly," Du Pont says, pointing to a tall man standing next to him. "Emile will be happy to settle up with you boys."

Emile moves quick, jumping from Du Pont's boat onto the Spider Dog's foredeck. Three shots from an automatic pistol take any future worries away from the Everett brothers and their friend Clarence "Buckshot" Thomas.

Emile grabs one of the auxiliary gas tanks and spills it around the Spider Dog. He jumps back to Du Pont's boat, grabs another pistol – a flare launcher, and aims it into the Spider Dog. As Du Pont's vessel pulls away, Emile fires the flare into the puddle of gasoline.

The flames are intense, lighting up the face of Du Pont, Emile, and another man in a wetsuit who has one of those familiar faces I can't place.

Their boat moves a safe distance away from the inferno. Du Pont stands on the foredeck, absorbing the glow from Emile's handy work.

We watch from behind the mangroves as the Spider Dog burns. Another gas tank aboard catches fire, creating a gigantic roar. Somewhere in the inferno, the remains of the Everett brothers and Clarence "Buckshot" Thomas turn into ashes. The smell of burning flesh and gasoline drifts through the air. The flaming boat drifts off in the direction of Key West, slowly approaching Du Pont's vessel. In a couple minutes, it stops.

The fire dies down to a glow from charred wood and melting fiberglass.

What's left of the Spider Dog sinks, sending clouds of steam into the night air.

Du Pont spits toward the sinking boat.

"So much for Florida dirtbags," he says. "Quickly, Emile, let's get our treasure to Key West."

Chapter 50

Emile guns the powerboat past the mangroves.

DuPont sits in the stern next to the guy in the wetsuit with the familiar face I can't place.

I figure they'll get to Key West in an hour or so. They have the strongbox that Valerie tossed overboard while arguing with Ronnie Nolan, the all-around gigolo rat residing in the Dade County slammer.

"On arrival in Key West, several things will happen," Jimmy says. "They'll take a welding torch to the two padlocks Valerie put on the strongbox. When they open it, they'll realize that Christopher Columbus's sex slave's skull has magically turned into an old plow anchor and an assortment of rusty chains."

"Yeah, the ten million buck fortune will turn into an eighty buck Saturday garage sale bargain," Captain Elmo says.

I nod in agreement, thinking that two possibilities will present themselves to Du Pont and his crew at that point. One would be setting a plan to arrange for someone at the jail to shiv Ronnie Nolan. The other will be to come back to find us, thinking that we have the inside track to the emerald-encrusted skull of Esmeralda.

"We've got to get it together and find the ice chest with Esmeralda," Captain Elmo says. He rises from the quarter berth with four bandages on his face. "We don't want to deal with a monster like that Emile."

"You sure you're okay? Jimmy says.

"I'm ready to go," Captain Elmo says. "Don't let a few scratches on my face tell you anything different."

"Okay," Jimmy says.

"Esmeralda is close," Valerie says. "I tied her down with that yellow nylon line. We should be able to pick it up in our spotlight."

"You heard the lady," Captain Elmo says. "Let's go get Esmeralda."

I look around the Maroon Key II. The boat is a mess. The tinted plastic porthole on the starboard side has bullet holes in it. There are bullet holes in the fiberglass beneath the porthole near the waterline.

"It'd be great if this rain stopped," Valerie says. "Make it easier to spot Esmeralda."

"From your lips to God's ear," Captain Elmo says.

The steady shower comes to a sudden halt as if someone pushed the off button.

"Give me a break," Jimmy says. "I bet you two can't do that again."

"Haven't you learned not to bet against smart women and the untamed seas?" Captain Elmo says.

The night is clear of clouds. At least a million stars are visible. The only sound is the gentle lapping of waves on the stern of the Maroon Key II.

Somewhere under this beautiful sky is Esmeralda.

"She should be over toward that group of mangroves," Valerie says.

She stands barefoot on the foredeck, pointing to port. "I think we should shine the spotlight over there."

The engine comes to life with a roar. The running lights are on, and the spotlight is ready.

Jimmy aims it where Valerie points. Sure enough, there's a long tangle of yellow nylon line stuck to a large mangrove root.

"That's it," Valerie yells. "We need to get over there and rescue her."

The spotlight shows that getting Esmeralda won't be easy. Mangrove roots and small branches stick up all over the shallow cove we're sitting in.

"There may not be enough water under the keel to move in that direction," Captain Elmo says. "Maybe we can get the Zodiac over there."

Jimmy turns the spotlight slowly in a circle.

"I don't like this," he says.

"I don't like this at all," Captain Elmo says.

I have to agree. We're surrounded by mangroves. Somehow, the storm surge deposited the Maroon Key II into a small lagoon with no visible way out.

The small ten-horse motor on the Zodiac comes to life. We follow the spotlight beam toward the yellow nylon tangle of line. There's a way through to where Esmeralda sits somewhere in this maze.

Jimmy stays behind on Maroon Key II. Valerie and I are at the Zodiac bow pushing branches out of the way as Captain Elmo steers us through. We're about fifty yards from the tangled mess of nylon line when the spotlight on Maroon Key II goes out.

I'm about to yell back at Jimmy when Captain Elmo says, "Quiet."

I look back at Maroon Key II. All lights are off. Through the mangroves, I can see the running lights of another boat.

"Grab paddles," Captain Elmo says. "I'm shutting down the motor. We've got company."

I turn to Valerie. She's not on the Zodiac. She's wading through shoulder-deep water, drawing close to the tangle of yellow nylon line.

The other boat is on the other side of the mangroves. I can hear their engine idling.

Voices carry. I hear Du Pont.

"I like the way our new partner thinks, Emile. The strongbox is probably a ruse. They weren't out here to dive for anything. They're still here looking for where that trollop hid the treasure."

"You are right, boss. We're letting them lead us to it."

"Hell, fellas, it was a logical conclusion," the third voice says.

I know that voice.

It's the guy in the wetsuit with the familiar face. When we first met him, he was standing behind the bar at Spider Dog Tap, telling us only fools would get involved in treasure hunting.

It's the Everett boys' brother-in-law Herman.

What he says next cinches it.

"Like we say in Madison, that's a slam dunk worth a drink on the house."

Chapter 51

Stay calm, I tell myself. This can be handled without any of us getting killed.

Du Pont's boat is over the next clump of mangroves.

I hear their conversations, and I get brief looks at their running lights.

We left Jimmy onboard Maroon Key II to aim the searchlight toward the tangled yellow nylon line in the mangroves.

I'm hoping that Jimmy has taken cover on the boat, or maybe he's taken to the water.

Valerie starts to wade the rest of the way to Esmeralda, leaving Captain Elmo and me to paddle our way through the heavy mangrove maze.

The searchlight from Du Pont's boat sweeps over the Maroon Key II. It briefly crosses over our ducked heads and continues its slow sweep of the area.

"They may not be getting a view of where we are," Captain Elmo says. "That bunch of mangroves is helping us. They may think we're all still on the boat where Jimmy is."

I'm considering this when I hear splashes from behind the Zodiac. It's Jimmy wading through chest-deep water. Captain Elmo grabs his left hand, and I take his right to hoist him aboard.

"Jesus, I didn't know what to do," Jimmy says. "They lit up the boat like broad daylight. I didn't want to be a sitting duck. I saw what Emile did to those Spider Dog guys."

"Okay," Captain Elmo whispers. "Keep it quiet. We might be hard to see where we are."

Jimmy nods.

"Where the hell is Valerie?"

Splashing sounds come from off the bow of the Zodiac.

"Help me up," Valerie says.

Jimmy grabs her hands and pulls her up.

"We need to figure out how to do this," Valerie says. "I can cut the ice chest loose from all the nylon line with a good knife and maybe float it over here with Esmeralda inside. I don't want to stand up and attract attention. Those bastards would shoot me once they know where the treasure is."

We duck down as the searchlight from Du Pont's boat sweeps overhead, moving from the Maroon Key II through the mangroves. They're looking for us.

They're looking for us to find Esmeralda.

Once we find Esmeralda, they're going to kill us.

Captain Elmo reaches into the carryall bag next to him and takes out a diver's knife.

"This'll help with the cutting," he says. "Du Pont and his boys might wait for us to find the treasure. They'll move in after we do the work. Maybe we can use that to get an advantage."

The four of us sit huddled down in the Zodiac, jerry-rigging together what can best be summed up as a Hail Mary plan.

If we all do our part.

If Du Pont and his partners Emile and Herman are greedy and dumb enough to take the bait.

If the storm doesn't come back, the tide doesn't rise, and sharks don't attack.

We might get out of this one alive.

Esmeralda?

Oh, yeah. We might get what's left of her, too.

Valerie leads the way through the mangrove jungle. I'm a few steps behind her in the waist-deep water. Somewhere up ahead is the autographed skull of Christopher Columbus's sex slave Esmeralda, sitting in a large ice chest labeled "Maroon Key II."

Slogging through water in the dark brings unpleasant images to mind. I think about Henri Boyer and his Tonton Macoute hotshots, who lost it all in a bloody shark attack. I also think about Du Pont's man Emile, who doesn't hesitate to shoot first and cremate afterward.

I've moved my gun from my waistband into the front pocket of my shorts. Please, no jokes about a Glock in my pocket, or am I glad to see someone.

I know it's soaked with saltwater. Still, I'm hoping that all the boasts I've read about how wonderful Glocks behave under trying conditions have some truth. Will it make any difference firing salty wet bullets?

I'm getting ahead of myself. I'm second-guessing myself, and that's not good. I tell myself not to go down the what-if track. What's done is done. It's the here, and now that counts.

Our trudge through the mangroves comes with pests above water and below. The mosquitos and other insects love what I'm offering them. They're the least of my worries. The bumps I'm getting from creatures below the water are bothering me more.

Valerie stops and turns toward me.

"Esmeralda is just ahead," she whispers. "If you look closely, you'll see the tangle of nylon line hanging from the trees."

I stare at where she's pointing, but nothing comes into focus.

"How far?" I ask.

She's about to whisper back when the searchlight from Du Pont's boat makes a slow pass over our heads and sweeps past mangroves just ahead of us. I see the yellow nylon line. The searchlight moves along, then turns back to focus on it.

"Herman," Du Pont says. "You have a wetsuit. Swim over and take a look. This could be our ten-million-dollar payoff. We'll keep the searchlight on you. If any of that bunch from the Maroon Key are still around, we have more than enough firepower to take them out."

"You heard that," Valerie whispers. "We can't let them do this."

The intense beam from Du Pont's searchlight stays on the tangle of the yellow line. I can make out the top of the ice chest sticking up from mangrove roots. Luck is with us. We're outside the beam of light, hidden behind leafy branches.

I'm about to reassure Valerie when a burst of bullets from automatic gunfire rattles the Maroon Key II and sweeps over us, busting through mangrove branches and skipping over the water.

"Stay down," I say to Valerie, but there's no need. She's under the water already.

I reach for her, but she's gone.

I look back toward the Zodiac. I can't see it.

Laughter comes from Du Pont's vessel.

"Yes, Emile," Du Pont says. "I wondered when we were going to hear from your Uzi."

Chapter 52

I reach again for Valerie beneath the water.

Again, I come up empty-handed.

Has she been shot?

Did she duck just before the bullets from Emile's Uzi hit the water around us?

I hear splashing coming from the direction of the yellow tangled nylon line. I'm about to stick my head out to look past a clump of mangroves when someone grabs me from behind. A hand covers my mouth. Before I can react, I hear a low voice.

"Cool it, Nick," Valerie whispers. "That Herman guy is splashing his way toward Esmeralda. He's getting close. You got it?"

I nod, and she releases her grip on me.

Splashes come from the direction of the Maroon Key II. I'm hoping they're coming from Jimmy and Captain Elmo paddling the Zodiac like we planned.

"We can't let that guy get hold of Esmeralda," Valerie says. "If it wasn't for that searchlight, I'd swim up and use this knife on him."

I look at her. She's serious.

"Val, when's the last time you killed someone?"

"With a knife, you mean?"

"With anything."

"Uh, Burmese pythons. I've killed a mess of them."

"Those don't count. If we have to stop that asshole, I'll use this," I say, drawing my Glock from my pocket and holding it up.

Water pours from the barrel of the gun.

Valerie grimaces.

"Nick, is this your way of saying we're in deep shit?"

Before I can answer, Du Pont's voice booms from his boat.

"Herman, snap our cable onto the ice chest. We can winch you and the treasure back to the boat."

"Yeah," Herman says. "There's a lot of tangled line to cut."

"Do your best," Du Pont says. "You're about to become a very wealthy man."

Through the mangroves, we can see Herman stand as he reaches the small key where Esmeralda sits. He kicks off his fins, takes off his dive mask, and staggers toward the ice chest.

"This looks like what we're looking for," he says. "It's got 'Maroon Key II' stenciled on it."

"Very good," Du Pont yells. "You see any of that blonde bitch and her crew?"

"No, just me and about a hundred yards of a tangle to cut through."

"Emile. Be ready with the Uzi," Du Pont says. "If you see any of them, shoot to kill."

Herman stumbles through roots protecting the ice chest. He loses balance and falls after tripping.

"This is like a web of a drunk spider," he says, stumbling and catching his balance. He keeps hacking to find a way through.

I shake the Glock to see if there's any more water in it. This show is about to come to a rousing finish.

Herman cuts away at the nylon line with his diver's knife. It's tough going. I think he's opted for the bargain bin variety of knives.

I trace the strands of the line. One section leads from the ice chest and over some small mangrove roots. From there, it falls into the water, pointing to where we're hiding.

Something doesn't make sense. The yellow nylon line should be floating.

"Was there something stuck on the end of that line?" I ask Valerie.

"You mean that heavy green plastic mushroom thingy?"

"A heavy mushroom thingy?"

"Yeah, I couldn't get it off, so I tied up everything and tossed that end into the water."

"I think that's an old anchor for the Zodiac. How far away from the ice chest did you toss it?"

"Maybe ten or twelve feet? I was in a hurry to get out of there."

She looks at me, then at the line coming from the ice chest handle.

"I think I can find it," she says.

I follow the yellow line again, tracing it from the ice chest to not far from where we're hiding. It could be doable.

I look back at Valerie. All I see are her feet and her bottom going underwater. She's headed toward the yellow line and the mushroom thingy.

"What's taking so long over there?" Du Pont's voice booms from his boat.

"I've got a few more strands to cut," Herman says. "Then we'll have her free."

"Have you got our line attached to the chest so we can pull you off with the treasure?"

Herman stumbles toward the chest holding a heavy cable with a spring-loaded shackle on end. He drops it next to the chest and moves to cut the last of the tangled yellow line.

"The last one," he yells as he moves to cut the line with the mushroom thingy on its end. "And we're ready to go."

"You heard him, Emile," Du Pont says. "Herman says he's ready to go."

The long burst from the Uzi makes it a slam dunk that Herman is not only ready to go, but he's gone before he hits the shallow water next to the mangroves.

"We have it," Du Pont says. "Steady ahead, Emile. Let's pull the treasure out of that mess."

The electric winch on Du Pont's vessel comes to life with a grinding sound.

The chest begins to move. Only it doesn't move toward Du Pont's vessel.

It moves past the bullet-riddled body of Herman, face down in the water with bare feet still next to a mangrove root onshore.

Valerie surfaces next to me. She's holding the mushroom thingy.

"Help me pull her to safety," she says.

We tug together, trying to get Esmeralda off the sand spit and out of Du Pont's searchlight beam.

"The chest is moving, Emile," Du Pont yells. "It's moving to the side. Don't we have it on our line?"

The chest skids along the sand toward Valerie and me.

Another burst of Uzi fire rattles the mangroves and the water around us.

I look at the chest that has Esmeralda inside. The top and part of the side have been riddled with bullets from Emile's gun.

"Pull harder," Valerie says.

The chest makes it past the bloody remains of Herman and begins to float towards us.

Another burst from the Uzi has us ducking under the water.

"It's not on our line, Boss," Emile says, shutting off the winch on Du Pont's boat. "It's that crazy bitch causing trouble. We need to get it from her. "

"You think that Captain Elmo guy is dead like that Buckshot said?" Du Pont asks.

"Yeah, Boss. He probably killed the other guys, too."

"So, it's only the crazy blonde bitch giving us some trouble?" Du Pont says. "She may need a hard lesson from little Francois, eh?"

Emile laughs.

"Or the Uzi, too," he says, firing another burst toward where we were seconds before.

We wade through the waist-deep water, pulling the ice chest past the mangroves. I'm worried about the next barrage of bullets from the Uzi.

I'm also worried about the bumps from something under the water.

I look at Valerie. She points at something in the dark water.

"Sharks?" It comes out of her with a squeal and a shake.

"I feel them, too," I say. "We need to keep going. They're after what's left of Herman."

Chapter 53

A short burst from Emile's Uzi rattles the ice chest and the surrounding water. We duck below the surface. When we come up and tug on the line, something is wrong.

The yellow nylon line has gone slack. One of Emile's bullets has cut through it.

"The chest is floating free, Emile," Du Pont yells. "We need to get it."

"Yeah, wait, Boss. Don't reverse the motor. The winch for the cable...."

It's too late.

The engine stops.

"What happened?" Valerie asks.

"Du Pont just backed over that steel cable," I say. "There's probably five feet of it wrapped around his propeller."

"We can fix it, Boss," Emile says. "We just need to get the boat into water where I can stand up and try to untangle the cable."

Something solid and coarse rushes past me in the water, rubbing against my leg. I look at Valerie. She's felt it, too. Her face is screwed up like she's accepted that she'll be dead from a shark bite any second.

I grab her.

"Stay quiet. If you go hysterical, Emile will kill us. They're interested in Herman's blood. We have a better chance with sharks."

"Okay, okay."

The sounds of a paddle splashing in the water come from DuPont's boat. Emile is trying to move the small cruiser toward the key, where Herman's bleeding body dips into the water.

Du Pont aims the searchlight beam to the water just aft of his boat.

"What do you think, Emile? Can you repair the propeller? Get into the water and get us going."

"Yeah, Boss, and I'll try to get us going."

The boat bounces in the foot-high waves near the sand spit.

"I can fix it, Boss. Maybe you can get in the water and hold the boat steady while I cut the cable away."

"Yes, hurry. The chest is floating away."

Emile moves down the swim ladder into the water. He has a diving mask tilted over his forehead and a cutting tool. Du Pont follows down the ladder and stands, holding the boat with both hands on the stern as it bounces in the waves. The Uzi is on a strap over his shoulder.

The whine of the ten-horse motor on the Zodiac comes from somewhere ahead of Du Pont's boat. Jimmy and Captain Elmo have decided it's time to make their move.

"Do you hear that, Emile? There's a boat approaching. If it's that blonde bitch...."

"You'll have to take the safety off the Uzi first, Boss."

"Of course. I'm no fool, you know."

Du Pont's boat bounces in the waves. He tries to hold it in place with both hands as the Uzi slides off his shoulder toward the water. He grabs for it and lets go of the boat.

The boat swerves toward the sand spit. What's left of Herman is waiting there, dangling over a mangrove root, head down in the shallow water.

Emile grabs the boat, trying to steady it in the waves, but it's no use. The boat turns sideways and heads toward the mangroves. Du Pont and Emile look toward the sound of the loud engine. It's the Zodiac, coming at them at top speed.

Du Pont fumbles with the Uzi, aiming at the oncoming vessel.

Emile grabs the gun from him and pulls the trigger.

Nothing happens.

The magazine is empty.

The Zodiac bounces into Du Pont and runs over Emile. He gets to his feet, choking on seawater, but there's blood pumping out of his arm, and now something in the water is dragging him down.

The Zodiac turns and heads back to sea.

Du Pont pokes his head above water. He sees the shark thrashing Emile and tries to get back aboard his boat. He gets a hand on the side of the swim ladder and one foot onto the lowest step, but that's as far as he gets. Something has him by the other foot.

"Oh, my god," Valerie says as the shark drags Du Pont into the water.

"Hurry."

I grab her by the arm.

"We've got to get back to the Maroon Key II without getting killed."

With Du Pont and his crew out of the battle, we don't have to duck bullets in waist-high water. We can walk in the shallows near the mangrove roots and avoid sharks in the deeper water.

Halfway back to the Maroon Key II, the Zodiac pulls up and grabs us.

"Get in, you two," Jimmy says, idling the motor. "I've had to take the helm from Captain Elmo. You saw what a reckless driver he is."

"I wanted to make sure the marine life got plenty to eat," Captain Elmo says. "Let's go find the ice chest and save poor Esmeralda."

"It shouldn't be that hard to retrieve her," Valerie says. "The ice chest got loose a few minutes ago when that thug shot a million bullets at us."

"Yeah, old Esmeralda's got to be somewhere around here close," I say.

"She gets around pretty well for an old sex slave," Jimmy says. He points a large flashlight at something floating on the other side of the mangrove roots.

"Let's go," Valerie says. "How'd she get through all the mangroves to the other side?"

"I figure she fit through with the rising tide," Captain Elmo says. "A little more water can make a big difference."

"Can we find our way to get her?" Valerie asks.

"Yeah, we found a way out past where the Maroon Key II is aground in shallows," Jimmy says. "I think we better hurry, though. I saw the way that maniac was shooting at the ice chest. We don't want her to sink before we get to her."

The Zodiac swings out of the mangrove maze, headed to where we last saw Esmeralda in her floating home. Captain Elmo hands me another flashlight out of a rucksack. Together we scan the horizon looking for our elusive woman of the night.

What starts out as a few minutes' search turns into several hours. Occasional glimpses of the elusive Esmeralda turn our search into a game of hide and seek.

We're tired, and it's getting cold.

"This was supposed to be easy Valerie says. "Get Esmeralda back to Key West and have dinner. Now, what is it? Three in the morning, and we're chasing around like loonies in the dark. If those Du Pont guys weren't already dead, I'd go back and kill them with my bare hands."

I share her frustration. We've chased Esmeralda in her ice chest carriage into open waters to the northwest of the Keys. Captain Elmo says the tidal current is partly to blame.

"Relax," Jimmy says. "She's somewhere between here and the Everglades. We'll get her."

"Starlight's giving us a problem," Captain Elmo says. "Every wave top sparkles. She'll be harder to find if she's riding low in the water."

The wind kicks up. The air turns cooler.

"She's out here somewhere," Jimmy says, waving the flashlight around.

"Wait. Stop," Valerie says. "Move the light off to your left. Over there. Look."

The stenciled words "Maroon Key II" show up in both flashlight beams. Esmeralda is off our starboard bow fifty yards away.

"Let's go get her," Jimmy says, goosing up the throttle on the ten-horse motor.

There's no doubt that we've found her. The engine cuts out as we approach alongside. Captain Elmo grabs one handle of the ice chest, I grab the other, and we haul her aboard.

"Omigod, Omigod, Omigod," Valerie says. "This is wonderful."

I pop the lid off the ice chest and point the flashlight into it. A hundred points of green shine back at me from inside the small iron cage that Esmeralda rests in. The coqui frog is carved into the top of her skull and circled with emeralds. And there below is the carved-in autograph of the guy we've given credit to for discovering America.

"We got her," Captain Elmo says. "How great can that be? Hemingway would have pissed in his pants over this one."

"So great, Jimmy," Valerie says, tears running down her cheeks into a wide grin. "The way you motored up and cut the engine when we got beside her. I'm going to put that in my book."

I look at Jimmy. He's got one of those looks on his face. The kind he gets when the third horse in his trifecta-– the favorite comes home out of the money.

He shakes his head and shrugs.

"Val," he says. "I'll tell you the truth. I didn't cut the engine. We're out of gas."

Chapter 54

Out of gas in the middle of nowhere.

We scan the horizon with our extra-large flashlights and see nothing but water. It's dark. We're wet and getting colder. We've all had more terror shoved into our lives in the last half-day.

I think about how that thug Emile can fire so many bullets and only manage to kill his partners. Or that druggie Clarence "Buckshot" Thomas firing hundreds of rounds from an automatic rifle and missing us all.

"We're damn lucky," I say.

"We are. We have Esmeralda," Valerie says. She hugs the small iron cage that holds the emerald-covered skull of Columbus's sex slave. "That's at least saying something, isn't it?"

She huddles under a large tarp that Captain Elmo has found in the oversized duffle bag.

The four of us each take a corner of the tarp and huddle together to keep warm.

"Hang onto the tarp," Captain Elmo says. "Don't let the wind take it. We might need it to shelter from the sun in the morning. Or maybe we can fashion a make-shift sail out of it."

I have questions, but I don't ask them. I'm pretty sure what the answers are, and I don't want to upset the rest of our crew. They need a rest.

I lean back under the tarp.

We have no water, except for three cans of diet soda rattling around near the motor well.

If there's any food on board, it's the candy bar and chewing gum variety that someone has stashed on their person.

We're out of gas.

Our battery has some juice, but we have no radio.

"We'll stay afloat until we run into something," Captain Elmo says as he drifts off. "That's what they call survival."

I think about how long it might take to die of starvation and thirst as I fall asleep.

In my dream, I'm floating on a large air mattress in my pool in Vegas. I look to my left. Jimmy is next to me on one of those floating pool chairs.

"Why can't they come out of the water and have dinner?" My five-year-old daughter Molly asks my wife.

"They're waiting to run into something," Dawn says. "That's how Daddy and your Uncle Jimmy are. They're really good at running into things."

I look up from my floating mattress. A large mass of black fur has launched itself toward me. Zorro, Jimmy's Labradoodle, is doing his backflip and landing with a big splash.

Water hits me in the face.

I feel a bump.

I'm awake.

It's a sunny morning.

We've just run into a large piling where a cormorant sits shaking water from its wings next to a solar-powered navigation light.

I grab for the piling and hold onto it. I get the painter line around it and start to tie up when someone yells.

"The feds don't like it when you tie up to their precious markers," the voice says. "They don't want anyone interfering with their bird shit collectors."

I turn to look.

Detective Jerry Cohen leans out of a Florida Marine Patrol boat.

"Nick, what are you doing way out here?" he asks.

"And what the hell happened back near Content Key?" another voice says.

It's Detective Alberto Cortez.

Jimmy pokes his head up from under the tarp.

"It's complicated," he says. "We could give you the lowdown on it over breakfast if you could tow us back to Key West."

"More like lunch when we get there," Cohen says. "Could you at least estimate how many bodies we should be looking for near your bullet-riddled boat?"

"Uh, six," I say. "The Everett brothers and Clarence Thomas bought it from some guy called Emile. Emile also killed Herman, the Everetts' brother-in-law. Du Pont and Emile were dumb enough to get into the water during a major shark festival."

"Knowing you two, it couldn't have happened any other way," Cortez says.

"Can I ask how you managed to find us?" Jimmy says.

"Sure," Cohen says. "A charming French lady named Colette told us that the Zodiac had a 'gadget for the position global.' It turns out all the Maroon Key vessels have them."

We get a line tossed from the patrol boat, and soon we're moving south toward Key West. Like some spectacular magic trick, the buildings start to grow out of the sea as we approach.

"Just like I said," Captain Elmo says. "Sooner or later, I knew that we'd run into something."

After getting cleaned up and refreshed, we get to lunch at the Oceanfront Suites. Corinne, our waitress, has given us our favorite table overlooking Key West Bight.

Cohen and Cortez make it easy on us. We explain how Du Pont and the Spider Dog Tap crew were convinced that we knew where some buried treasure was.

"They followed us out from Marathon," Jimmy says, "We went out looking for lost equipment from the Maroon Key II."

I nod.

"Things soon got dicey," Captain Elmo says. "They first tried to kill us over the non-existent treasure. Then they ended up killing each other. The sharks took what was left of them."

"What was the lost equipment you were looking for out there?" Cohen asks.

"A ten-horse outboard, a missing anchor, some nylon line and chain," Jimmy says. "There was an ice chest, too. We found that floating away from where those six nuts killed each other."

"Anything of interest inside of it?" Cohen asks.

"Not anymore," I say. "Back when Ronnie Nolan took it out from Marathon, it was filled with food and cold beers. From what Valerie says, he went crazy out there, tossing stuff off the boat."

"You're talking about the late Ronnie Nolan," Cortez says. "Du Pont never cared to have Ronnie around. Once Ronnie spilled the beans about where this treasure was, he was useless to Du Pont. He was going to be a pain in the ass. Dear old Ronnie somehow got strangled with an electrical cord while sitting on the can in his cell last night."

"What a way to go," Jimmy says. "No pun intended."

"None taken," Cortez says. "The guy who did Ronnie couldn't keep his mouth shut. One of our confidential informants called us. We found out that Du Pont was the one who ordered the hit, so we came down here to arrest him. From what we gather from you, there may be not enough left of Du Pont to put a collar on."

"This is the third time Ronnie's been declared dead," I say. "You think it will take this time?"

"He's cooling off in a body locker at the morgue," Cohen says.

"I'm glad he's dead," Valerie says. "He was scum. The people he hung out with were scum."

"I'll drink to that," Cortez says, raising his bottle of Beck's.

"Well put, Ms. Masters," Cohen says. "You think you might write a book about any of this?"

"Not immediately," Valerie says. "I've been working on a book about Christopher Columbus."

"Good luck with that," Cortez says. "I thought most of that subject has already been covered."

"Perhaps covered-up might be a better term," Valerie says. "The so-called Discoverer of America was, among his other atrocities, a serial sex monster."

“That alone should sell a lot of books,” Cohen says.

Chapter 55

October 2019

Detective Cohen was right. Valerie would sell a lot of books detailing the sleazy activities of "America's Discoverer." She had a good story filled with sex, drugs, and violence. She also had evidence of Christopher Columbus's penchant for life on the dark side.

Two months after our recovery of Esmeralda, Valerie Masters introduced her book in a packed ballroom in the Galloping Dominos Casino. In attendance were writers and critics from around the world.

Captain Elmo was listed on the program as the leader of the Esmeralda Quest Expedition. He described how Esmeralda was found in international waters by tracing the route of the ill-fated Levant ship from Haiti toward its intended destination, New Orleans.

My wife was next to speak to the large crowd. Dawn announced that EQE directors planned to keep Esmeralda on permanent display at the well-guarded Galloping Dominos Museum of Natural History. She and Valerie then led the procession of notables to where Esmeralda's skull sat, glowing under glass in subdued lighting.

"How did you find her?"

"Is that really how Columbus signed his name?"

"Columbus carved that in her skull?"

"Those emeralds, are they real?"

"What's with that frog carving?"

The questions came, and experts were standing by to answer all inquiries.

Or at least obfuscate enough to keep the champagne party on high-test controversy.

The next day, Valerie and Esmeralda were all over the news.

Headlines read, "**Columbus a monster?**" and "**Columbus carved woman's skull, book says**."

Reactions to the Columbus headlines were swift in coming. Organizations defending the great Christopher denied that he had ever carved anything into a woman's skull. In fact, some of the Columbus defenders proposed sainthood for the explorer.

One defender, Henry Pesci of East Fairmont, New Jersey, broke into a Manhattan TV newsroom to attack Valerie while she was being interviewed. His small-caliber revolver managed one shot. It struck Pesci in the foot.

Reaction to Pesci's attack brought more controversy.

"Valerie Masters gets attacked because she's a woman who's tired of taking crap from a male-dominated society," Meg Saunders, president of Women Get it Right, said. "For centuries, men have said terrible things about women like Anne Boleyn. You don't see women trying to shoot their way into the headlines over that."

Science also checked into the controversy.

"We've done tests on the skull," Professor Arnold Cotter, head of UCLA's Forensic Medicine Program, said. "It belongs to a Taino woman who lived about five hundred years ago. She appears to have been malnourished."

"Typical of the way White men have been treating the rest of the world," said Jesse Standing Tall, leader of Red Arrow Rising, upon hearing Cotter's report. "Look at the pictures of Columbus. You don't see anyone who's missed a meal but the poor Taino woman? Columbus used her for a sex toy."

"This Jesse Standing Tall needs to shut his mouth," said Anthony Di Prima, head of the Christopher Columbus Canonization Foundation. "He's got no proof that Columbus did anything wrong. The man was a saint, a good Italian saint. Someday the church will honor him."

The controversy continued as sales of Valerie's book skyrocketed. Bookings for women's groups at the Galloping Dominos went way up, too.

I should have been riding high.

"What's the matter, Nick?" my wife asks. "You and Jimmy seem a little removed since you got back from the Keys. It's like you left something of yourselves there."

We're sitting poolside at Jimmy and Cassandra's house. We're sipping coffees and B&Bs beneath gas-powered torchlights while watching Molly and Zorro swim laps. The evening's barbecued shrimp, baked potatoes, and watermelon are gone.

"It takes a while for things to sink in," Jimmy says. "We went to South Florida for a real estate deal. Twenty people we never met start killing each other over a treasure that only became real after someone accidentally found it."

"It's true," I say. "If Valerie had shut her mouth about what she found with Ronnie Nolan, all those people might still be around. Letting Billy Teller know that Ronnie was raving about some treasure when he beat her up got things started. Right away, she realized it was a mistake. She tried walking it back, adding it was probably bullshit. But Billy and his partners liked getting suckers into a treasure hunt worth millions."

"At first, they were trying to get enough money to bail Billy out of the Sea Change," Jimmy says. "They could pay off the loans, sell the joint, and split the profits."

"That's the dump that burned to the ground overnight?" Cassandra asks.

"With a little help from our friends," Jimmy says. "Then they realized the scam they were working could make them all rich. They didn't count on Billy's homicidal wife, Bonnie. She got a trio of high-roller bums competing for the inside track to the treasure."

"So, it escalated from there?" Cassandra asks.

"Yeah," Jimmy says. "Most of it was people in the hunt killing each other. None of them knew where Esmeralda was."

"Did you have to...?"

"No," Jimmy says. "I didn't have to fire a shot."

Dawn looks at me with that look.

"One," I say. "Self-defense, some drugged-up hitman that Bonnie sent after us."

She nods and sends me that smile I'd fight dragons for.

"What else?" she asks.

"I should be happy," I say. "I'm home safe with the people I love. I am happy. There's a part of me, though, that can't settle. Something's missing."

"Like you left something down there?" Cassandra asks.

I sip my coffee. It's one of those beautiful desert nights. Stars are visible in the sky, and there's a light breeze cooling us.

"It's like that," I say. "We came back with a prize much bigger than we expected. We won a big battle while everyone else was losing the war."

"I know, Baby," Dawn says. "We all feel it. It's like no one is in charge. Anyone who has any sense that is."

"She's right," Cassandra says.

"Damn right," Jimmy says.

I think about the Keys and what Brewster said as he wiped the countertop at his restaurant.

"You want the real beauty of the Keys?" he said. "It's out there in the flats. That turquoise-colored water that you can see forever through. That's the real treasure."

I look at our group gathered around the table. Forever might be running out of time.

I look at the pool and five-year-old Molly. There are things my daughter needs to see before the three-piece suits fuck it all up.

"Florida is slowly drowning," I say. "The Keys are going under. We need to see the beauty before it's too late."

Dawn and Cassandra nod.

"We're ready to go when you guys are," my wife says.

"Nick's right," Jimmy says. "It's a beautiful treasure."

"It is," I say. "And so are all of you."

Dawn reaches over and wipes under my eyes with a clean napkin.

"A tough guy like Nick," she says. "So many allergies."

THE END

Epilogue

After Christopher Columbus stumbled upon the island we know as Haiti in 1492, he wrote of the Taíno people who inhabited it, "They never refuse anything that is asked for. They even offer it themselves, and show so much love that they would give their very hearts."

It was this perceived generosity and goodwill that Columbus thought would make it easier to seize the giant island, with its "fine, large, flowing rivers" and forests "full of trees of endless varieties, so high that they seem to touch the sky." Years later, the Taíno would be reduced to a tiny fraction of their population of approximately 300,000— and Haiti would lose 98 percent of those trees Columbus coveted.

There was nothing trivial about Columbus' violent destruction of Taíno people. While the sailor and his crew are sometimes lumped in with all the other conquest-crazy Europeans of their era, their particular cruelty can't be so easily exonerated and shouldn't be ignored.

Natives were regularly whipped for what Columbus considered minor offenses — but stealing a vegetable or animal could result in cutting off a Taíno's nose, ear, or hand; the offender was sometimes forced to walk around with their severed body part in shame. Columbus took and gifted Taíno women to his crewmen, who would violently beat and rape them. Pregnant Taíno women who were taken captive gave birth to babies who were sometimes thrown to hungry dogs. Columbus established a business in the sale of 9- and 10-year-old Taíno girls for sexual slavery. He also kidnapped and enslaved Taínos themselves — personally initiating the transatlantic slave trade in his voyage back to Europe.

What followed was centuries of oppression — to the human beings who lived there, and to the land they lived on. Spain cleared land for massive tobacco plantations, beginning a long process of deforestation and soil erosion. After France came into possession of Haiti, it cleared more land, and brought enslaved Africans to grow sugar for European palates. The destructive practice of monocropping for overseas consumption had already taken hold.

Columbus is responsible for launching an ecocide as well as a genocide. The wealth from resources like sugar, tobacco, and cotton ushered in the start of the Industrial Revolution, which began emitting carbon at an unprecedented record level.

Haiti remains the poorest country in the Americas; the European Union region is one of the wealthiest in the world. This isn't because of some innate curse on Haiti. It's because its peoples, their labor, and their resources have long been embezzled without reparation. The colonization of the Americas, which started in Haiti, not only terrorized the people who lived there; it also created a system that kept indigenous peoples in slavery or perpetual poverty, while Europe basked in wealth.

By Aura Bogado, Grist https://grist.org/

Sources: ***Atrocities, Massacres, and War Crimes: An Encyclopedia,*** by Alexander Mikaberidze; ***The Rediscovery of North America***, by Barry Lopez; ***Blessed Unrest: How the Largest Social Movement in History Is Restoring Grace, Justice, and Beauty to the World,*** by Paul Hawken; ***The Spanish Frontier in North America,*** by David J. Weber; ***Columbus: The Four Voyages, 1492-1504***, by Laurence Bergreen; ***A History of Jamaica from Its Discovery by Christopher Columbus to the Present Time***, by William James Gardner.

About Author

Ray Pace is a member of the Authors Guild. He lives in Waikoloa Village on the Big Island of Hawaii.

His works of fiction are:

Disappearing Act, A Las Vegas Love Story, Sort Of...,

The Babylon Deception,

Sea Change in Crimson,

Hemingway in Hawaii,

Bearstone Blackie, Detective,

Captain Mike's Honolulu Fright Night Tour, a ghost story.

Hemingway, Memories of Les, a memoir, deals with Pace's friend, Leicester Hemingway, author of ***My Brother Ernest Hemingway.***

More on Ray Pace's books at www.raypacewrites.com

Made in the USA
Middletown, DE
23 April 2022

64638043R00146